Andrew said, "Do you understand

what I'm telling you?"

"My God," exclaimed Sarah, for whom the penny had finally dropped with the efficiency of a cement-covered body thrown from a great height. "You're having an affair with Hyacinth!"

Andrew corrected her gravely. "I'm in love with Hyacinth."

Sarah, feeling as if she'd been hit in the solar plexus, took a slug of her champagne. "Isn't that the same thing?"

"No," said Andrew. "One is a transitory experience based on sexual desire, the other is a meeting of minds as well as bodies."

Sarah stared at him for a few moments and then smiled. She felt the relief coursing through her veins. "Andrew Stagg, I almost believed you!"

"Sarah," Andrew said. "I'm not joking."

Sarah looked at him in disbelief. "I don't know what's worse," she said at last, "the fact that you're having an affair or the fact that you believe all that stuff you just said."

THE
EX-WIFE'S
SURVIVAL GUIDE

DEBBY HOLT

doWn
tOwn
press

NEW YORK   LONDON   TORONTO   SYDNEY

An *Original* Publication of POCKET BOOKS

 DOWNTOWN PRESS, published by Pocket Books
1230 Avenue of the Americas
New York, NY 10020

Library of Congress Cataloging-in-Publication data is available.

ISBN-13: 978-1-4165-1329-2
ISBN-10:   1-4165-1329-9

This Downtown Press trade paperback edition February 2006

10 9 8 7 6 5 4 3 2 1

DOWNTOWN PRESS and colophon are
trademarks of Simon & Schuster, Inc.

Manufactured in the United States of America

Designed by Jaime Putorti

For information regarding special discounts for bulk purchases,
please contact Simon & Schuster Special Sales at 1-800-456-6798
or business@simonandschuster.com.

For Joan Skinner,

the best aunt in the world

Acknowledgments

This book would never have been written if I hadn't been lucky enough to receive the support and inspiration of three great writing friends, Crysse Morrison, Emily Gerrard, and Jill Miller. Fenella Kemp and Angie Moss gave me great advice. I am incredibly lucky in my publisher, Simon & Schuster, and my agent, Teresa Chris. Special thanks to my children and especially my youngest son, Charlie, whose whole-hearted enthusiasm kept me going. Very, very special thanks to my husband, David, for just about everything.

Alcohol Does Not Encourage Clear Thinking

Sarah's father always said amateur dramatics was a dangerous pastime.

The danger, when it finally appeared, came in the shapely form of Hyacinth Harrington, who was the first new member to have joined the Ambercross Players in years. Audrey Masterton, the company's self-appointed director, took one look at her flaxen hair and her baby blue eyes and gave her the main part in the forthcoming production of *Dear Octopus,* thus gravely offending Harriet Evans, who had played the romantic lead in every production for the last eighteen years and had expected to go on doing so for the next eighteen.

Sarah, despite her father's grave misgivings, had never been concerned about the dangers lying in wait for her husband. Andrew had been a member of the Players for fifteen years and had never shown a disposition to stray from the marital path, even when the horrible wife of poor Martin Chamberlain had done her very best to lure him into her web with the now legendary invitation, "Martin and I have an open marriage, if you know what I mean." As if, as Andrew said to Sarah when recounting the episode, poor old Martin would know what an open marriage *was*.

When Andrew came home and told Sarah he at last had a credible leading lady, Sarah was glad he would no longer be irritated by Harriet Evans's simpering imitation of youth. When Andrew returned from rehearsals, enthusing about Hyacinth's charismatic stage presence, Sarah said with genuine sincerity that she couldn't wait to meet her. When Andrew came home from rehearsals in the early hours, she didn't bat an eyelid. When she watched the final performance she was moved by the intensity of Andrew's scenes with Hyacinth, and when she said this to Martin Chamberlain at the after-show party, she assumed his discomfort was due to painful memories of his now ex-wife's performance in the same role twelve years earlier. Sarah went up to Hyacinth and told her how wonderful Andrew thought she was and Hyacinth told her the feeling was mutual, which at least, Sarah thought later, cringing at the memory, was truthful.

Sarah had an inkling that something was not quite right when, driving home after the party, Andrew asked why the twins hadn't come. He sounded as if he'd only just noticed their absence, which was odd because this was the first time they had ever missed one of their father's plays. Sarah said they'd felt dreadful about missing the big night but had forgotten that it was their friend's eighteenth birthday party. The boys, with characteristic absentmindedness, had only recalled the engagement an hour before the play and Sarah had dreaded telling Andrew. It was a family ritual that Andrew would return home like a victorious warrior, where they would all enjoy a celebratory bottle of champagne. Andrew merely asked if they'd be out for the night. He wasn't angry; he didn't even look disappointed. Sarah did glance at him then and wonder at the reason for his unaccustomed equanimity in the face of such provocation.

She found out, during her second glass of champagne. He was, he told her, glad they were on their own. He had something difficult to tell her, something he never thought he would have to say, and he wanted her to know he still cared for her and would never stop caring for her and that . . .

"Oh my God!" Sarah exclaimed. "Don't tell me: you want to be a proper actor! I always thought you'd say this one day. Andrew, of course I'm with you. If the money's a problem, I'm sure I can find ways of earning more."

"Sarah," Andrew broke in irritably, "What on earth makes you think I want to be a professional actor?"

"Well, you did," Sarah said. "After *Move Over, Mrs. Markham,* you said you did."

"That was eight years ago! I wasn't a partner then. Now you've made me forget what I was saying."

"You said you still care for me and that"—Sarah squeezed his hand affectionately—"you always will."

"That's right. And of course I will. You've been a great friend to me as well as a wife and I hope we'll always be friends. . . ."

"Of course we will," said Sarah. A terrible thought struck

her. "Andrew, are you trying to tell me you have some horrible illness?"

"No, I am not! How much did you drink at the after-play party?"

"More than I meant to. Dear old Adrian kept filling up my glass. He's so sweet."

"He's a boring old idiot," said Andrew brutally. "I'm finding this very difficult, Sarah, and it doesn't help that you keep interrupting me."

"I'm sorry."

"The thing is, as you know, I've spent the last few months rehearsing with Hyacinth. . . ."

"She was terrific tonight," Sarah mused, "but she made me feel so old. Do you know she could be our daughter?"

"Don't be ridiculous," said Andrew, adding for no obvious reason, "She comes from Surrey."

"She could be. She can't be more than twenty-three."

"She's twenty-six."

"Exactly. If you and I'd had children at seventeen, she could be our daughter."

"We didn't know each other at seventeen. Honestly, Sarah, your habit of going off on some hypothetical tangent is extremely irritating. Will you please shut up and listen? The thing is, there's no easy way to tell you this. . . . In fact, in your present state there's no easy way to tell you anything . . . but the thing is that Hyacinth and I have become very close." He glanced at Sarah, who smiled encouragingly. "We've become very, very close." Andrew looked significantly at Sarah. Sarah looked back blankly at Andrew. Andrew rubbed the back of his neck with his hands. "Do you understand what I'm telling you?"

Sarah didn't say anything. Nothing could be heard but the wheezing of the old fridge. She stared steadily at her husband.

She stared steadily at her husband and then, with a flash of inspiration that even Sherlock Holmes might have admired, pointed an accusing finger at him. "My God!" she exclaimed, "You're having an affair with Hyacinth!"

Andrew corrected her gravely. "I am in love with Hyacinth."

Sarah, feeling as if she'd been hit in the solar plexus, took a slug of her champagne. "Isn't that the same thing?"

"No," said Andrew. "One is a transitory experience based on sexual desire, the other is a meeting of minds as well as bodies."

Sarah stared at him for a few moments and then smiled. She felt the relief coursing through her veins. "Andrew Stagg, I almost believed you!"

"Sarah," Andrew said, "I am not joking."

Sarah looked at him in disbelief. "I don't know what's worse," she said at last. "The fact that you're having an affair or the fact that you believe all that stuff you just said."

Andrew smiled. It was a very annoying smile and it made Sarah long to hurl her champagne at him. Since the urge to drink her champagne was even greater, she said nothing and filled her mouth with bubbles instead.

"Sarah," Andrew said gently, "I expect you to be bitter. I understand you are hurt and resentful and I want you to know I think you have every right to be."

Sarah stared at him. "That's very big of you," she said.

Andrew gave a sympathetic nod that was even more annoying than his annoying smile. "I have one question for you," he said, craning his head toward her. "Do you love me?"

"Funnily enough," Sarah said, "at this precise moment, not at all."

Andrew sighed. "If you are going to be flippant," he said, "we won't get anywhere."

Sarah folded her arms. "Where do you want to get? Do you want me to say I love you? Do you want me to say our marriage is a farce, a passionless farce? Well, pardon me, but when we made love last week, you gave a pretty convincing performance for a man in a passionless farce."

Andrew raised his hands in the air and dropped them again. He had used exactly the same gesture to great effect in act 1, scene 5 of *Dear Octopus*. "You see, I talk to you of love and you respond with a smutty comment about sex. It's what I'm trying to show you. We don't speak the same language anymore."

"I agree with you there," Sarah said. "You sound like you've eaten and inwardly digested every romantic novel in the library. Is this Hyacinth's influence? Does she talk like this?"

Andrew put his elbows on the table and pressed his fingertips together. "Hyacinth and I are in love with each other. I knew you'd find that ridiculous. You've never been happy to talk about love, have you, Sarah? Don't get me wrong. You've been an excellent wife and you're a wonderful mother."

Sarah frowned. One moment he was a sugar-drenched love story and the next he was an end-of-semester report card. She swallowed her observation with more champagne and assumed an air of polite interest.

"The point is . . ." Andrew paused as if he'd temporarily lost the point and was waiting for it to show itself. "The point is . . . and I am not in any way trying to denigrate your contribution to our life together"—which meant of course he was trying to denigrate her contribution to their life together—"I don't think you ever really loved me."

The rank injustice of this comment cut through Sarah's champagne-muffled brain like a knife. This was revisionist history with a vengeance.

"Do you know something?" she exploded. "You are just like Stalin! I mean, you are not exactly like Stalin because you haven't created a man-made famine or sent people to labor camps or grown a silly mustache, but in every other way you are just like Stalin!"

Andrew stared at Sarah and then, meaningfully, at the bottle of champagne. "Sarah," he murmured pityingly, "what are you trying to say?"

"When Stalin came to power, he had Trotsky's image removed from all the photos of the Russian revolutionary leaders. He made it look as if Trotsky hadn't been there. That's what you're doing, only you've started a revolution of your own, a revolution with you and Hyacinth, and you're wiping me out. You're obliterating me from your past and I won't have it because it's not true!"

"Perhaps," said Andrew, whose sympathetic tone was sounding like a piece of plastic wrap that had been stretched too far, "I should talk to you when you're sober."

"If you talk to me when I'm sober I could give you year by year evidence to refute what you said. Be glad, be very glad I am not sober. How dare you say I haven't loved you! How can you say I haven't loved you!"

"I think," said Andrew carefully, "you thought you did and I think I thought I did too. It's only since I've met Hyacinth that I realize I didn't know what love was."

Sarah, knowing it would annoy him, poured herself another glass of champagne. "How very convenient," she said. "So what do you want to do?"

For the first time that evening, Andrew seemed to be at a loss for words.

"Well?" she demanded, daring him to make things worse. "Are you leaving me?"

Andrew hesitated. "I'm so sorry," he said, "but I think I am."

Be Ready to Accept New Challenges

Sarah and Andrew had moved into Shooter's Cottage when the boys were three. They had been looking for a village with its own school, playground, and grocery shop. Ambercross fulfilled all three requirements. Unfortunately, the only house for sale was on Finn Street, which ran straight through the village and formed part of a major artery to the South West.

The real estate agent had been almost apologetic about mentioning Shooter's Cottage. Its owner, an eighty-year-old widow, was a virtual recluse and lived in the L-shaped house with six cats. Downstairs, there was a grimy little kitchen and a dark dining room with an archway into another small room, which had been given over entirely to the animals. There was a long sitting room with an enormous fireplace.

On the day Sarah and Andrew visited, there was a dead crow in the grate.

The other rooms downstairs formed the bottom part of the L. They comprised a bathroom with the brownest bathtub Sarah had ever seen, a small bedroom in which the widow resided, and at the end was what the realtor euphemistically called the utility room. This last was crammed from head to foot with boxes, broken furniture, garden implements that looked as if they'd been there when the Romans invaded Britain, and some curtains that were home to a multiplicity of insects.

Upstairs, there were five bedrooms and a bathroom. When the realtor opened the door to the bathroom, he went very pale and after looking at his clients for confirmation, closed it again very quickly.

By this time, Andrew and the realtor were ready to go. Sarah, however, had noticed some very important advantages. The house might smell like cat litter but it was far bigger than any of the other places for sale in their price range. The garden might be a jungle but it was safe enough for her to leave the children playing there while she and Andrew were in the house. Shooter's Lane ran parallel to Finn Street but was separated from it by a cornfield. Few cars went down Shooter's Lane because it was simply a link between the two roads that ran either side of the field, and the widow's home was the only house in the lane. At the back of the house, the garden looked out onto fields and woodland as far as the eye could see.

Andrew thought Sarah was mad to even consider it but eventually gave way to her enthusiasm. When they moved in, it took Sarah three months to exorcise the smell of the cats.

After completing the Herculean task of cleaning the place, she set about decorating it.

Now, the house was almost as Sarah had originally imagined. In place of the overgrown drive and tangled bindweed, there was a sturdy white gate and a stone path with grass and rosebushes on either side. One of the upstairs rooms had been changed into a big bathroom and the three rooms of the bottom L were now one vast kitchen with a red cast-iron stove at one end and an enormous cupboard that faced the door into the back garden. Best of all, the old dining room and cat room had been transformed into Sarah's studio, with its very own wood-burning stove.

Sarah had often said to Andrew that there was nowhere she would rather live. They had planned to build a conservatory in the spring and then the place would be perfect. Here on Shooter's Lane they were in their own private little world with only cows for company.

Now, Sarah didn't even have the cows for company, since they'd been taken in for the winter. In the three days since Andrew had left, she felt as if everything she'd loved about their home had been turned inside out. The peaceful solitude had become an isolated hermitage in which Sarah would soon be the lone occupant. Perhaps she too would become a mad old recluse with smelly cats all around her.

Now, the generous space of the cottage seemed to mock her single status. Last night, she and the boys had sat in front of a roaring fire and watched a *Die Hard* video. The sitting room still smelled of pine cones. Would she even bother to light a fire when the boys went away? How would she feel, alone in this house, night after night? Even her beautiful studio had now become a source of anxiety since Andrew had somehow packed her enthusiasm and inspiration along with his clothes.

The house was no longer her refuge and she had changed too. For more than two decades, she'd lived happily in Andrew's handsome shadow, deriving her confidence from him. Andrew Stagg loved *her*, and as Andrew's beloved she was confident, outgoing, and cheerful. Her entire perception of herself had been based on their relationship. What if Andrew had stopped loving her long ago? Perhaps he found her dreary and dull. Was it just a coincidence that he left her a few months before the boys were going away? Did he panic at the idea of living out his days with only her for company? Did he look at her and wonder why he ever found her attractive? Sarah tried to imagine herself in the tight little silver number that Hyacinth had worn to the after-show party. She'd never have got it past her hips. She stared fiercely at herself in the mirror and a faded woman with nondescript hair, sagging breasts, and a waist that could be sued under the Trade Description Act stared back at her.

And yet . . . In the last few days, that "and yet" had made her feel she was conducting a game of Ping-Pong inside her head. She didn't know herself at the moment. She seemed to have the emotions of a weather vane. One moment she would be raging at the brutality with which Andrew had dispatched her, the next she would be weeping uncontrollably. She'd lost count of the number of times she'd picked up the phone. Thus far at least she had the sense to know that any attempt to speak rationally to Andrew would degenerate after a few seconds into ugly hysteria. The one constant feeling was fear: fear for the future, fear of the dark hole into which her husband had cast her.

None of this made any sense. They had always been so happy. How could Andrew want to throw away the mountain of shared experiences and memories? She knew him better than anyone else. He knew *her* better than anyone else. How could he want to go and live with a girl called Hyacinth who could never know the Andrew she knew? Surely this was just an aberration, a panic-stricken reaction to the looming cloud of middle age? She and Andrew had talked about the next stage of their lives. There would be no empty-nest depression for them, oh no. They would improve their house, they would travel, they would have fun!

The rest of the world did not know Andrew had left her. Sarah had what she knew was an irrational belief: if she told no one, perhaps Andrew would change his mind and come home before there was any need to say anything. It was always possible.

REACTIONS OF THE REST OF THE WORLD

1: *The vicar*

Sarah's paintbrush hovered over her palette. Should she, or should she not, paint the client's eyelids the color of frozen peas? On the one hand the client had covered her eyes in frozen-pea eye shadow, so presumably she thought frozen-pea eye shadow was incredibly attractive. On the other hand, the color did not look good against the mustard yellow background of the sofa on which the client was sitting and the client had insisted that the sofa should be shown in all its glory since it was the sofa on which she and her husband had created what the client described as the crowning achievement of their lives. The three-year-old crowning achievement had a nose that produced record levels of snot, the color of which was an exact match of the sofa, a fact which Sarah found pretty spooky if not aesthetically attractive.

Sarah had just decided that if the client truly felt her three-year-old son was a crowning achievement, then she would probably want her makeup to be immortalized on canvas, when, as her brush dipped into the emerald green, the doorbell rang.

It was the vicar. The Reverend Michael Everseed was an eager young crusader with a fresh-faced wife and two sweet little boys when he had taken on the parishes of Ambercross and Gassett ten years ago. His wife was now a fierce-looking mathematics teacher, his sons were devastatingly dangerous predators, the biggest threat to female virtue in Wiltshire, but the Reverend Michael had retained both his enthusiasm and his faith. He was a good-looking man whose patent goodness denuded him of any sex appeal. Two years into his residency, Sarah had stopped accompanying Andrew to church when she realized, during a particularly stirring reading of the second lesson by her husband, that she had long since stopped believing in the hereafter. The Reverend Michael had never reproached her with her defection but his presence always provoked in her a Pavlovian sense of guilt. This feeling invariably manifested itself in an effusive case of hyperactive chatter. So now, Sarah greeted him as if he were the answer to prayers she had long since stopped making.

"Vicar, how lovely to see you! Do come in and I hope you'll excuse my appearance. I must look a sight. I've done no work for a week and I'm terribly behind with everything, so I've been painting madly. I was just going to put the kettle on. You'll have a cup of tea, won't you? I'm afraid the kitchen is in a terrible mess. I was just about to start doing a clear up, but you know what it's like when you start painting, you lose track of all time. . . . Well, I suppose you don't know, but believe me it is true. Now let me move my bag and the newspaper and you can sit down. Is Andrew supposed to be reading the lesson on Sunday? Because if that's why you've come, there might be a problem. . . ."

"Sarah," the vicar interrupted her gently. "I know about Andrew."

"Oh!" said Sarah. In the last few weeks, some malevolent badgers had been unearthing stones from the bank in her lane. Two days ago, Sarah's front left car tire had been neatly punctured by them. She knew just how that tire must have felt. "How do you know?" she asked faintly.

The vicar glanced hopefully at the kettle that a frozen Sarah was holding aloft as if she were posing for a painting. "Andrew thought I should know why he could no longer be on the list of church readers," he said. "It was good of him to remember his responsibilities to the church in his time of crisis."

Outrage defrosted Sarah. She put the kettle on the stove and went over to the cupboard to get two mugs. "I wouldn't feel too sorry for Andrew," she said acidly. "If he'd remembered his responsibilities to his family, he wouldn't be having a time of crisis in the first place."

The vicar took off his donkey jacket, unwound the long scarf from round his neck, and placed them carefully on the back of a chair. He sat down at the table and cleared his throat.

"You must be feeling very angry at the moment," he said, "and you shouldn't blame yourself for such feelings."

"I don't," Sarah muttered, reaching for the tea bags. "Believe me, I don't."

"Such feelings are a healthy response to a terrible situation." The vicar spotted a faded carrot lying on the floor. He picked it up and set it on the table. "You know, Sarah, in your situation, I'd be feeling exactly the same."

"Really?" Sarah placed the biscuit tin in front of him. "Won't you have a biscuit?"

The vicar lifted the lid and took out the one remaining chocolate digestive. "Actually," he continued apologetically, trying not to look at the white powdery surface covering the chocolate, "I think I'll just have tea."

Sarah whipped away the offending tin. "I'm sorry," she said. "I cannot get my boys to put lids on properly. Don't you find this with teenagers? They never put lids back on properly, so all my biscuits go soggy and my cakes go hard but they eat them anyway. They'll eat anything. Only yesterday, James made himself cheese and banana on toast. He said it was delicious."

"I don't know," the vicar sighed. "My boys seem to be remarkably unadventurous in their choice of food. They like pizzas, burgers, and fry-ups and crisps. We show them all the articles about the dangers of fast food. Angela is a wonderful cook. She does things with a blender you simply wouldn't believe, and do they appreciate them? No, they do not. It's upsetting for Angela. She takes their indifference very personally."

Sarah nodded sympathetically. "It must be hard for her. You must tell her that even if she was the best cook in the world, they would still prefer take-out. Adolescent boys are pro-grammed to reject everything their mothers do for them!"

The vicar raised his hands in mock despair. "Teenagers! As I say to Angela, we must remember we were all teenagers once!"

"Quite," said Sarah, taking the milk from the fridge. She couldn't imagine the vicar as a teenager.

The Reverend Michael cleared his throat. "I came here, Sarah, to tell you that, despite what you're feeling, this is not the end of the world."

"Right," said Sarah, pouring the boiling water into the mugs. She wished they could continue talking about teenagers.

"In fact," the vicar said, "I have some good news for you. Firstly, we said prayers for you in church this week." He stopped and looked at Sarah, like a dog that has dropped a bone at her feet.

"Did you?" responded Sarah, recalling her visit to the village shop yesterday. She had wondered why everyone had stopped talking as soon as she'd entered.

"Secondly," the vicar leaned forward, his elbows on his knees, his hands on either side of his face. "I know you are feeling abandoned, betrayed, and deserted at a time in your life when it is not so easy to make new friends and when you are conscious that your youth has gone. But, Sarah, now is the time to realize some things are more important than a flawless complexion or a perfect body. I have often felt you have an inner beauty and spirituality. Let that blossom! Don't turn to bitterness or hate! Andrew has been weak and selfish. . . . In-deed, I told him so, but he is not wicked or inhumane. Do you understand what I'm saying?"

Sarah swallowed a mouthful of tea. It was very hot and

made her eyes water but at least it stopped the impulse to burst into tears. "Yes," she said. "I do. You're saying I'm old and ugly and alone but it doesn't matter because I'm beautiful on the inside, although since nobody in the whole world can see me there, I don't find that particularly reassuring. You're saying if I make myself think sweet thoughts about my rat of a husband I'll feel better. And all I can say is if that's your idea of good news"—Sarah stopped to blow her nose—"I'd hate to hear what your bad news is like."

The vicar laughed. "There you are, you see! Smiling through your grief! You are a strong woman, Sarah, and a good one. You will be fine."

He did not, Sarah couldn't help noticing, deny that he thought she was old and ugly. The one chink of hope was that since he was wrong in thinking she was strong and good, he might also be wrong in thinking she was old and ugly. He was certainly wrong in thinking she'd be fine.

"I'll tell you something else," he said. "You live in a caring and loving community. The entire village is behind you!"

2. Clementine Delaney

Sarah was sitting in front of three boxes of Bargain Assorted Christmas Cards. The cards were pretty vile: a mixture of robins, Christmas trees, the sort of snowmen no one could make, and the sort of holly no one could ever find. Sarah had taken out the first card twenty minutes ago. It had a picture of a large baby Jesus and a startled-looking Virgin Mary. She had sat at the table for twenty minutes, pen poised, wondering what to write. In the past she had always written, "With love from the Stagg family." What should she write now? Perhaps "With love from Sarah, Ben, and James but not Andrew because he's buggered off" or "With love from Sarah and the children and Andrew can do his own frigging cards" or "With love from Sarah and the boys and, by the way, Andrew has left us" or possibly "With love from most of the Stagg family." She had just decided on "With love from Sarah and the boys" when the phone rang. It was Clementine Delaney.

Sarah did not like Clementine and the fact that she knew her antipathy stemmed from her own failings rather than those of Clementine only served to fuel her dislike. Clementine was a handsome woman. Tall and lean, with dark blonde hair that was always swept back into a tight chignon, she reminded Sarah of a thoroughbred racing horse. This was less to do with her long nose and high forehead than with the air of effortless self-belief that radiated from her. She was, indisputably, a good woman. She did the flowers in church, she made regular forays around the village, soliciting funds for the British Legion, the N.S.P.C.C., and the local dogs' home. She called on old Mrs. Cruickshank regularly and did her shopping for her. She was one of the prime organizers of the Midsummer Village Fete and the Christmas Bazaar. She was a valuable and valued member of the village community, unlike Sarah, who could leave tomorrow without causing a ripple. Sarah knew that one of the reasons she disliked Clementine was because Clementine's well-developed sense of community only highlighted her own apathy. But there was also a faint patina of superiority in Clementine's dealings with Sarah that was all the more annoying for the fact that it was justified. It didn't help that Clementine's husband was charming, as were her children. She was also a brilliant cook. And a superb gardener. And she made her own curtains.

"Sarah," Clementine said, "it's me. I won't take a minute but I had to ring and tell you how sorry I am. . . . I simply can't believe Andrew could do such a thing. I was so upset when I heard."

Sarah could well believe that. Andrew had always flirted outrageously with Clementine, but even as Sarah recalled Clementine's heightened color after one of Andrew's more outrageous compliments, she knew she was being unfair. Clementine was genuinely appalled.

"I want you to tell me," Clementine said earnestly, "if there's anything I can do for you, anything at all."

"That's very kind," Sarah murmured, "but . . ."

"I know. It's silly. What *can* I do? What are you doing for Christmas?"

Sarah had a horrible suspicion that she was about to receive an invitation to spend Christmas with the Delaneys. She moved quickly to forestall it. "My parents are coming down," she said. "They want to see the boys before they go off on their travels."

"Of course, your sons are going backpacking, aren't they?" Clementine gave a huge sigh. "And then, oh poor Sarah, you will be utterly alone!"

"Yes," said Sarah brightly, "I suppose I will be." She wished people would stop pointing out unpleasant facts to her.

"I'm sorry to be rude about your husband," Clementine said briskly, "but I would never have believed he could be so selfish. To leave you at a time when the children are flying the nest is too cruel."

"Don't apologize," Sarah said. "You can be as rude as you like." She was beginning to warm to Clementine.

Clementine laughed awkwardly. "I think you're fantastic. I'd be a complete wreck if it were me. Now listen, Sarah, you've probably forgotten. . . . In the circumstances I know I would have . . . but we had invited you and Andrew to dinner on Saturday. I felt I must ring and say I totally understand if you don't want to come. It's only that I'm doing my shopping list and I thought I should check with you."

Sarah put a hand to her forehead. "I'm sorry. You're quite right, I had forgotten. I think I can safely say that Andrew will not be coming."

"And neither will you, I completely understand. The last thing you'd want to do is join three happy couples at a jolly dinner party. And I'm crossing you off my Boxing Day party list. At a time like this you'll want to stay quietly at home with your family."

"Oh, I don't know," murmured Sarah, who'd seen the occasion as an opportunity to escape if only briefly from parental demands. "I think I could manage—"

"No, no, I won't hear of it. Believe me, I understand. There is nothing more depressing than surrounding yourself with happy party guests when you're . . . well, when you're depressed. I'm canceling you out as I speak. There! Now I've taken up enough of your time but if you ever wish to have a sympathetic ear, I'm at the end of the phone. Good-bye, Sarah!"

The phone went dead quite suddenly. Sarah stared at the handset and put it on the table. The image of Clementine crossing out her name was rather chilling. Was she expected to go into purdah now? Should she be floating round the village like a wraith, with a bell in her hand and a placard announcing Abandoned Wife: Keep Away? The fact that Clementine had rung off so quickly suggested various interpretations: one, she was so overcome by sisterly solidarity that she couldn't trust herself to speak anymore; two, that sensitive to Sarah's grief, she had not wished to intrude on her time any longer than was necessary; three, she had rung in order to prevent a deserted woman from inflicting her gloomy presence on Clementine's house and frightening the other women with visions of a fate worse than death. The fact that Clementine had rung off as soon as she'd guaranteed Sarah's absence seemed to indicate that the third alternative was the correct one. It was almost enough to make Sarah decide to turn up to the sodding parties. Almost.

3: *Jennifer Upton-Sadler*

Every morning since the beginning of September, Sarah had risen at six in order to give her sons a good breakfast before they went to work. Ben drove his brother in the creaking antique on which he had blown the accumulated savings of two years of holiday jobs. He dropped James at the chicken factory where James spent his day dismantling legs and bones, an activity which within the first forty minutes had transformed him from a cheerful carnivore into a committed vegetarian. Ben then drove on to Bath, where he had a job as a waiter, for which he had had to sacrifice what his girlfriend called the sexiest stubble in Wiltshire.

Since Andrew's departure, the boys had treated Sarah as if she were afflicted with a terminal illness. They had told Sarah they were quite happy to get their own breakfasts but, as Sarah assured them, at a time like this, she found routine reassuring. The facts that James always left half a piece of toast on his plate and Ben always spilled milk on the table were comforting in their predictability. So now on this morning, ten days before Christmas, Sarah smiled as she heard Ben's car give its habitual groan before tottering up the lane. She looked at the table with its usual early morning residue and felt momentarily over-whelmed with love for her handsome sons. Then she remem-bered that she must finish the yellow sofa painting today. It was destined to be a Christmas present for the client's husband and Sarah had promised to deliver it before the end of the week.

She was just wondering whether to make herself a coffee before starting work when she heard the front door open and a voice call out, "Sarah?" adding quite unnecessarily, "It's me!"

Jennifer Upton-Sadler had a low throaty voice that sounded as if it were perpetually on the edge of a cough. She and her hus-band, George, lived in the most beautiful house in the village, an eighteenth-century mansion opposite the church. Their garden, a pastoral idyll with its graceful weeping willows, great glassy pond, and rolling lawns, was a mecca for local horticulturalists.

Some friendships, like some love affairs, are inexplicable. Sarah and Jennifer had little in common apart from the fact that they both lived in Ambercross. Yet they had liked each other from the moment they'd met in the village shop five years earlier, despite the fact that Jennifer's Jaeger skirt and cashmere twinset seemed utterly incompatible with Sarah's denim trousers and Greenpeace sweatshirt. Jennifer's girls boarded at Bedales; Sarah's boys, until a few months ago, coasted at the public school. Jennifer's idea of a perfect Sunday was church in the morning followed by a point-to-point horse race in the afternoon. Sarah's was a couple of hours with the Sunday papers and an old film on the television after lunch. Yet Sarah never failed to feel uplifted by Jennifer's company.

Now Jennifer thrust a huge bunch of lilies into Sarah's arms and said, "These are for you. I haven't been here before because I've had my suicidal sister staying with me. She keeps going on about the pointlessness of life, and I say 'Why does everything have to have a point? Can't you enjoy yourself without having to have a point?' But of course she can't and it's all so exhausting and after a while I find she's got me starting to worry about points, so I thought I mustn't come near you until my sister's gone and I can start being myself again. And now I'm taking the girls to see Mummy for a couple of days before George's parents arrive for Christmas, so it's all too frantic, but I bought these for you last night. I have to tell you, Sarah, I always thought Andrew was a bit of a slacker, though if you get back together again I shall deny I ever said that."

Sarah breathed in the opulent perfume of the lilies. "These are beautiful," she said. "Why do you think Andrew's a slacker?"

"I don't know." Jennifer screwed up her face. "I suppose it's because he's so very good-looking. Men as good-looking as Andrew are always spoiled and it doesn't help that the Ambercross Players have always treated him as if he were a second Rudolph Valentino. And for a man of his age to go off with a woman of Hyacinth's age is unoriginal yet somehow not surprising. Do you know what I mean?"

"I'm beginning to," said Sarah. "Can you stay for coffee?"

"I'd love to but I must get back and wake the girls. It takes them two hours to make themselves presentable and I promised Mummy we'd be with her by lunch. I'll ring you when we come back. Are you going to the Delaneys' Christmas do?"

"Apparently not. Clementine says I would find it depressing."

"Really? How extraordinary! Though actually I do find Clementine terribly depressing. I must go." Jennifer shifted her shoulder bag. "Now promise me you won't go thinking this is all somehow your fault. I know you. You've been a perfect wife for Andrew. George has always maintained you're far too good for him."

"George," Sarah said warmly, "is a very sweet man."

"Well, he's very fond of you. He says Andrew must have a screw loose to let you go. I must say, I agree. I'm sure he'll see that for himself eventually. In the meantime, keep your spirits up: it's such a pity you don't ride. There's nothing like a horse between your legs to make you feel good. Never mind. Just keep reminding yourself of all the good things."

"Are there any?"

"Of course there are. You know how you always hated going to Andrew's business functions, being charming to loads of creepy people? No more! You can paint till you drop, you can eat when you like, you don't have to drop everything for Andrew, you've got the whole bed to yourself, and I bet Andrew was the sort who took all the bedclothes. And you can try being selfish for a change. I promise you, it's very seductive. My cousin, Ariadne, says she's never been happier since Rupert left her."

"Is that the cousin who's an alcoholic?"

"Well, yes she is," Jennifer conceded, "but she's a very happy alcoholic. Darling, I must go. Now remember, be positive. Enjoy your freedom!"

Sarah watched Jennifer drive off. I am very lucky, she told herself, I have the whole bed to myself. Caught between sleep and consciousness that morning, she had reached out instinctively for the husband who was no longer there. Most mornings, she would wake to find Andrew's hand roaming idly over her body. Sometimes, she fell asleep again: more often, she would respond and he would turn to her with a grin and she would smile and open her legs. She loved those lazy, almost inadvertent couplings. Remembering them now, she felt her throat constrict. She blinked back the ever-lurking tears, swallowed hard, and went back inside.

4: *The Ambercross Players*

"Sarah? It's Audrey Masterton. Be a dear and ring me back. It is important. I'll be waiting."

Peremptory, autocratic, infuriating, and impossible to disobey. Sarah switched off the answering machine and sighed. She had taken the yellow sofa painting to the client, endured an embarrassing argument with the client, who had tried to win a thirty-pound discount from Sarah on the dubious grounds that she had given Sarah's name to at least three friends who had vowed to use her. Then, on the way home, she had become snarled up in a lengthy traffic jam and when she had finally got back she discovered she'd left her scarf at the client's house. Sarah wanted a cup of tea before she did anything else but she knew she would not relax if she didn't first get the Audrey Masterton phone call out of the way. It was pathetic that at the age of forty-three she regarded Audrey with the same terrified deference she had once given to her first headmistress, Miss Turner. Sarah picked up the phone. "Audrey?" she asked with well-simulated enthusiasm, "It's Sarah Stagg. I've just got in and found your message. How can I help?"

"A great deal, I hope." There was a pause after which, sounding uncharacteristically hesitant, Audrey said, "I am so sorry about Andrew and Hyacinth. We could see what was going on, of course, and I did try to warn Andrew that if he and Hyacinth did not pull themselves together I would find it difficult to direct them in the next production. I am only sad that he found it impossible to heed my advice."

"So am I," said Sarah, "but thank you. Anyway . . ."

"Anyway, the point is," said Audrey, instantly recovering her equilibrium, "we are facing disaster. Our next production is going to be *Rebecca*. As a matter of fact it was Andrew's idea. He had always wanted to play the part of Maxim de Winter and I must say, he would have been perfect. And Hyacinth would have been the ideal young Mrs. de Winter. In fact I . . . Never mind." Audrey paused to sigh audibly. "It is no good to dwell on what might have been. I have agreed with both of them that it would be appropriate if they have a temporary break from the spotlight. Our problem is that all the programs for *Dear Octopus* had news about *Rebecca* and they have generated great enthusiasm. We can't possibly back out but we have no Andrew, no Hyacinth, and as of yesterday no Harriet Evans, since for some inexplicable reason that she did not choose to share with me, she has defected to the Frome Operatic Society. I am ringing everyone, Sarah, to say that the Ambercross Players is in a state of crisis and that it is up to the villagers of Ambercross to pull together and help their oldest society in its hour of need. Auditions are on January seventh and I hope I can count on you to attend."

Sarah sat down on her bed and threw off her shoes. "Well, of course I'd be very happy to design the posters and programs just like I always do. But I don't need to come to the auditions for that."

"I'm sorry, Sarah, but that won't be sufficient. I fully understand that it is not your fault that your husband has let us down but I do think in the circumstances you should at least attend our first meeting. Remember: it's January seventh. Write it down. I look forward to seeing you. Have a happy Christmas!"

The phone went dead, leaving Sarah unable to tell Audrey that there was no way she would attend auditions for a play that had been chosen in order to show off the talents of her husband and her husband's girlfriend. Of course, Sarah would never have dared to say any such thing but she could have thought up some convincing excuse, like "I'd love to come to the audition but unfortunately I'll be in the Outer Hebrides." At least now she could just write the excuse at the bottom of her Christmas card and Audrey would be unable to talk her out of it: "Happy Christmas, and by the way, I shall sadly have to miss the audition as I shall be visiting my therapist." That was more convincing than the Outer Hebrides.

Feeling she had successfully worked her way out of a fate worse than death, Sarah celebrated by opening a new packet of chocolate digestives.

5: Sarah's best friend

The first person Sarah rang after Andrew left home was Miriam. In the first term of her first school, Sarah had been fascinated by the truncated lavatory doors from which could be viewed the small feet of the occupants. While kneeling down to shout "Peek-a-poo!" at a classmate, she had been hauled off by a self-righteous prefect, one Monica Bennett, who had delivered Sarah, like a sacrificial lamb, into the hallowed portals of Miss Turner's office. Miss Turner had asked Sarah if she did such things at home. Sarah replied that she did not, since the lavatory doors there reached down to the floor. Miss Turner told her she was a disgusting little child who did not deserve to belong to an institution like Fairlawn School for Girls. Afterward, the classmate found Sarah crying and marched into Miss Turner's office and told her that she had been playing peek-a-poo with Sarah only moments earlier so she must be a disgusting little child too. Sarah had loved Miriam ever since.

Miriam was the first person to hear about Sarah's first kiss and Sarah's first period. After Sarah lost her virginity and decided she did not like sex, she told Miriam. When Sarah discovered she did like sex, she told Miriam. When Sarah lost her heart to the godlike but sadly uninterested Barney Melton at art school, she told Miriam. When Sarah fell in love with Andrew, she told Miriam. Their lives had followed very different patterns after Sarah's marriage. Sarah's life revolved around first Andrew and then around Andrew and her baby boys. Miriam traveled the globe, teaching English to students whenever she ran out of funds. Along the way she met

Johnny, bronzed and blond, with a smile that could have melted the heart of even Miss Turner. They settled in London and Miriam became an extraordinarily effective English teacher, all the more extraordinary since she found most children dull and depressing. When Johnny ran off with an equally bronzed and blond young man called Malcom, Miriam continued to teach. Ten years ago she had married Clive, a large man with a wandering eye, whom Miriam kept neatly tethered by the simple expedient of appearing at strategic intervals to consider straying herself. Sarah knew that if anyone could help to pull her from her slough of humiliation and misery, it was Miriam.

Miriam did not disappoint. When Sarah relayed her news, she said simply, "I break up on December twentieth. I'll come down for the night."

She arrived in time to bid a fond farewell to Ben and James, who were off for the evening. They embraced her warmly and warned her not to lead their mother astray.

"Nonsense," said Miriam, "why else do you think I've come?" And she insisted they be back by midnight to join the party. Sarah came out, took one look at Miriam, and burst into tears. Ben and James exchanged panic-stricken glances and with one accord leapt into Ben's car and disappeared up the lane. Miriam gave Sarah a hug.

"I'm sorry," Sarah breathed, "I promise I don't do this very often any more." She took Miriam's hands. "You look fantastic. I love the pinstripe trousers."

"One of the pleasures of not having children," Miriam said. "I can indulge my passion for clothes. And wine." She opened the trunk of her car. "I can't wait to open a bottle. The M25 was worse than ever. The thought of the Lirac in the trunk was the only thing that kept me sane."

Half an hour and two glasses of Lirac later, Sarah stood stirring the spinach and Gorgonzola sauce while Miriam grated the Parmesan.

"I must say," said Miriam, "I never thought you two would split up. You had so much in common."

Sarah nodded vigorously. "I know."

"I mean," Miriam continued, shaking the last of the Parmesan from the grater, "you loved Andrew. Andrew loved Andrew. It was a match of perfect understanding."

Sarah was shocked. "Are you saying you never liked Andrew?"

"Of course I liked Andrew. I like lots of conceited men. There's something rather sweet and trusting about them. He's made a big mistake, though, exchanging you for a younger model. No woman under thirty is going to put up with a relationship where she's expected to be the exclusive housekeeper, secretary, cook, and general factotum. I foresee some interesting discussions in the love nest. Delicious smells! What's in the sauce?"

"Spinach, Gorgonzola, a bit of milk and butter. All I have to do is cook the spaghetti."

"Wow! Now I *know* he was mad to leave you. Do you really want him back?"

Sarah nodded. "Yes."

Miriam stood up and took the wine over to Sarah. "It's not the end of the world, you know. When Johnny went off with Malcom I thought I'd die. I didn't want to see anyone, I couldn't eat, I even lost interest in *Friends*. And then I realized

I was getting hungry and bored, and one day I realized I didn't miss him so much and then another day I realized some bloke was chatting me up and I rather liked it. Life goes on."

Sarah poured the spaghetti into a large pot of boiling water. "When Johnny left you, you were a gorgeous woman of thirty-two with a tummy as flat as an iron. It's been twenty years since I slept with anyone but Andrew. My body has never been the same since I had the twins. I have bumps on my legs. I have a tummy that looks and feels like a balloon that's burst, my breasts have stretch marks . . . I am seriously damaged goods. I could never take my clothes off for another man even if another man was shortsighted enough to ask me. I am fat and forty-three. Who am I going to meet at forty-three?"

"You can meet people any time! My great-aunt married for the first time at eighty-two! You're an attractive woman. You have a lovely smile. . . ."

"I don't feel like smiling at the moment," Sarah interjected glumly.

"Then find things to make you smile. Don't watch any serious dramas on television. Keep to a strict diet of *Friends* and *Frazier* repeats. And don't read any Thomas Hardy novels. . . ."

"I haven't read a Thomas Hardy novel since I was fifteen."

"Good. Stick to authors like P. G. Wodehouse. He'll make you laugh." Miriam glanced abruptly at Sarah. "What was I talking about?"

Sarah's mouth twitched. "You were telling me how attractive I was."

"Exactly! You have beautiful, sparkling, hazel eyes. You are not fat, you are pleasantly rounded. You've got nice hair, good skin, and a great smile. So if you are saying you'd take him back because you couldn't find anyone else, then think again. Being alone isn't so bad. Sometimes," Miriam sighed a little wistfully, pouring the last of the wine into her glass, "I think it is rather good."

Sarah, noting with surprised pleasure that her own glass had been refilled, took a large gulp. "I don't want Andrew back because I can't face life on my own, though I have to say that at this moment I don't think I can face life on my own. I want Andrew back because I can't make sense of my life without Andrew. I have spent my entire adult life with Andrew. And now he's gone, and he's taken my past with him. My past has been kidnapped. All the relationships we've made together are all different and difficult. His family, our friends . . . everyone's different, no one knows what to say. I don't feel grounded anymore, do you know what I mean? And I can't believe, I really can't believe, we are not going to spend the rest of our lives together. Am I being stupid? What do you think?"

"I think," said Miriam thoughtfully, "I need to open another bottle of wine."

An hour and another bottle of wine later, Sarah sat at the table peeling a satsuma. "It's a very funny thing," she mused, "but I never liked hyacinths. Don't you think that's funny? I mean, I like daffodils, I like lilies of the valley, I like irises, I like lupins, but I never liked hyacinths."

Miriam frowned. "Why don't you like hyacinths?"

"Because," Sarah said slowly, "they have funny, false colors. They are perfectly pink, gorgeously green, resoundingly red. And they don't bend or flow like other flowers, they just stand straight in their bowls, like Hyacinth Harrington."

"Hyacinth Harrington doesn't stand in a bowl."

"No, but she doesn't bend or flow either. She just is. You know what I mean? I hate Hyacinth Harrington."

"Well, personally," said Miriam, "I can't take any man seriously who wants to go off with a woman called Hyacinth. Do you really want Andrew back?"

"I really, really do. I want him to grovel and be miserable and be sorry he was born but I want him back. The vicar's told me to nurture my inner beauty, Clementine Delaney thinks I should become a hermit, Jennifer Upton-Sadler told me to embrace my solitude, and Audrey Masterton wants me to join the Ambercross Players. I wish someone would tell Andrew what he ought to do."

Miriam stiffened. "Who wants you to join the Ambercross Players?"

"Audrey Masterton. She *is* the Ambercross Players. She's over eighty and strong as an ox. I get the feeling she holds me directly responsible for losing her star players. Apparently, Andrew and Hyacinth feel it would be tactful to bow out of the next production even though the next production is *Rebecca* and Andrew and Audrey think Andrew would have been the perfect Maxim in it. I think Audrey thinks I owe it to her to join. Perhaps I could be Mrs. Danvers? I could definitely act the part of a sinister, embittered woman who can't bear the hero's new wife. Anyway"—Sarah pushed back her chair and stretched her arms—"there's no way I'm going to go."

"But you must!" exclaimed Miriam. "If you are certain you want Andrew back, then you must listen to me. If you want Andrew back you have to show him you don't need him. Men find women who can't do without them very unattractive. So, one, you show him you're having a brilliant time without him. Go to lots of parties!"

"No one wants to invite me to any parties. Apparently abandoned wives don't make good party guests."

"Only in the eyes of an insecure hostess. Never mind. You can pretend you're going to parties. Two, you join the Ambercross Players. Take the Mrs. Danvers part, make it your own! Andrew will be furious, of course. You will show him you've moved on, you've become someone he no longer knows. He will be furious, frustrated, intrigued. From being sad old Sarah, you will be stupendous Sarah! You have to join. You must join."

Sarah smiled. "You're not serious!"

"Never more so. From now on, you tell everyone, including your sons, that you're fine. And get a haircut. . . ."

"What's wrong with my hair?"

"You've had the same style for thirty years. It looked great on Shirley Temple but she was a five-year-old actress. It needs shortening and shaping and you might even consider highlights. And wear makeup and perfume and join the Ambercross Players. I have not stayed married to a serial womanizer for eight years without learning how to keep a man interested."

Sarah bit her lip. "Do you honestly think I can get Andrew back?"

"If you do what I say. Do you promise you'll join the Ambercross Players?"

"Supposing they gave me a part? I have a lousy memory. You know I have a lousy memory. . . ."

"Then this will be a very good discipline for you. Now promise me you will join."

"All right, I promise." Sarah reached for the wine. "And now I want to hear *your* news. How are you getting on with your new headmaster? Is he still being horrid to everyone?"

Miriam's eyes sparkled. "You wouldn't believe the plotting that's been going on this term!"

"Tell me," Sarah said. She settled back in her chair and was soon absorbed in the heady tales of Machiavellian strife in the staff room.

6: *Andrew's sister-in-law*

Every year, Andrew's brother, Jeremy, and his wife, Rachel, included a photocopied résumé of their lives in their Christmas card and every year it made Sarah wish she had the nerve to make up her own newsletter: "You'll be happy to know Ben's off the heroin now and James came out of prison last month. . . ."

This year, Sarah felt the need for a very black coffee before she opened the holly-bedecked sheet of paper. As usual, it began with a cheerful salutation.

> *Hello, you guys!*
>   *We hope you are having a joyful time celebrating the birth of Christ. It's so easy to forget the "reason for the season," what with all the commercialism these days. We try to remind Tamzin and Edward of the real reason for Christmas and why we celebrate it. What with school bazaars and a Bring and Buy Sale, the children and I are very busy making and baking. Edward and a friend decided they wanted to do a Bring and Buy Sale for this year's school charity appeal, which is to help people with leprosy. So*

their headmaster has given them permission to have it in the school and we've made some Christmas decorations and cakes to sell. It's nice to see that there are still some eight-year-olds who want to do something to help others. The children are just great to have around at the moment, growing in size, confidence, and charm. Tamzin won the school prize for most helpful girl in the school. She has also discovered a gift for netball and her games teacher says she has never seen a ten-year-old with such strong arms. Edward won the first prize in the summer fete's handicraft competition for his potato man. We were delighted! Jeremy's business is going from strength to strength. He has only had to let three people go this year and is thrilled to find out that the rest of his team are now determined to work as hard as he does. On a less positive note, we have been saddened by the news that Jeremy's brother, Andrew, and his wife, Sarah, have separated. We pray they will find it in their hearts to resolve their difficulties and discover the delights of mutual, unselfish love. Jeremy and I have always been aware of the dangers of taking love for granted and we regularly renew our vows in the privacy of our bedchamber. The garden is looking good: we had a good crop of spinach, onions, and mange-tout this year. The beans and carrots didn't do too well. Over the winter we plan to plant a new front border with some conifers and herbaceous plants. Jeremy is planning to lay a sycamore hedge along the front garden. It promises to be hard work but will hopefully be worth it!

Festive greetings to you all,
Jeremy, Rachel, Edward, and Tamzin

Select New Challenges with Care

Miriam had done her work well. On January 2, she rang Sarah and delivered a lecture on the Unattractiveness of Being a Victim. She had answers to all of Sarah's remonstrations. No, attending an audition would not be humiliating, attending an audition would show she was unbowed by Andrew's craven desertion. No, attending an audition would not make her the subject of ridicule because, she, Miriam, knew that Sarah could act very well, having witnessed her sensitive portrayal of the innkeeper in the Fairlawn nativity play thirty-five years ago. No, the thespians would not compare her appearance unfavorably with that of Hyacinth bloody Harrington because Hyacinth bloody Harrington was obviously a typical blonde bimbo, whereas Sarah had real style and by the way had she had her hair cut yet? On January 3, Miriam rang Ben and James and told them to make sure that their mother went to the audition, that it was incumbent on them to ensure that Sarah recovered her self-confidence before they went off on their travels, and that the audition was the first step toward that recovery. On January 6, Miriam rang to say she would wash her hands of Sarah if she did not go to the audition. On January 7, Sarah went to the audition.

The Ambercross Players always met in the room above the Fox and Hounds. Sarah, together with her new haircut, walked into the pub, bought half a pint of cider, and took a remedial gulp. She felt horribly self-conscious. Her hairdresser, an arresting beauty with pink hair, had cropped her locks until they only just covered her ears and had completed the transformation by giving her bangs, ruthlessly overriding her client's hesitantly expressed doubts.

Sarah hardly recognized herself. Also in line with Miriam's strictures, she had visited the sales and purchased a pair of navy blue jeans. She was wearing them now. They were smart and well-cut and obviously new. She wished she had more time to adjust to her new persona before confronting her husband's fellow actors. She climbed the stairs with a sinking heart. There was a momentary silence before everyone greeted her with a great display of spontaneous enthusiasm. Audrey's voice rose effortlessly above them all. "Sarah! Come on in!" She clapped her hands and cleared her throat. "I know all of you will be pleased to welcome Sarah into our little band. I asked her to come because in this time of crisis we need anyone we can get."

Sarah smiled vaguely. She was 75 percent certain that Audrey did not mean to be as rude as her words sounded.

Howard Smart, an old friend of Andrew, said, "Sarah, how very brave of you to come." Margaret Simmons, an elderly lady with improbably auburn curls whose unfortunate tendency to spit when emoting on stage had always rendered her an object of fascination to Sarah's sons, bounded up to Sarah and cried, "Lovely to see you! Did you have a good Christmas?"

"Christmas?" Sarah repeated, and a kaleidoscope of recent memories cartwheeled round her mind: her mother sighing wistfully at least twice a day, "It's not the same without Andrew"; her father prefacing most of his remarks to his grandsons with, "I'm sorry to speak ill of your father but . . ."; the boys reacting with guilty relief when Sarah told them they could escape whenever they wanted; Sarah and her parents watching *The Longest Day, A Bridge Too Far,* and *The Great Escape;* Sarah realizing that she would never again look forward to Christmas.

"Christmas," Sarah said, "was fine."

Margaret's well-powdered face could not conceal a sudden crimson flush. "Oh dear, how silly of me! Of course it must have been difficult. Oh dear, I'm so sorry."

She and Sarah were rescued from mutual embarrassment by the authoritative tones of Audrey. "All right, now, let's sit down, we don't want to waste time! The production will be taking place at the end of April, just after Easter, and while you may think that's a long way off, believe me, it isn't. Rehearsals won't begin until February and there will be no rehearsals during half-term as I have promised to look after my great-grandchildren in Milton Keynes. Add to that the Easter break and you can see what I mean. So please, sit down now!"

The chairs were arranged in a semicircle around their leader's seat. Sarah sat down at one end and tried not to notice that everyone else had gravitated to the other side. Audrey passed round copies of the play, arranged herself on her chair like a mother hen settling on her eggs, and pulled out a notebook and pencil from her capacious jacket pocket. "Now," she began happily, "I think the best way of—"

She was interrupted by the arrival of Martin Chamberlain, waving a glass of beer in one hand and his glasses case in the other. "Happy New Year, everyone! Sorry I'm late, Audrey." He caught sight of Sarah and said with gratifying enthusiasm, "Sarah! How nice to see you. Can I sit next to you?"

Sarah only had time to smile graciously before Audrey said testily, "Sit down quickly, Martin, I want to be finished by nine if I can. Now I assume that everyone here knows the story of *Rebecca,* so I don't need to go over it other than to say that Maxim de Winter, our hero, is a tortured, sexually magnetic male, unable to express his feelings to his sweet young wife. He brings her to his ancestral home in Cornwall, which is dominated by the embittered housekeeper, Mrs. Danvers, who runs the place as a shrine to Maxim's first wife, Rebecca, who is of course"—Audrey paused for dramatic effect—"dead." She took a deep breath, puffed out her bosom, and continued. "Encouraged by the evil Mrs. Danvers, our child wife becomes convinced that Maxim still loves his dead wife and only discovers in a powerful scene, bristling with sexual chemistry, that he did in fact hate Rebecca. It all ends happily with Mrs. Danvers dying and the house burning down. So we will start with a scene between Mrs. Danvers and young Mrs. de Winter. Any takers for the latter?"

Claire Battersby put up a hand. "I'll have a go."

Claire Battersby had been with the Players for five years. A tall young woman, she was blessed with a beautiful voice and a flawless complexion. She was also fat, a fact of which she seemed oblivious to judge by the clothes she wore, since they invariably revealed every generous roll of flesh.

"Thank you, Claire." Audrey put on her glasses. "Anyone for Mrs. Danvers?"

Sarah took a deep breath and raised her arm. She had already worked out how she could embody the role. By dint of imagining Hyacinth as the young bride, she could, she felt certain, bring out the requisite hatred, bitterness, and frustration needed for the part. It would, she thought, be very good therapy. For the next few minutes, Sarah threw herself into the character. She loved being Mrs. Danvers; indeed, she felt she really *was* Mrs. Danvers.

There was, she felt, an appreciative silence when the scene finished. Audrey took off her glasses. "Thank you both," she said. "Beautifully read, Claire, and a very interesting interpretation from you, Sarah. Moving on . . ."

Sarah saw Howard exchange a smirk with Claire and knew instantly that Audrey's use of the word "interesting" had been kind rather than complimentary. She could feel her face flush crimson. It was crazy to think she could encroach on Andrew's territory like this. She must have been mad or subconsciously masochistic. She would never speak to Miriam again. Why did she always let Miriam bully her into doing stupid things, and why hadn't her boys pointed out to her how foolish she was being? She would never speak to them again either.

Sarah did not raise a hand again. She sat mute, barely listening, planning a rapid retreat and a subsequent hysterical phone call to Miriam. She visibly jumped when Audrey called out her name. "Page twenty-seven, Sarah, you can read Mrs. de Winter. Howard, you try Maxim."

Once again, a fleeting grimace crossed Howard's face and Sarah felt her stomach muscles shrink. She bit her lip, stared at the script, and stammered her way through the next few pages. Finally, oh blessed relief, Audrey said "Thank you" and shut her eyes for a few moments as if communing with the dead. "Well!" she said, "I have no wish to keep you in suspense. Martin, you will be my Maxim."

Beside her, Martin reacted like someone who'd been given an electric shock. "Look here, Audrey, I'm not a Maxim sort of person. I thought I could be Frank. Frank, I can do. Maxim's supposed to be romantic and brooding. I don't think I can do brooding and I certainly can't do romantic."

"Nonsense, Martin, you'll be marvelous. And besides, there isn't anyone else who can do it. Howard is perfect as Jack Favell and Adrian and Malcom are too old. Sarah, you will be Mrs. de Winter, our sweet young bride. Claire, I want you to be Mrs. Danvers. . . ."

"Excuse me, Audrey," Sarah said, "did I hear you say I would be Mrs. de Winter?"

"You did," Audrey said, smiling. "You will be our heroine."

"But I don't want to be!" Sarah was aghast. "I can't! Audrey, your heroine is supposed to be a child bride. I'm forty-three years old. In September I'll be forty-four years old."

"Yes, dear, but you don't look it as long as we keep the lights off you, and you captured the heroine's hesitancy and timidity perfectly and you're so small you'll make Martin look tall. Now, as to the other characters . . ."

Sarah gulped desperately. "Martin doesn't need me to make him look tall."

"Hear, hear!" said Martin. "I'm five foot ten."

"Precisely," Audrey said. "Sarah will make you look tall. Now, if I may proceed . . ."

Sarah and Martin exchanged despairing glances. "Don't worry," Martin muttered grimly, "I'll talk to Audrey."

Sarah couldn't help feeling that talking to Audrey would be like trying to cross the M25 in rush hour. She returned to her seat and studied the floor while Audrey allotted the remaining roles. When Audrey at last announced the end of the meeting, Sarah accepted the congratulations from the rest of the company with a face as red as a beetroot. She could see Martin approach Audrey and as soon as the others had gone she joined him.

"But seriously," he was saying, "I really don't think I could do it. I mean I've never done a big part before and I don't look anything like Laurence Olivier."

"And I certainly don't look like Joan Fontaine," Sarah added.

Audrey put her notebook and pen into her bag and hoisted it onto her shoulder. "That was the film," she said. "We're doing the play. You'll be fine, Martin. Think arrogant. Think aristocratic. Think mysterious! And, Sarah, I want you to think innocence, think youth, think adoration! And perhaps you should think about getting a haircut." She put on her glasses and smiled. "I must dash. See you in a few weeks. You must learn your lines straightaway."

"But, Audrey," Martin beseeched, "I really think . . ."

"Let me do the thinking," Audrey boomed. "I am the director, after all. See you both at the next rehearsal. Learn those words!" She proceeded down the stairs like the *Titanic* sailing blithely toward its iceberg.

Martin and Sarah stared at each other in dismay. "Think youth," said Sarah glumly.

"Think aristocratic," responded Martin. "I mean, look at me. Do I look aristocratic?"

Sarah looked. Martin had a broken nose and the sort of hair that looked as if it would kill a comb on sight. "Well," she retorted, "do I look like youth?"

"You look more like youth than I look aristocratic. This is terrible."

"This is catastrophic," corrected Sarah. "I can't possibly do it."

"Neither can I."

"At least you wouldn't be a laughingstock. I mean Maxim is meant to be quite old, isn't he?"

"He's also the hero and I don't look like a hero. Andrew should be playing him. . . . Oh, Lord, I'm sorry, Sarah, that was incredibly crass."

"Don't worry." Sarah stretched her arms in front of her. "You're quite right. Andrew should be Maxim and Hyacinth should be Mrs. de Winter. I could kill Andrew. It's all his fault I'm here."

"You mean," Martin asked doubtfully, "he wanted you to come tonight?"

"No. My stupid friend thought I might win him back by becoming a star of the Ambercross Players. I know. I don't understand the logic either. I don't know why I listened to her."

"I see." Martin's momentary silence seemed to imply agreement. He picked up his empty glass. "I'll tell you what," he said, "let's go down and have a drink. I'm dying of thirst and perhaps we can make a plan."

They sat downstairs in a corner of the pub, sipping their drinks and failing to think of a plan. Sarah gave a deep sigh. "I don't see how you can get out of it. You'll be fine and Audrey is right: there is no one else except Howard and Howard was born to play the part of Jack Favell. Jack is the ultimate rotter. It's perfect type-casting. As for me"—she shook her head—"there is no getting away from the fact that I'm twenty years too old."

"Perhaps," said Martin hopefully, "most people nowadays don't know the story. Perhaps they'll think you're meant to be, well, not that young."

"My being young is mentioned in virtually every page! I can't do it. Claire read it far better than I did and at least she doesn't look as if she's ready for her bus pass."

Martin put down his drink. "Can you imagine me having romantic scenes with Claire? I'd look like an undersized dwarf! You couldn't do that to me."

"Actually," said Sarah apologetically, "I could. In fact, come to think of it, it's the only answer, because nothing in the world will make me do that part."

Martin shook his head. "I always thought you were a kind woman."

"Being a kind woman hasn't got me very far. In this world," Sarah said portentously, "it's dog eat dog."

"Look here," said Martin, taking a pen from his pocket and scribbling something down on the beer mat, "this is my number. Think about it overnight and ring me tomorrow if you change your mind."

Sarah put the beer mat in her cardigan pocket. "I won't change my mind."

"If you won't do the part, then Claire will have to do it and I'm not going to be hero to Claire's heroine. If you won't do it, then neither will I."

"Well, don't tell Audrey that or else she'll blame me for sabotaging her production."

"I'm afraid," said Martin primly, "I can't promise anything. In this world, it's dog eat dog."

Sarah was in bed, reading her favorite Georgette Heyer when the telephone rang.

"Sarah," said a familiar voice, "how are you?"

Sarah glanced at her alarm clock. "Andrew? What's wrong?" The flicker of hope, always too easily ignited, made her heart race.

"Nothing's wrong. I just rang for a chat."

"It's eleven o'clock!"

"That's all right, I'm not tired. I gather you went to the audition tonight."

Sarah sank back against her pillows. "News travels fast."

"Howard rang. He thought I ought to know that Audrey bullied you into taking the main part. She's completely out of order."

"It was rather a shock."

"I can imagine. To expect someone like you to take on a part like that! It's grossly unfair. Would you like me to give her a ring tomorrow and tell her you can't do it?"

"That's very kind of you."

"It's the least I can do. The thought of you making a spectacle of yourself on stage with everyone sniggering behind your back . . . No, it's not fair. There's no need for Audrey to make all these panic decisions. And to give poor old Martin the part of Maxim! If Audrey postpones it till the autumn, Hyacinth and I can do it. Her evening course finishes in June. Don't worry, I'll handle Audrey. The trouble with you is you can never say no to people."

Sarah sat up straight. "I thought you and Hyacinth were keeping away from dramatics until all the gossip had died down."

"Well, of course that was a factor. But I assumed Audrey would do a different play. It was obvious she couldn't cast it without us. She only chose the play because she knew I'd be the perfect Maxim. And to take you on! You've never even acted before."

"Actually," said Sarah, "I had a starring role in the school play once."

"Sarah, I know you. You'll be terrified. You'll be a disaster. And anyway, you're far too old. I can't bear to think of it. I'll ring Audrey in the morning."

"Thank you," Sarah said coldly, "but if anyone's going to ring Audrey, it will be me. This has nothing to do with you and I'd be very grateful if you'd keep out of it. Now if you'll excuse me, I'm very tired and want to go to sleep. Good-bye."

Sarah slammed down the phone and picked up her Georgette Heyer. She could imagine Andrew and Hyacinth sitting in bed. Andrew would be raging at the idea that his wife and Martin could take on the roles that he and Hyacinth were born to play. Hyacinth would be lying seductively against the pillows in some vile silk nightie. "Don't worry, darling," she would croon, "even Sarah wouldn't be silly enough to think she could play Mrs. de Winter."

Sarah put down her Georgette Heyer, reached across to the end of her bed, and pulled the beer mat from her cardigan pocket. Then she picked up the phone and rang Martin. She heard a sleepy voice say "Hello?"

"Oh, Martin, I'm sorry!" Sarah was instantly contrite. "I've woken you up!"

"Not at all." Martin yawned. "The thought of playing opposite Claire was keeping me wide awake."

"You don't sound wide awake. I just wanted to tell you. I'm going to do it."

There was a pause. "Do what?"

"Be your wife. I don't care if I'm a laughingstock."

"You won't be a laughingstock."

"I have it on excellent authority I will be and I don't care. Nothing in the world will make me turn the part down."

"Jolly good." Martin yawned again. "Is that all?"

"I just wanted you to know."

"Jolly good. That's wonderful. Good night, Sarah."

"Good night, Martin." Sarah put down the phone, picked up her Georgette Heyer, and read to the end of her chapter.

Think Twice before Acquiring New Companions

The boys were going. They had received their inoculations, had bought their rucksacks into which they could pack, they assured Sarah, everything needed for six months in India. They had had a farewell lunch with their father, about which Sarah had heroically refrained from inquiring, and a farewell party for their friends, into which Sarah had made occasional self-conscious forays before retreating to the sterile peace of her bedroom.

Throughout all the preparations, Sarah concealed her shrinking soul beneath a carapace of cheerful excitement. She bought a vast map of India, which she fixed on to the fridge door, and she poured over her sons' guidebooks. She told them she couldn't wait to start getting their e-mails and letters, it would be such fun to follow their travels, she could imagine she was doing it herself but with none of the discomfort, it was so exciting, really it was so exciting.

On their last night, she poured a reckless amount of prawns into their favorite supper, fish pie. She opened one of Andrew's better bottles of wine and made a toast: "To India!" she said. "And mind you be careful about the water."

The boys raised their glasses and cried, "To India!"

She was so proud of her dashing sons. They had inherited their father's good looks, although James did at least have her mouth. On her, it had always seemed grossly disproportionate to the rest of her face, sitting as it did above her apology of a chin and her equally inadequate nose. On James, it coordinated perfectly with his chiseled features.

He put his glass down and took Sarah's hand. "You will be all right, won't you?" he asked. "Dad says you like being on your own and you'll be able to concentrate on your painting but . . ."

"Your father," Sarah said, mentally consigning him to everlasting hell fire, "is absolutely right. Give me a paintbrush and I'm happy. And, believe it or not, I am quite capable of looking after myself!" She gave her son's hand a brisk squeeze. "Besides, I shall be far too busy to be lonely, doing stupid things like pretending to be a sweet young girl in front of the entire village of Ambercross. And you never know: by the time you come back, your father might just have decided to come home." She saw her boys exchange significant glances, like two surgeons who are wondering whether to let the patient know the truth about her condition.

James said carefully, "I don't think you should count on that."

"No, of course not," Sarah said, "but your father and I have been together for our entire adult lives. We know each other better than anyone else. Sooner or later he's going to miss all that."

"Yes, but Mum . . ." James paused. "Perhaps he likes being with someone who doesn't know him as well as you do. . . . Hyacinth doesn't have the first idea about him. She thinks he's perfect."

"Well, that won't last," Sarah said tartly. "I don't suppose," she added with exaggerated carelessness, "he's said anything to you about his plans?"

"No, but he doesn't look like someone who thinks he's made a mistake."

"Well, of course he wouldn't," said Sarah, spearing a prawn with her fork. "Andrew never looks like he's made a mistake, that's why he's so successful. Anyway, the point is," she said quickly, not wishing to spend their last night bitching about their father and realizing she was perilously close to doing just that, "I will miss you very much but I do have a life of my own: I've got lots of commissions, I have my friends, and I have this stupid play, for which I thank you most insincerely."

James grinned. "I'm really sorry we're missing that."

Sarah snorted. "I bet you are."

"Ruth says she'll go," Ben said.

"Oh well, that makes me feel a whole lot better. Your girl-friend can see Sarah Stagg pretending to be twenty-one. Great. The whole thing is going to be the biggest farce Ambercross has ever seen. Your father will be delighted." She was doing it again. She would not be seeing her boys for another six months and their last impression of her would be of an embittered old cow. She felt as if she were driving an enormous lorry, continually having to maneuver it out of cul-de-sacs. She said, "Poor Ruth is going to miss you terribly!"

Ben shrugged. "She'll be all right. She's going to Greece in May and she spends most weekends at the rescue home in Bath. She'll be fine."

"I bet she won't be," said Sarah. "How long have you two been together? Two years? And now she won't see you for months."

"We always knew we'd be doing different things this year. Her life doesn't revolve round me. It's not as if we're looking for a church wedding and happy ever after."

Was there an implied criticism here? Probably not, since Ben was already moving on to discuss tomorrow's arrangements with his brother. Sarah was well aware that in her raw and wretched state, she tended to read murky meanings in the most commonplace exchanges. Only the other day, the postman had greeted her with, "Good morning, Mrs. *Stagg*," and she had actually spent half an hour wondering if the inflection had been ironic. Besides, whether Ben's comment had been aimed at her or not, was he not right in his view that people who let their lives revolve round those of their partners were sad, sorry souls? Perhaps if she'd had a dynamic rather than a stuttering career and a sensationally independent social life, Andrew would not have lost interest in her? Miriam would say she was now showing Andrew that she *could* make a very successful life for herself. But if she was showing Andrew that she could make a very successful life for herself by attracting universal ridicule for her ludicrous role in *Rebecca,* might he not decide that her success was even more alienating than her failure? Sarah reached for the bottle of wine.

She went to bed at eleven and lay, savoring the sounds of her sons. She could hear them say good night to each other, heard the music of Gomez coming from James's room. Ben, whose musical taste had apparently been formed in the womb, was playing Prince's *Sign o' the Times*. Only when the house was silent, did Sarah drift off to sleep.

Keeping busy, that was the answer. As soon as she returned from the airport, Sarah donned her overalls, retired to the studio, and put on the *Ultimate Baroque Collection* at full volume. She was not a great fan of classical music but today she needed an orchestra in all its bombastic excellence to drown out her last sighting of her boys as they waved cheerily before disappearing into another realm, another continent, another world. She would not let herself think of them flying away from her, she would not think of all the dangers that might be lying in wait for them. She would concentrate on the subject at hand, which was, at the moment, a truly remarkable dog, a Cavalier King Charles spaniel called Raffles.

Raffles belonged to a couple of retired doctors in Shaftesbury who had commissioned the painting as a joint present for their thirtieth wedding anniversary. Raffles was a subject worthy of Sarah's talents. According to the doctors, he had saved both their marriage and their lives. Six years earlier Mrs. Doctor had retired on the understanding that her husband would shortly do likewise. When he failed to do so, she felt aggrieved, acquired Raffles as an alternative companion, and planned her exit from the marital nest. Raffles, however, developed a passionate attachment for Mr. Doctor, who grew increasingly upset by the puppy's anguished cries when he departed for work. Realizing the error of his ways, Mr. Doctor retired.

Sarah was very impressed by this story. She was even more impressed by its sequel. For Raffles's finest hour had come three years later when the Doctors were driving to the Lake District in the pouring rain. Raffles, for no discernible reason, had suddenly begun to bark in an ever more frenzied manner. Mr. and Mrs. Doctor had pulled on to the hard shoulder and then watched in horror as the cars they'd been following and the ones that had been following them plowed into each other in a horrendous tangle of smoke and metal. Raffles, meanwhile, unfazed by his extraordinary prescience, curled up in the backseat and went to sleep.

It was a fascinating story and Sarah enjoyed painting him. After two hours of work on the heroic hound, Sarah called it a day and went through to the kitchen to make a cup of tea. She caught sight of Ben's woolly hat on the cupboard, swallowed a large lump in her throat, walked over to the tea caddy, and found she was out of tea bags. She was out of tea bags. This suddenly seemed the biggest calamity in the world. To her horror she realized she was actually about to cry because she didn't have any teabags. She blinked rapidly, grabbed her coat and her purse, and walked out of the house.

The wind, cold and harsh, made Sarah's eyes water. The beech tree at the end of the lane was waving its branches like a disco dancer on speed. Thick ribbons, the color of ink, were forming patterns across the sky. Soon it would be dark. Sarah quickened her step and maintained a brisk pace until she reached the village shop.

Clementine was there, chatting animatedly to Amy Griggs,

the shop's proprietress and the disseminator of all news in Ambercross. "Oh, Sarah, hello," Clementine said, in the special voice she had adopted toward Sarah since Andrew's departure. "How are *you?* Have you heard the news? There's been another break-in: John and Barbara Lintern. While they were sleeping! Barbara came down this morning and found all the silver gone. Apparently there was a cigarette butt in the fireplace and a smell of tobacco. I think Barbara's more upset about that than she is about the silver. You know what poor Barbara thinks of tobacco. And they left dirty footprints on the new carpet."

"How terrible!" Sarah said. "Poor Barbara! You'd have thought their dogs would have made a noise."

Amy Griggs shook her head. "They sleep in their bedroom. Mrs. Lintern said she was glad they slept through it. If they'd woken the colonel, he'd have got out his air rifle and then anything could have happened."

Clementine frowned at Sarah. "I hope you lock your door at night, Sarah. You're rather isolated on Shooter's Lane, aren't you? When are your boys leaving you?"

"I took them to the airport this morning," Sarah said brightly. "I can't wait to hear from them. It's so exciting!"

"Well, you make sure you lock your door tonight," Amy said. "Don and I keep a garden fork under our bed."

"Really?" asked Sarah, wondering if she should do the same.

"Poor Sarah, you must be bereft," said Clementine. "You really must come and have a meal with us soon. I'll ring you."

Lately, Clementine had developed two very irritating habits. One was to spell out Sarah's predicament whenever she saw her, just in case Sarah might have forgotten. The other was to announce that Sarah must come over for a meal, when both she and Sarah knew that she had no intention of inviting her to anything. Sarah turned to Amy. "Can I have some tea bags?" she asked. "I'm completely out."

"Thank heavens for the village shop!" said Clementine brightly. "Where would we be without it?"

"In my case," said Sarah, leaving her money on the counter, "without a cup of tea. Bye now!" She smiled cheerily at the two women and walked quickly out, looking, she hoped, like a woman who had things to do and people to see.

At home that evening, Sarah wandered upstairs to the boys' bedrooms. Both were in a state of utter chaos, with clothes covering the floor, open drawers revealing a tangle of sweatshirts and sweaters. On Ben's bulletin board there was his *Far Side* calendar with today's date circled in red and the rest of the month covered with the one word, "INDIA!" Above it was a photograph of Ben and Ruth, taken at the Glastonbury music festival. Both of them were laughing uproariously at the camera. Sarah wondered what it was that had amused them. She turned away and on an impulse pulled off the bedclothes and organized the drawers. A few minutes later she wished she hadn't, since the neatness transformed the room into a horribly empty space. She went downstairs and poured herself a glass of wine. Pull yourself together, she thought. You've often been on your own, you like being on your own. But of course she liked being on her own because it provided a contrast to the moments when she was not on her own.

The boys had gone to Glastonbury last summer. She could remember the weekend very well. On the Friday night she and Andrew had sat in the kitchen. She'd been worried about the rain because Ben had forgotten his waterproof jacket.

"For heaven's sake," Andrew had said, "they're big boys now. They're away for one weekend. What are you going to be like when they're in India?"

"I shall hate it," Sarah had admitted. "What will we do without them?"

"We ought to go away when they do," Andrew had said. "Remind ourselves of the advantages of life without them. Take off just because we can. We could go to Paris, sit in Aux Deux Magots, watching the world go by. I think we should do it. I always wanted to show you Paris."

Sarah sat down at the kitchen table and drank deeply from her glass of wine. She wished Hyacinth had never been born, she wished Andrew were here, she wished they were going off to Paris tomorrow, she wished the boys were here at home, she wished she could rid herself of the feeling that at the age of forty-three her life was effectively over, she wished she wasn't weeping into her wineglass. The phone rang, making her jump. She reached for the handset, knocked over her glass, and swore.

"Sarah?" It was Andrew. He sounded concerned. "Are you all right?"

"No," Sarah said. "I've knocked over my wine."

There was a pause. "How much have you had to drink?"

"Gallons," said Sarah. "I'm about to open my fifth bottle."

"I'm sure that's not true." Andrew didn't sound sure at all. "I just rang to see if you were all right now the boys have left."

"Andrew, that is so thoughtful of you. I'm overwhelmed by your thoughtfulness."

"Don't be sarcastic, Sarah, it doesn't suit you."

"Being on my own doesn't suit me either."

"If it's any consolation," Andrew said, "I worry about you a lot."

"Now that is a consolation. Thank you, I feel quite all right now."

"If you're going to take that tone," Andrew said testily, "I don't see how I can help. I knew you'd be missing the boys tonight. I wanted to talk you through it, help you to see the positive side, but if you persist in being so . . . so negative . . ."

"Do you know something?" Sarah hissed. "I am fed up with people telling me to be positive. I am fed up with people telling me what to feel, and if there is one person on this planet who has absolutely no right to tell me anything at all, that person is you!"

"I'm not going to try to talk to you when you're like this," Andrew said. "I will just say one thing to you. . . ."

"I thought you might," Sarah muttered.

"Alcohol is not the answer. That's all."

"Thanks for the advice," Sarah said. "I have to go. I need to open my fifth bottle."

After she'd cleared up the wine, she went over to the fridge. She took out the remains of the fish pie. There was some salad left as well and she put it on the table. Sarah put the fish pie in the microwave and stood with her back to the stove. The house was so silent!

She went over to the cutlery drawer, took out a fork and knife, and set them on the table. This was it then. Here she was, on her own. Her boys had gone. It seemed like yesterday that she'd sat, frowning with concentration as she'd spooned into their mouths some spinach concoction that she'd spent hours making for them.

They'd been such jolly children. Eight years ago, she and Andrew had been celebrating the success of Sarah's latest money-making scheme. The card company she'd been pestering for ages had finally agreed to use her latest piece, *Girl with a Flute,* offering her the princely sum of one hundred and fifty pounds together with royalties of 5 percent. She and Andrew had been so excited, convinced she'd become a household name once stationers started selling postcards of her painting throughout the land. The boys came down in their pajamas to find their parents waltzing round the kitchen table while the Animals belted out, "Let the Good Times Roll." The boys had joined in and the four of them had ended up dancing crazily, singing along to the chorus. Then James had stood on the table in his Superman pajamas and had made a speech in honor of his brilliant mother, with Ben yelling exuberantly, "Hear, hear!"

She looked at the table. Why had she put a fork and knife there? She blinked and went over to the microwave. The fish pie had shriveled into an unappetizing blob. She took it out, went over to the table, and heaped the limp lettuce onto her plate. She wondered what Andrew was doing now and then wished she hadn't because she could imagine only too well. He and Hyacinth were probably sitting over some candlelit supper. "I'm worried about Sarah," he was saying. "I think she's falling apart. It's so sad."

"It's not your fault," Hyacinth would say. "She's a grown woman."

Sarah ate a mouthful of the fish pie and decided to stop eavesdropping on her husband and his mistress. Outside, an owl hooted. Sarah looked out toward the darkness of the night.

She had never bothered to hang curtains over the kitchen windows or the glass-paned door into the back garden. There was no room for them by the window over the sink and a curtain in front of the door would only pick up dirt from the floor. It had never bothered her until now.

She picked up her supper, put it on a tray, went through to the sitting room and switched on the television.

Thirty minutes later, she decided it was probably not a good idea to watch a film about a lone, blind female being terrorized by intruders in her own home. Best to go to bed and read her Georgette Heyer.

She went back to the kitchen and did the washing up. Then she poured herself a large glass of water and switched out the kitchen lights. She began to make her way upstairs when she remembered the conversation in the village shop. She returned to the kitchen and for the first time ever, locked the door. In the distance, some animal, a badger perhaps, made a screech and the outside light went on, illuminating the front garden. There was nothing to be afraid of; the light often did this. It was probably a badger or a fox or just possibly a couple of burglars. If she went out to the garden shed to collect her garden fork, the burglars would see there was someone there and would go away, unless they were nasty, violent burglars in which case they would knock her out. But if they were nasty, violent burglars they would break in anyway and knock her out in the bedroom. At least, since she was a sad old woman of forty-three, they would not do anything worse to her, unless they were undiscriminating burglars as well, in which case they might well do something worse, in which case it was essential she armed herself with the fork. Sarah unlocked the front door and went out to the garden shed, singing tunelessly as she went on the grounds that if she sounded happy and confident she would not sound like a woman whose husband had left her, she would sound like a woman whose husband was striding around the house, just waiting to protect his wife from any unseen menace. She found the garden fork and, still warbling, hastened back to her house. She locked the door, grasped the fork with one hand and her water with the other, and went upstairs. She tried to open the door to her bedroom while pushing the fork under her arm, felt the fork slip and impale itself on to her calf. She yelled with pain, dropped the glass of water, which broke neatly in half on the wooden floorboards, depositing its contents as it did so. Sarah stumbled toward the bed and sank down on to it, clutching her leg. Things, she thought miserably, could only get better.

She was wrong. At half past six the next evening, the doorbell rang. Sarah hobbled to the door and found Ben's girlfriend on the other side. Ruth, a pretty girl with a determined jaw, was holding a supermarket bag in one hand and a leash on the other. At the end of the leash was possibly the ugliest dog she had ever seen: a thickset, black beast of indeterminate origin, panting heavily with an unattractive skein of saliva hanging from its mouth.

"Ruth!" Sarah said, "how lovely to see you. Won't you come in?"

"I'd better not." Ruth directed a significant glance at the Ford Escort outside the front gate. "My mother's waiting for me and she's not feeling too good."

"Oh, dear. Nothing serious, I hope?"

"Just a headache. Jacko barked all the way here."

"Jacko?" Sarah stared at the hound. She felt Ruth was expecting some positive response and tried to oblige. "What a nice dog!"

"Isn't he?" Ruth said brightly. "He's for you. Ben and James were worried about leaving you on your own. They thought you'd be lonely. They asked me to bring you a dog from the rescue center."

Sarah could feel her smile freeze to her face. "Did they?" she murmured faintly.

"I thought Jacko would be perfect for you. He has a very loud bark and he looks fierce, so he'll be a great guard dog." A faint shimmer of something that could be conscience flitted across Ruth's face. "To be honest, he's been at the center for quite a while now. No one seems to want him."

"Really?" asked Sarah. "Why do you think that is?"

Ruth hesitated. "To be honest," she said again, the three words reverberating like a bell of doom in Sarah's head, "he's had a difficult time. You'll be perfect for him. I think he was treated very badly by his original owners, so he has a few problems with human beings. He needs a lot of love."

"I know exactly how he feels," said Sarah.

"Well, there you are," said Ruth hopefully.

"Which is why I don't feel up to looking after a maladjusted dog at the moment. Besides I know nothing about dogs."

"I've got his menu in the bag and some dog food. Ben and James were determined you should have a pet."

Sarah looked at Jacko. The word, "pet," seemed singularly inappropriate.

"I appreciate the thought," she said, "really, I do. Jacko's a lovely dog but—"

"I knew you'd like him! And anyway, Mum won't have him back in the car. She says he's given her one of her migraines. And Ben will be really upset if you don't have him. Ring me if there are any problems but I know you'll be brilliant with him." She thrust the leash and the bag into Sarah's hands. "I must go. Have fun with him. He's very sweet really. He just needs some love."

"Don't we all," Sarah muttered, but Ruth had already retreated to the waiting car. Sarah stared into Jacko's eyes. Jacko had yellow eyes and if there was one word that did not describe them, it was sweet.

"Well, Jacko," Sarah said, "shall we go inside?" She pulled lightly at the leash. A low growl emanated from Jacko and his upper lip receded slightly, revealing a row of dentally challenged teeth. Sarah bit her lip. Perhaps she could just leave him outside and hope he'd wander out into the road and get run over. Ruth would never forgive her. In Sarah's present mood that prospect presented no anxiety but the boys were a different matter. Sarah yanked again at the leash, did her best to ignore the ominous noises rumbling like thunder from the beast's throat, and led him into the kitchen. He stood, gazing, like the hound of the Baskervilles' big brother, a few drops of saliva falling silently onto the floor. Sara pulled out the contents of the supermarket bag. There were a couple of tins of dog food, a blue plastic bowl, and a sheet of paper onto which Ruth had written his feeding times and meals. Perhaps he was just hungry. Sarah opened a tin of dog food and emptied it into the bowl. "There you are, Jacko!" she said, setting it on the floor as near to him as she dared. "Good dog!"

He stared at her with disdain for a few moments, approached the bowl, sniffed at it, then swallowed the contents in a matter of seconds before raising his head and resuming his unblinking and extremely unnerving scrutiny of his new mistress.

"That's all right," Sarah told him. "I don't like you either." She opened the back door. "Do you want to go outside?"

Jacko didn't move. Sarah opened the back door and went out onto the lawn. It was freezing.

"Come on," she said. "Come and see the nice garden."

Jacko straddled the doorway. What would she do if he didn't let her back in? She might die of hypothermia. A brief vision of a repentant Andrew failed to render the idea attractive. Sarah said with as much authority as she could muster, "Look here, Jacko, you need to spend a penny or something. Come *on!*" Jacko lowered his head for a moment and lumbered out into the middle of the lawn, onto which he promptly uncoiled a massive, steaming turd. He immediately straightened himself, stamped his feet on the grass, pulling up great wads of turf as he did so, and waddled back into the kitchen, his immense posterior lurching from side to side. Sarah shivered and followed him back in. Something told her this was not the beginning of a beautiful relationship.

That night when Sarah went to bed, Jacko began to bark. After twenty minutes, Sarah went downstairs with the vague intention of providing some comfort. From the corner of the kitchen came a low, furious growl. Sarah scuttled back upstairs, heard the barking resume, and threw a pillow over her head. At least, she thought, he'd deter the nasty, violent burglars.

Twenty minutes later, the dog sounded different. Now he was howling rather than barking. In fact, Sarah thought, he sounded just like she felt. Moved to pity, she hurried down-stairs and opened the door. She and Jacko were two of a kind, really: unwanted, unloved, and alone. She knelt down. "Come on, Jacko, old boy," she said. "What do you say to being friends?"

"Grrrrrrrr!" growled Jacko.

"It's all right," Sarah said, "I understand."

"GRRRRRR!" roared Jacko. His teeth gleamed in the moonlight, a perfect row of lethal daggers. Sarah quickly es-caped to the other side of the door and raced upstairs. She hoped, she really hoped, the nasty, violent burglars would break in and she hoped, she really hoped, they'd kill Jacko.

A Man's Best Friend Is Not Necessarily a Woman's

Sarah had never liked horror films. She had tried to watch *The Shining* three times and had never progressed beyond the first twenty minutes. A boyfriend had once taken her to *The Pit and the Pendulum* in a creaky old cinema in Lewisham. At the first sight of the pendulum she had flung up her arms in terror, hitting the boyfriend on the chin. Her watch had flown off her wrist and she'd lost it forever, along with the boyfriend.

She was therefore fundamentally ill-suited to her present situation in which she had a starring role as a lone woman tormented by the malevolent presence of Jacko, whose character appeared to comprise all the more terrifying aspects of Jack Nicholson, Vincent Price, and Freddy Kruger.

During the day, Jacko grudgingly allowed her into her kitchen, staring at her with unforgiving eyes. At night, the kitchen belonged to him. If she stepped out of her bedroom, even to visit the bathroom, Jacko would let out an unearthly howl that would set her heart pounding.

The postman and the milkman refused to come to the door now and left their letters and milk by the gate. When she took Jacko for walks, neighbors would cross the road rather than face the hound's terrifying teeth. When she left her favorite cardigan in the kitchen for a few minutes, she returned to find Jacko tearing it apart with unrestrained glee: she would not have been surprised had he thrown back his great head and let out a manic laugh. Sarah rang Ruth and begged her to come and rescue her. Ruth warned her that Jacko would be irretrievably damaged if Sarah were to forsake him. Sarah tried to point out that if things carried on as they were, *she* would be irretrievably damaged. Ruth told her that she knew she was far too kind to snub such an unhappy soul and furthermore, said Ruth, did Sarah realize that if she gave up on Jacko she would probably be signing his death warrant since the center couldn't keep him indefinitely? Sarah, who was beginning to seriously dislike Ruth, agreed to be a little more patient.

When Jennifer invited her for lunch, Sarah accepted with alacrity. If anyone knew about dogs, it was Jennifer. She had two Labradors and a dachshund, all of whom greeted Sarah with a gentle affection that only underlined the psychopathic nature of her own animal. Jennifer settled Sarah down with a glass of wine and a plate of Salade Niçoise and told her it was all about leadership. "Dogs are pack animals," she said. "They will always respond to authority."

"Well, there you are," Sarah responded. "If there's one thing I've never had, it's authority."

"It's never too late to acquire new skills," said Jennifer. "I've just taken up swimming."

"Well, bully for you," Sarah retorted. "You can't compare gliding up and down a pool with being terrorized in one's own house by a hound from hell. Andrew rang me yesterday in a foul mood. He'd come round, while I was out, to collect his dinner jacket and Jacko wouldn't let him in."

"Good for Jacko," said Jennifer.

"That's all very well," said Sarah, "but the dog is forcing me into the life of a hermit. No one will come near the place. I have to get rid of him."

"Is that what Andrew said?"

"No, he didn't. He did say I should take him to dog-training classes. He was pleased I'd acquired a companion."

"Was he?" Jennifer raised an eyebrow. "How surprising. Perhaps it makes him feel less guilty. Did he mention the fragrant Hyacinth?"

"No. I have my first rehearsal for *Rebecca* tomorrow and he asked me to bring his dinner jacket along and give it to Howard, who is apparently going to supper with them on Friday in order to give a blow-by-blow account of my humiliation. Do you ever feel your life is spinning out of control?"

"Constantly," said Jennifer. "Would you like some more wine?"

"Better not. I have to finish a painting this afternoon."

"I haven't," said Jennifer, helping herself to the bottle. She sighed. "I'm worried about George."

Sarah looked up in alarm. "What's wrong with George?"

"Oh"—Jennifer waved a dismissive hand—"he's so boring."

"What about?" asked Sarah, helping herself to a piece of

bread. She could feel all the tensions of the last few days melting away. The food, the wine, the company, and the setting all combined to soothe her fractured nerves. Jennifer's kitchen was a temple to Jennifer's culinary expertise. The huge American fridge, unlike her own antique, hummed gently in the background. A gleaming twin Belfast sink nestled in the middle of a pristine granite countertop, covering milk-colored Shaker-style cupboards. At the other end of the kitchen was a huge oak cupboard on which was displayed Jennifer's collection of Victorian china. Sarah glanced at the dogs sleeping peacefully on the smooth ash floor and sighed happily.

Jennifer turned her lettuce over with her fork. "George is boring. I am bored by George. I find him boring."

Sarah picked up the olive she had been trying unsuccessfully to spear with her fork and swallowed it. She had no idea how she was supposed to respond to such an admission. She very much hoped Jennifer was being flippant.

"I'm not sure what I should do about it," said Jennifer. "I mean, I wish I didn't find him boring but I do. The man is like an automaton and not a very sophisticated one at that. He has a finite number of responses to every situation. When I give him his meal he says, 'Lovely grub!' and when we watch the news he says, 'Idiots!' When he wants some sex he says, 'You look as if you're in need of a seeing-to,' even though it would be obvious to anyone else that I am *not* in need of a seeing-to."

"Yes, but we're all like that," Sarah protested. "Take my grandma. Every time my brother and I argued, she would always say, 'Little birds in their nests should always agree.' Come to think of it," she mused thoughtfully, "it was very irritating."

"It *is* irritating. I am permanently irritated. When I heard

Andrew had left you, do you know what I felt? I felt jealous! I wished that George had gone off with Hyacinth."

Sarah sighed. "I wish George had gone off with Hyacinth."

"You see?" Jennifer crowed. "You agree with me!"

"No, I don't. George is kind and thoughtful and he loves you and I'm sure he has hidden depths."

"Believe me, I've spent a very long time trying to locate them. After twenty-four years of marriage, I've given up. What you see is what you get. George is kind, George is thoughtful, George is boring."

"He must have had something to make you fall in love with him in the first place. Why did you marry him?"

Jennifer shrugged. "I fancied the pants off him and my dragon of a mother made sure I never did get the pants off him until we were married. And he was fun. That was before the record got stuck. If he would just occasionally surprise me, it would be something. He never surprises me."

"Surprises," Sarah said with feeling, "are overrated."

"Poor Sarah, I'm sure you think I'm being hopelessly self-indulgent. I suppose I can live with feeling vaguely irritated whenever I'm with him. On the other hand, the prospect of years of vague irritation is rather depressing."

Sarah put her hands on her head and shrugged. "Quite honestly, I'm not the best person to tell you. From my point of view, predictability seems very attractive. And what's the alternative? You eject poor, blameless George from the marital home, you devastate your daughters, you devastate George, just so you no longer have to listen to his jokes. You wait until you find out just how much fun it is being on your own the whole time. I bet you'd start to appreciate him then."

Jennifer stood up and waved an impatient hand. "The difference between you and me is that you still love Andrew. Also, of course, you think he'll come back and so you are not even trying to adjust to a solitary life. If you did, you might enjoy it."

Sarah looked wistfully at the bottle of wine and poured herself some water. "You don't think Andrew will come back, do you?"

Jennifer frowned. "I don't know. Andrew's so vain that if he thought you were losing interest in him he might be goaded into coming back just to prove he could."

"That's very like something my friend Miriam said. She was the one who told me to do this stupid play."

"In which, I'm sure you'll surprise us all."

"Yes," agreed Sarah. "That's what I'm afraid of."

Sarah had not expected to enjoy her rehearsal but neither had she thought it would be an unmitigated disaster. She had even, she realized afterward, nurtured some barely unacknowledged fantasy in which the Ambercross Players would gaze with awe on her amazingly perceptive interpretation and tell her a star had been born.

Audrey had said all lines should be learned in time for the first rehearsal. Sarah had made some efforts to do so but, remembering Andrew's cavalier approach to this task, had assumed Audrey was not serious. Within minutes of arriving, Sarah realized the full gravity of her mistake. In all matters relating to the Ambercross Players, Audrey was deadly serious. As Sarah stumbled painfully through a scene in which Howard and Claire knew their lines with an almost eerie precision, the atmosphere grew thick with the promise of thunder. Finally, in front of the entire cast, Audrey told her that she, Sarah, an un-tried novice, had been given over a month in which to learn her script. If there was some reason why, Sarah, alone among the cast, should be exempt from this task, Audrey would love to hear it. When Sarah opened her mouth to speak, Audrey re-minded her that everyone else had equally busy lives. Claire and Howard, for example, unlike Sarah, both had extremely demanding full-time careers and poor Claire was also subject to extremely unpleasant bouts of allergic rhinitis. Yet Claire and Howard had learned their lines and were already inhabit-ing the parts of Mrs. Danvers and Jack Favell with consum-mate ease. Did Sarah feel similarly confident?

Sarah, blushing furiously, assured Audrey that she didn't but that since Andrew had always taken a long time to learn his words, she had assumed she could do the same. Audrey's re-splendent bosom seemed to expand before Sarah's eyes and her face became positively puce. Andrew, she reminded Sarah, was the tried and tested star of *Move Over, Mrs. Markham, Season's Greetings, When We Are Married, Pride and Prejudice, Salad Days,* and others too numerous to mention. Andrew had noth-ing to prove. Sarah, on the other hand . . . Audrey left the sen-tence hovering in the air. It didn't help that Howard and Claire stood smirking like the horrid little good-goodies they were. Sarah could almost see Howard's mental tape recorder whirring happily away inside his horrible, self-satisfied head. She heard her voice promising with impressive conviction to have the en-tire first act at her fingertips in time for the next rehearsal.

"Then we will say no more," Audrey announced. "We've wasted enough time already. Let us do the scene again."

So they did, and every time Sarah paused to find her place

in the script or stumbled over a word, Howard would assume the expression of a man struggling painfully and nobly to control his impatience. To make matters worse, Audrey kept telling Sarah to move upstage or to move downstage and Sarah was too cowed to admit she had no idea what such terms meant. Consequently she kept darting all over the place like a bee that's been zapped with fly spray and that didn't please Audrey either.

The final indignity came at the end of the rehearsal when Audrey took Sarah aside. Lowering her voice to a subdued shout, she advised Sarah that she couldn't help noticing she had put on weight. "The trouble is," said Audrey, "you are supposed to be a little slip of a thing. I mean, Maxim would hardly be interested in a woman who's podgy, would he?"

Sarah gasped. "You think I'm podgy?"

Audrey raised her eyebrows significantly. "The signs are there. You must take yourself in hand. Now, go home, learn your lines, lose some weight, and all will be well." The simplicity of the prescription evidently cheered her, for she added benevolently, "This is all about having fun, Sarah. We want you to have fun!"

If this was fun, Sarah thought savagely, then she was a banana. Or rather, she was an apple, a gross, podgy apple. With flaming cheeks, she managed a valedictory nod to the cast, picked up her bag, and fled into the night.

Back at home, a bored Jacko had knocked over the kitchen bin and apparently played football with the contents. Sarah cleared up the mess, made herself a cup of tea and, reaching for the biscuit tin, ate three chocolate digestives in a row.

The next morning, Sarah realized she had made a momentous discovery. For the first time since Andrew had left her she had gone to bed without being conscious of the aching absence of Andrew. Perhaps she should write an article for women like her:

Ladies! Have *you* been abandoned by your husband and your children? Do *you* feel you have discovered the true meaning of loneliness for the first time in your lives? Well, don't despair, because Sarah Stagg has the answer! Involve yourselves in the most humiliating activity you can find and then take into your home a hound who hates you. Hey presto! You'll be too busy feeling crushed and frightened to worry about being lonely!

Ridiculous but true. She had no time to dwell on her miserable future. When she wasn't busy dreading her next rehearsal, she was busy trying to avoid Jacko's evil eye.

In fact, an article was not enough. What she ought to do was write a manual, a guide to survival for all abandoned wives. She could imagine herself on television, chatting with huge animation to Richard and Judy. "Oh, goodness," she would laugh softly. . . . She would have to practice laughing softly. . . . "You ask why I wrote the book? Because no one else has! There are guides for pregnant women, widowed women, newly married women, but *nowhere* is there a guide for abandoned wives. And yet we are the most crushed, humiliated, vulnerable, unhappy group in the world. What should we do? How should we behave? Why has this happened? How do we get ourselves off the floor?"

Judy would lean forward, impressed by Sarah's passionate sincerity. "Very briefly, Sarah, what sort of advice would you give?"

Sarah would pause briefly. "One: Get out there and exercise. You can't cry when you walk up a hill and you can't spend money either. And exercise produces endorphins and endorphins produce energy and energy zaps depression. Two: Let the world see you enjoy your new independence. Ration your self-pity. The world tires very quickly of misery. Three: Since men never value what they have, make yourself unavailable, find other men who desire you. Four . . ." She would smile winningly here. "Well, to find out more, read my book!"

Richard would nod gravely. "So, Sarah, after following your own advice, what has happened in *your* life?"

And that, of course, was why Sarah would never be able to write a best-selling handbook. The truth was that she was *still* plump, *still* lonely, and still deeply, and probably eternally, sad.

On Friday, Sarah returned from a calorie-reducing canter to the postbox and back to find a surprise awaiting her. Not only was there a man in her kitchen, sitting calmly at the table, with pen and paper, but the man in her kitchen had all his limbs intact. Sitting at his feet, good as gold, was Sarah's own little fiend from hell.

The man turned round and smiled. It was Martin Chamberlain. Why wasn't he dead?

"Why aren't you dead?" Sarah asked.

"Sorry?" Martin looked puzzled and then embarrassed. "Look, if this is about the rehearsal, I'm sorry I didn't spring to your defense but I know from experience that you just have to let Audrey get things off her chest. . . ."

"And it's a pretty big chest," Sarah couldn't resist adding.

"Quite so. If I'd intervened, she'd have gone on all night. But I am sorry. . . ."

"I'm not talking about that." Sarah pointed at her hound. "How did you get past the door without being savaged by Jacko?"

Martin was clearly mystified. "I just walked in. I've been writing you a note."

"Didn't he growl? Didn't he do anything horrid?"

"He barked a lot at first, didn't you, old boy?"

Martin patted the dog's head. Jacko wagged his tail. Sarah, watching, fascinated, took a sharp intake of breath. "I don't believe it," she said.

"What?" asked Martin.

"This is the first time I've seen Jacko wag his tail. I didn't even know he *could* wag his tail." She gazed at Martin with awe. "Perhaps you're a reincarnation of Saint Francis of Assisi or something. You may not realize this but I have just witnessed a miracle. Ever since I've been saddled with him, this dog has turned me into the pariah of Ambercross. No one will come near me because of this dog. He terrifies everyone. He terrifies me."

"Why did you get him then?"

"I didn't," Sarah said bitterly. "He was foisted on me by my son's girlfriend on the spurious grounds that the boys didn't want to leave me without a companion. In fact, I strongly suspect the rescue center people were about to execute him and the only person Ruth could think of who might be stupid enough to take him in was yours truly. And now you wander in, cool as a cucumber and—"

"I didn't wander," Martin corrected her hastily. "I knocked first. The door was unlocked."

"I didn't think I needed to lock it with Jacko here. You wander in and Jacko does nothing. You know"—Sarah stared at him with genuine respect—"I shall look at you in a completely different light from now on."

"Thank you," said Martin, "I think."

"No, seriously, I am overwhelmed. Why are you here?"

"I should have rung. I'm sorry."

"Not at all, it's good to see you. Would you like a cup of tea?"

Martin checked his watch. "A quick one. I'm due to meet a blocked drain in twenty minutes." He put his pen in his jacket pocket and cleared his throat. "You left the rehearsal very suddenly the other night. You looked upset."

"Upset? Wouldn't you be if you'd just been told you were"—Sarah could hardly bring herself to say the word—"podgy?!"

"That's the point," Martin said eagerly. "I wanted to tell you that you're not the only one."

"Thank you, Martin. I feel a lot better knowing that."

"What I mean is," Martin said quickly, "and let me say right away that you are not the slightest bit . . ."

"Podgy?"

"Yes. I mean, no. You're not. But the thing is, after you went, Audrey had a go at me as well. She said Maxim was a lean and tortured soul. She said lean and tortured souls don't have spreading midriffs."

Sarah glanced at him suspiciously. "You're making this up," she said. "You're trying to make me feel better."

Martin sat back in his chair and folded his arms. "I have to tell you," he said, "I'm really not as thoughtful as you seem to think I am."

Sarah set two mugs down on the table and studied Martin. "Anyway, you don't have a spreading midriff."

Martin made a face. "Would you describe me as lean?"

"Well, no," Sarah conceded. "I'd describe you as . . . sturdy. Do you want a biscuit?"

"Definitely not. Audrey wants me to lose ten pounds."

"That's ridiculous!"

"Not really. I wouldn't mind losing a bit of fat. Anthea could never bear me to eat between meals and ever since she left I've been eating for England."

"Me too. It seems so unfair. Most people lose their appetite in times like this. Not me. I've eaten two bananas just this afternoon."

"They're very good for you."

"And a king-size Mars Bar."

"Not so good."

"I know." Sarah filled the mugs with boiling water and proceeded to stir the tea bags with great care. "Martin, tell me if you want me to shut up, but I'd really like to know. Did it take you a long time to adjust to living on your own?"

"No," said Martin. "I found it very peaceful."

"Not lonely?"

"No. But things hadn't been right for a long time . . . as of course you know." He caught Sarah's eye and smiled. "Did you think I wasn't aware of all the gossip? You must think I'm incredibly stupid."

"Of course I don't." Sarah knew she was blushing and wished she wasn't. "It's only that, well I suppose I'm surprised that, I mean, I think you are, or rather you were, very tolerant." She could almost hear her spade digging a deeper hole with every word. She opened the door of the fridge and, welcoming the blast of cold air on her face, took out the milk jug.

"I suppose," said Martin stiffly, "other people's marriages can seem a bit bizarre to those who don't know what's going on."

"I'm sorry," said Sarah, passing him his tea. "I wasn't trying to pry."

"It's all right. But I do need to lose some weight. So I'm going to embark on a campaign. I'm going to do a couple of brisk walks every weekend. And I'm going to stop buying crisps."

"I don't suppose," Sarah said, glancing at Jacko, "you'd like some company on your walks?"

Martin grinned. "Jacko? Yes, all right, I'll be happy to take him."

"Thank you. But actually, I'd like to come along too. I don't want to be podgy."

"You are not podgy!"

"You heard Audrey. The signs are there. Can I come?"

"I'd be delighted. We can practice our lines while we walk."

"All right," said Sarah. "Just as soon as I learn them."

"Oh Lord, I'm going to be late." Martin took a sip of his tea. "I'm sorry, I shall have to leave this." He gave Jacko a final pat and stood up. "Shall we start tomorrow? Shall I come round at ten? Or are you busy?"

"No," said Sarah, thinking of the long emptiness of the weekend ahead, "I'm not busy."

After Martin had left, Sarah drank her tea and looked at Jacko. "So," she said, "you can be a civilized dog when you want to be. What do you say, Jacko? Shall we be friends now?"

"Grrrrr!" growled Jacko.

"Fine," said Sarah. "I didn't want to be friends with you anyway."

Take Regular Exercise

It was soon apparent that Martin and Sarah had radically different ideas as to what constituted a good walk. For Sarah, it meant stopping at the first stile in order to appreciate the myriad colors of the stream, stopping at the top of the hill in order to appreciate the rolling hills and the splendid skyline, and stopping at the top of the next hill in order to recoup physical reserves for the walk back. Her itinerary also allowed for sundry breaks in order to study unusual birds, interesting cloud formations, wild flowers, and any other wonders that nature might choose to display that day.

When Sarah was a child, Miriam's quietly spoken father had invited her to join them for a day's sailing in Southampton. Once aboard his boat, he had turned instantly into a Captain Bligh, shouting incomprehensible commands at Sarah and generally reducing her to a gibbering wreck.

Walking boots, Sarah decided, had the same effect on Martin as boats had on Miriam's father. "If we keep resting," he said, "we won't be achieving the desired objective. You can admire the scenery any time. We are here to lose weight."

"I don't see why we can't do both," Sarah grumbled. "At this rate I'll be unable to move tomorrow." She seized his arm suddenly. "Oh, Martin, stop! There's a deer. Look."

Ahead of them at the top of the hill, the small animal paused, one foot raised. Then he was off, leaping elegantly over the fence and disappearing through the undergrowth.

"There!" Sarah said. "Wasn't he beautiful? You'd have missed that. Wouldn't it be glorious to be as graceful as that? To be able to skim over fences and glide through the trees!"

"If you listen to me," Martin responded, "in a few weeks time, you'll be able to do just that. Come on!"

Sarah, striving to catch her breath as she followed him up the hill, would have liked to point out that she did not literally want to emulate the deer by cavorting over bushes and that furthermore she was disappointed to find that he was someone who clearly had no sense of the beauty of the natural world. She would have liked to say all this and more but was too busy gasping for air in order to keep up with him and Jacko. Jacko, having glanced back at Sarah with an expression that Sarah could only interpret as smug, was in his element, surging ahead and clearly anxious to give his mistress a heart attack.

Finally, at half past one, they reached the Oak and Anchor. Sarah crumpled onto the bench while Martin tethered Jacko's leash to the post.

She did feel better when they entered the pub. The warmth of the fire wrapped her limbs with its heat and the smell of fish and chips hovered in the air. Martin dived for the bar and Sarah was about to follow him when a voice like a foghorn called her name. She turned and smiled at the portly presence of Colonel John Lintern.

"Sarah!" he exclaimed, giving her a wet kiss on the cheek. "How very nice to see you. Look, Barbara, it's Sarah. How are you? You're looking very healthy! Been for a walk? Good girl, good girl. We've just dropped in for the old fish and chips after a hard morning at the wine merchant. No one does chips like these people. Melt in your mouth, they do." He stopped to clap his hands against his thighs. "We were sorry to hear about Andrew. Terrible business, terrible. Some people have no sticking power. In my day we believed that when you get married you grit your teeth, you stiffen your sinews and stick at it, no matter how bad it is. You stick at it! That's what I do, that's what Barbara does. I've no patience with slackers."

Barbara Lintern, as large as her husband and with an equally piercing voice, said approvingly, "Absolutely!" She wound an enormous yellow and purple scarf round her neck. "The man's a bounder and if he shows his face in Ambercross I shall tell him so. The vicar tells me he's living in Warminster with his young woman. As far as I'm concerned he can stay there. I was unpleasantly surprised by his behavior. He always reads the lesson so beautifully. Not that you can tell. Our daughter, for example, looks like an angel and behaves like a trollop; in fact I would go so far as to say she is a trollop."

"It's true," sighed the colonel, "our daughter is a trollop. A very pretty one but a trollop nonetheless." He shook his head and then brightened at the sight of Martin. "Hello, there, Martin. How are you? I keep meaning to ring you about our dishwasher. The dratted thing doesn't work properly! What are you doing here? Keeping our young Sarah company? Good show!"

Sarah, aware of Barbara's sharp eyes, said quickly, "Martin and I are both in Audrey's play. We've been trying to learn our words."

"Excellent!" boomed the colonel. "You must let us know when it's on and we'll be there. We never miss one of Audrey's productions. Amazing woman. She's as old as the hills and as loud as ever. She gave us an extraordinary plate on our golden anniversary. Quite hideous. The burglars took it. Did you hear we were burgled?"

"Yes," said Sarah. "I was so sorry."

"Bloody refugees," grunted the colonel. "They come over here, steal our valuables . . ."

"Really, John," said Barbara, "I don't think there are any refugees in Ambercross. The police said the burglars were probably drug addicts. . . ."

"Exactly! They come over here, steal our valuables, smoking their opium pipes. . . ."

"I don't think it's opium," said Barbara. "I think it's proba-bly pot. Sarah will know, won't you, Sarah? What is it they all smoke these days?"

Sarah was flattered to be regarded as an expert on anything, although she was aware that her credentials in this area were pretty poor. She had never been tempted to try mind-altering substances, since her mind was chaotic enough without them. "I think some of them smoke cannabis," she said cautiously, "or it might be marijuana. Or perhaps marijuana *is* cannabis . . . or grass. I think that's what it is . . . grass!"

"Grass!" expostulated the colonel. "We went to war so the kids could smoke bloody grass. Give me good old-fashioned tobacco any day . . . or rather," he corrected, catching his wife's eye, "please don't!"

Barbara fished out from her bag a violet-colored hat and fixed it on her head. "The burglars left a cigarette butt behind. I found it. Benson and Hedges."

"Bloody nerve!" said the colonel. "All I can say is, thank God I was at home. If they'd thought Barbara was on her own, there's no telling what might have happened. My God, it makes the blood boil!"

"They didn't come near the bedroom, dear. And anyway, Bobby would have stopped them."

"Huh," snorted the colonel. "Bloody Bobby slept on our bed and never made a sound. Neither did Digby! And anyway, you know what bloody Bobby's like. . . . If there's any rumpy-pumpy going, he wants some too. Very odd like that, Bobby . . . Never mind! The point is, Sarah, you should be very careful where you are, all on your own on that lane."

"I keep a garden fork under my bed," Sarah said. "And I have my own dog now. Have you heard about my dog?"

The Linterns exchanged glances. They had, it was obvious, heard about the dog. "If you want any tips on dog management," Barbara said kindly, "I am always on the end of a phone. John, we must let these good people have their lunch. So nice to see you both."

The colonel shook hands with Martin. "I'll be in touch about the dratted dishwasher." He smiled at Sarah. "Nice to see you having fun, my dear." He glanced significantly at Martin. "Life's too short and all that. And you're still young!"

"Come along, John," scolded his wife, taking him by the arm. "Oh, and Sarah, there's a very good dog lady in Gassett. I have her address at home."

"Thank you," said Sarah faintly. She watched the couple proceed toward the door and murmured, "Whenever I talk to them I feel as young as Mrs. de Winter. You realize they think you and I are an item?"

"Really?" said Martin. "I'm flattered. I've got us a table in the corner. They'll bring our lunch over to us."

Lunch turned out to be cheese sandwiches and orange juice. Sarah tried not to look at the three women eating fish and chips next to them. She sat down and bit into her sandwich. "Thank you," she said, adding pointedly, "If we ever do this again, I'll get lunch."

Martin sat down opposite her. "Tell me," he said, "do you really have a garden fork under your bed?"

"I'm sleeping on my own for the first time in twenty years and there've been three burglaries in the village in as many months. Of course I have a garden fork under my bed."

"If someone burst into your room," Martin pointed out, "you wouldn't have time to reach for your fork."

"A burglar wouldn't burst in. Burglars prowl. They'd prowl up the stairs and I'd have time to arm myself."

"As a matter of interest," said Martin, "what would you do with it?"

"I'd wave it about, I expect. I don't know. Anyway, I'm all right now, because Jacko would tear them to shreds before they'd even started to prowl . . . that is"—Sarah frowned suddenly—"unless they had freaky powers of dog control."

Martin assumed a pained expression. "Don't look at me like that. I can't help it if your dog likes me."

"If I were you," Sarah said cuttingly, "I'd be a little worried that a psycho hound has decided you are his soul mate. If I were you, I'd wonder what it is about you that he likes so much."

"My sweet-natured personality?" suggested Martin.

Sarah snorted. "Until this morning I might have agreed with you."

"Are you telling me you don't feel better for a brisk walk?"

"My feet are hurting, my whole body is hurting, and that's before we've even walked home again. At this rate, I'll be a broken woman before we even get to the next rehearsal."

"Yes, but you'll be a slim, attractive, broken woman."

Sarah grimaced. "Thank you."

"At the risk of embarrassing you," Martin continued, "I think you are already a very attractive woman, and after a morning in your company, I'd be surprised if Andrew doesn't come home very soon, begging you to forgive him." He smiled and then, instantly contrite, pulled out a handkerchief from his pocket and held it out to her. "I say, I'm sorry, that was stupid. I didn't mean to upset you."

Sarah blinked rapidly. "No, it's all right. I'm quite all right until people are kind to me and then for some reason I want to cry. I'm sorry."

"I wasn't trying to be kind," said Martin. He looked helplessly at her. "Would you like another drink?"

"No, I'm fine now, honestly. Thank you."

He picked up his glass and downed his orange juice. He assumed an air of slightly forced jollity. "Now! About tomorrow. Are you up for another walk?"

"A short one," said Sarah. "Much shorter."

"Fine. I can only spare an hour or so in the morning anyway. Have you learned scene one yet?"

"I read through it last night. I can't even imagine saying 'I'm twenty-one' with any conviction."

Martin grinned. "It's called acting. Try and learn the last bit where it's just you and me, then we can practice it while we walk."

"By tomorrow? That's impossible!"

"All right. Now imagine I'm Audrey and you're explaining why you haven't learned your words. . . ."

"All right, I'll learn it. I had no idea you were so bossy."

"I'm sorry."

"No, you're not," said Sarah. "You're enjoying yourself."

Martin smiled. He had a very nice smile. "You're right," he said, sounding a little surprised. "I am."

And so, thought Sarah, was she. Who'd have thought Martin Chamberlain would be such good company?

Boost Your Morale by Planning a Holiday

By the time they arrived back at Shooter's Lane, even Jacko was beginning to flag. Sarah said, "Do you want a cup of coffee? I have just enough energy to put the kettle on." She stiffened suddenly at the sight of the red Toyota in front of Martin's van. "It's Andrew," she said. "I wonder what he wants?"

"Perhaps I'd better leave you here," said Martin. "Do you want to take Jacko?"

"I never want to take Jacko," Sarah said, "and there's no need for you to rush off just because Andrew's dropped in. If he wants to lecture me about the play, you can tell him how superb I am."

"It would only be the truth," said Martin gallantly. "When you did that scene with Howard the other night, you were

89

really convincing. You looked so nervous and uncomfortable, it was great."

"That wasn't acting. Howard always makes me feel like that." Sarah opened the gate and knelt down to collect her post from the crate. She pulled out a postcard and smiled. "It's from the boys!"

She heard her front door slam and looked up. Jacko instantly sprung into action, tugging desperately at his leash and barking and snarling with a fervor that was little short of miraculous after such an epic expedition. Martin held on to him grimly while Andrew, clutching a painting, backed warily toward the rosebushes.

"I'll take him on in," said Martin. "Come on, Jacko, old boy." He pulled him toward the door and nodded at Andrew, who had retreated to the fence.

Sarah walked forward to meet her husband. He was, she noticed, looking slim and svelte in navy chinos, matching V-neck sweater, and the glimpse of a pristine white T-shirt. Adultery, she thought acidly, clearly suited him. Aware of her windswept hair and rosy cheeks, she said coldly, "I see you're taking the Matisse." She had given him the print on his birthday over a decade ago. She had no idea he liked it so much.

"You don't mind, do you? I did ring this morning. I rang you two or three times."

"We've been walking. You take it. It's your picture after all."

"Thank you. So you've been out walking with Martin? That's nice." He sounded as if she'd been swallowing some medicine.

"We're trying to lose—" Sarah corrected herself quickly. "We're trying to learn our words."

"Poor old Martin," said Andrew. "I'm afraid he's not cut out to be a Maxim. Panic-casting on Audrey's part. It's a pity because he'd be the perfect Frank: solid, dependable, a bit of a bore."

A pleasant image floated into Sarah's mind in which she grabbed the Matisse and broke it over her husband's head. She'd forgotten how patronizing he could be. She said, "I don't find Martin boring and I think he's going to be a very good Maxim. He's never had the chance to play the hero before."

"For the very good reason that he's not hero material. Don't get me wrong, I'm very fond of old Martin. The man's a brilliant plumber, of course, but—"

"What's that got to do with anything?"

"Nothing at all." Andrew lowered the Matisse and propped it against his legs. "I don't want to talk about Martin. How are *you?* I hope Audrey's not bullying you too much."

"Not at all," said Sarah. "In fact," she added, warming to her lie, "I'm enjoying rehearsals. *Rebecca* is such a good play."

"I'm looking forward to seeing it."

"You're coming to see the play?"

"Of course I am. You know you have my full support."

Sarah was saved from making a less than charitable response by the return of Martin. "I've put Jacko in the back garden," he said. "I'd better go. I've things to do."

"Thank you for saving me from a fate worse than death!" Andrew gave an I-was-never-really-worried-chuckle and smiled benignly. "Sarah tells me you're doing great things with Maxim."

"That's very kind," Martin murmured. "I'm certainly doing something with Maxim." He put his hands in his pockets and started stamping his feet, like a horse waiting for the starting pistol.

Andrew smiled. "I'm sure you're doing very well. It's a difficult balancing act: Maxim has to be unkind and insensitive while retaining the sympathy of the audience. Very tricky. I'm sure you'll manage it."

"Thank you." Next to her tall, debonair husband, Martin seemed smaller, awkward, diminished. The confident leadership he'd shown on the walk had melted away. Sarah felt cross with both men: with Andrew for being so superior and with Martin for being so overawed by Andrew's presence.

"I must go," said Martin. "Thank you for the walk, Sarah. Good-bye, Andrew."

"Good-bye," said Andrew, "and good luck."

Martin nodded and walked toward his van with all the energy of a man who can't wait to be somewhere else.

"Good old Martin," Andrew said without much conviction. He caught sight of the postcard in Sarah's hand. "Is that from the boys? I had a card yesterday. They'd got to Goa and made friends with some other travelers. James was going to be best man at their wedding."

Sarah turned the postcard over and quickly perused its contents. "Oh my God," she said.

"What is it?" asked Andrew sharply. "Is anything wrong?"

"It's from Ben. Listen. 'Goa is great and we've been to a wedding. James has gone off with the bride but I'm staying in Goa for a while. Hope you like your dog. Love, Ben.'"

Andrew took the card. "It's a joke," he said. "It must be."

"Ben doesn't do jokes. What can we do?"

"Nothing. There's nothing we can do. We can hardly fly

out to Goa and say sorry to the bridegroom. There are all sorts of explanations and anyway the boys are adults now. We have to let them sort out their own lives. You mustn't worry. Sarah? Promise me you won't worry." He put his arm round her and for a moment she allowed herself to lean against him. She was appalled by the sheer physical longing she felt for him. "You're right," she said, pulling away. "There's nothing we can do. Would you let me know if you hear any more?"

"Of course I will and you do the same." He picked up the print. "I'd better go. You are all right?"

Sarah nodded. "I'm all right."

"Good." Andrew paused. "It means a lot to me that you are. I hate the fact that I've hurt you."

Come home then, she wanted to say, come home and we'll forget it ever happened. The sound of Jacko's grating bark, which had the same effect on her nerves as chalk being scratched up a blackboard, reminded her of the full extent of Andrew's infamy. "I'm sure you do," she said coldly. "Goodbye, Andrew."

"I'll be in touch," he said. "We'll have lunch sometime so we can discuss future plans. I'll ring you."

"Fine." She walked back to the house without looking back. How typical of Andrew to be so sweet and kind and then, quite casually, deal a killer blow. What did he mean by future plans? Did he want an instant divorce or was he just punishing her for not collapsing into the pathetic wreck he'd expected her to be? Somewhere in Goa there was a poor bridegroom whose heart had been broken by her son. Not only had she married a bounder, she had also, apparently, produced one too. And furthermore, she thought as she opened the door into the back garden and surveyed the upturned plant pots, she was the owner of the worst dog in the world.

In the kitchen, the phone was ringing. Sarah retreated indoors, shutting the door on her loathsome hound, and picked up the handset.

"Sarah? It's Miriam. How are things?"

Sarah told her. "And the worst of it is," she concluded, "the play will be a disaster, Ben's on his own in Goa, James is goodness knows where with someone else's bride, my dog continues to hate me and I hate him, and now my husband is talking about 'future plans.' I have to say that your clever plan to lure him back to me is not looking too clever at the moment."

"Well, actually, I have another idea," said Miriam, and it was only then that Sarah perceived that the bounce had gone from Miriam's voice. "I'm going away at half-term and I thought you might like to come too."

"Miriam," said Sarah, sitting back in her chair and resting her feet on the table, "has something happened?"

There was a pause. "A friend's offered me her flat in Puerto d'Andratx. It's near the harbor. Great position. You'd like it."

"Miriam," said Sarah again, "what's happened? I've driveled on and on about my own silly problems until I'm even boring myself. I know something's wrong. What is it?" Another pause and now Sarah knew something was very definitely wrong because Miriam's conversation usually flowed like Niagara Falls.

"I might be wrong," Miriam said carefully, "but I don't think so because I recognize the signs. Clive's started taking his mobile into the garden, he's late back from work, he only comes to bed when I'm asleep. So I thought a week in Majorca and a small holiday romance . . . we can make up the details while we're out there . . . would do the trick. What do you think?"

"I think you're overreacting. It sounds to me as if he has problems at work. Andrew never wanted sex when he was worried about work. Clive loves you. I'll never forget him telling me how lucky he was to have found you."

"He told you that at least five years ago," Miriam said shortly. "A lot can happen in five years. A lot has happened to my body in five years. I'm beginning to look old."

"Absolute nonsense," Sarah said robustly. "You look fantastic. You're tall, slim, elegant, and given that I'm short, fat, and apple shaped, I think it's very decent of me to be friends with you. You don't look remotely old. In fact, you look disgustingly young."

"Well, I feel old. And anyway, Clive might appreciate me more if I leave him for a few days. Won't you come with me?"

"I really shouldn't," Sarah said. "I really must set about getting more work."

"It would do you good to get away. And . . ." Miriam hesitated. "I could do with the company."

That settled it. It was a long time since Sarah had heard Miriam sound so deflated. "I'll come," said Sarah, "so long as I can have a holiday romance too."

"All right. You can have Antonio Banderas, I'll have Marcello Mastroianni."

"He was Italian and anyway he's dead."

"I'm not fussy. You do want to come? I'm not bullying you into it?"

"At this particular moment I feel as if you've thrown me a lifeline."

"Great," said Miriam. "We'll share it. Is your play really going to be a disaster?"

"Yes, and Andrew says he's going to come and see it."

"Of course he will. He'll be eaten up with curiosity. I have a good feeling about this play."

"Tell me," said Sarah, "do you have a good feeling about Majorca?"

"Yes," said Miriam, "I do."

"Right," said Sarah. "Now I'm really worried."

When Martin arrived the next morning, Jacko erupted into a frenzied welcome, wagging his great tail with such enthusiasm that it lashed against Sarah's shin, causing her to trip over his half-empty water bowl, thus drenching the Sunday papers she had just been about to put on the table.

"You see?" Sarah demanded. "You see the mayhem this dog creates? It wouldn't be so bad if this enthusiasm was directed at *me* but it's *you* he loves!" A sudden, wonderful idea came to her. "Would you like to have Jacko? Martin, let me give him to you. He'd be a brilliant companion and I'll even throw in his dog bowl and leash."

"I'd do many things for you," Martin said, picking up the papers and shaking the water from them, "but taking Jacko is not one of them."

"I don't see why not. He loves you, you like him. It's the obvious solution."

"No it isn't. He'd be on his own all day. I couldn't take him to work with me. He'd go mad."

"He already is mad," Sarah pointed out, "and meanwhile

he's destroying my sanity too. Would you like to look after him for a week when I go away and see how it goes?"

"No I would not. Where are you going?"

"To Majorca. In a few weeks. My friend Miriam asked me yesterday. We're going to make our husbands jealous with Spanish lovers."

"Very good," said Martin politely.

Sarah put on her jacket and handed Martin the leash. "Is that 'very good' implying that I'm unable to find a holiday romance or that I won't make my husband jealous?"

"Neither." Martin opened the door. "Where shall we go today?"

"Why don't we go along to the recreation ground, through the field, and down past Halldown Farm. That's quite enough for a Sunday morning."

"All right. Easy, Jacko. Heel, boy!"

"Look at that!" Sarah observed. "He's almost obeying you. Are you sure you don't want him?"

"Quite sure."

They walked to the end of Shooter's Lane and turned left onto Gassett Street, alternating their memorized lines with impressions of their cast mates. Martin did a particularly devastating version of Audrey. In the meantime, Jacko stopped growling and even appeared to be good-humored until they reached the crossroad, when he began to pull at his leash.

"Heel, Jacko," Martin said authoritatively and, taking Sarah's arm, shepherded both woman and dog across Finn Street. Jacko trotted beside them like a lamb. They walked past the row of terraced cottages and turned left into the recreation field.

"Martin," Sarah said, "why did you dash off yesterday?"

"I thought you'd like to be alone with Andrew."

Sarah glanced up at him. "You don't like Andrew, do you?"

Martin relaxed his grip on Jacko's leash. "All right, old boy," he murmured. "We're nearly there." Conscious that Sarah was waiting for a response, he said blandly, "I don't know him well enough to say."

"You've been acting in plays with him for the last fifteen years! It doesn't worry me if you don't like him." Sarah paused while she negotiated the stile and waited while Martin let Jacko off his leash. Jacko immediately streaked across the ground past the dilapidated swings to the other end of the field, where a group of rabbits were about to be pulverized. "I know," Sarah said, "that Andrew has his faults. You probably think I'm mad to want him back." She glanced at him for some reaction. "Do we have to walk so fast?"

"This is not fast, this is brisk. We're supposed to be losing weight, remember? Did you learn scene one last night?"

"Some of it. I'd have learned more if you hadn't worn me out. I fell asleep at the bit where you kiss the top of my head."

"Feeble excuse," said Martin ruthlessly. "Let's start at the bit where I come in and find you crying."

At first, Sarah was hesitant and stumbled over the words. Martin was better but uttered his words in a flat monotone. By the time they reached Halldown Farm they were both enjoying themselves. Martin's diction was beginning to resemble that of Colonel Lintern and his air of superior, even savage impatience made it easy for Sarah to say the line "I love you so much" with a genuine tremor.

"Cool!" sniggered a voice, and the thespians were instantly transported back into reality. Sarah, looking around, located the source of the snigger to Luke Everseed, the vicar's younger son, who was sitting on the village bench with a cigarette in one hand and an arm round the local siren, Tracy Endover.

"We're learning our lines," explained Sarah quickly, "for the Ambercross Players."

"Cool!" said Luke again. Tracy giggled.

"We're performing it in April," said Sarah. "You should come and see it."

"Right," said Luke. Tracy giggled again.

"Good-bye, then," said Sarah brightly, moving forward quickly. "Now where were we, Martin?"

"You were telling me," Martin said levelly, "that you loved me."

Behind them the teenagers were laughing freely. "What are *you* smiling at?" Sarah hissed at her companion.

Martin grinned. "You've gone bright red," he said.

Sarah squared her shoulders. "It's all right for you but I was the one sounding pathetic and feeble. Luke thought I was being *me!* I hate to say it, but Mrs. de Winter is an utter wimp. And what does she see in a bully like Maxim? She'd be far better off with his nice friend, Frank. Frank's so kind and reliable. Everyone likes good old Frank."

Martin shook his head. "Women never go for good old Frank. They always go for the bastards."

"No we don't!"

"Yes you do. Look at history. All the great womanizers: Napoleon, Charles the Second, Byron, James Bond: they all treated women appallingly. Women love a bastard."

"I don't." She saw Martin raise a skeptical brow. "I knew it! You think Andrew's a bastard!"

"You're putting words into my mouth."

"You're right. He is a bastard but he's a bastard with redeeming qualities. It's just that at the moment I can't think what they are."

"He'd have been a terrific Maxim," said Martin.

"I think you're an excellent Maxim," Sarah protested. "In fact when you're Maxim, you're really rather sexy. What is it? Why are you looking like that?"

Martin grinned. "Has anyone ever told you," he said, "that you have a wonderful way with compliments?"

Do Not Be Surprised by Surprising Sexual Urges

Until Sarah's participation in *Rebecca*, her meetings with Martin had been restricted to the after-play parties. She always enjoyed talking to him on these occasions since he seemed to be the only person there who didn't treat the Ambercross Players as the last word in culture. He was so kind and courteous and so utterly unsuited to his wife, who flaunted her charms with such enthusiasm and who, in her dealings with the opposite sex, had all the subtlety of a Venus flytrap. Martin never seemed to notice her outrageous behaviour. Sarah had suspected he was the sort of man who simply ignored anything unpleasant. When Anthea had left him, he dropped out of the next production and on his return had kindly and courteously deflected any attempts by others to express sympathy.

So Sarah liked him but never felt she knew him. She didn't

quite understand, therefore, why after two walks in his company, she felt sufficiently relaxed to tease him about his sex appeal. Perhaps it was because they had both been publicly humiliated by their more flamboyant spouses.

She had only become irritated by Andrew's inability to refer to Martin without adding the prefixes "poor" and "old" since she had acquired the same labels. She had become poor old Sarah now and if that was why Martin was more at ease with her and she with him, she didn't care. She was grateful to spend time with someone who understood.

The weekend walks had also lessened her dread about rehearsals. She knew she had an ally now, if not a very outspoken one. So, today, despite the fact that she had a rehearsal in the evening, she was able to concentrate on her work without thoughts of the evening ahead damaging her concentration.

In fact, this afternoon, Sarah was happy. She was well aware that in her present circumstances such a feeling, however transient, should be savored and she was doing just that. The house was quiet, so heaven knew what Jacko was doing, but with any luck he was exhausted by the walk Sarah had given him before lunch. The studio was warm and sweet-smelling as a result of the pinecones Sarah had thrown into the wood-burning stove. Best of all, as Sarah sat back from the easel and gazed at her work, she had the satisfaction of knowing she had completed the best painting of her life.

After taking hundreds of photos of Raffles and then playing around with different poses, she had finally decided on a very stark and simple design in oils. Raffles's black and brown features from the neck up dominated the canvas with just a hint of olive paint in the background. His nose shone, his fur glistened, and his beautiful, big eyes suggested a wisdom and intelligence far beyond the constraints of his species.

At times like this, Sarah loved her studio. When work was going badly she would pace around her easel, chafing at the confines of the room, impatient with the chaos. When she was pleased with her work, she appreciated the soothing glow from the wood-burning stove, the cheerfulness of the bright yellow walls, and the uninhibited mess of paintbrushes, canvases, and discarded palettes.

From somewhere within the uninhibited mess, the bracing tones of the telephone could be heard. Small gray handsets and uninhibited messes did not live comfortably together. Sarah eventually found it underneath last Sunday's papers and said a little breathlessly, "Hello?"

Jennifer's low voice responded immediately. "Sarah, thank goodness you're here. Can you come to dinner next Saturday, not this coming Saturday, but next Saturday? I need you to come. You're not doing anything, are you?"

"I don't think so," said Sarah, knowing very well that her social calendar was completely blank. "Is this one of your informal supper parties where you only produce about four courses or is it one of your banquets?"

"No, it's just you and the Delaneys and the Everseeds. But I am very keen that you come. I want you to pay very close attention to George. I shall sit you next to him at dinner."

"Why?" asked Sarah warily. Recalling their last conversation, she wondered if Jennifer planned to off-load poor George onto her.

"I think it's possible," said Jennifer in a tone of immense

satisfaction, "that George might be having an affair. Your job is to find out if my suspicions are correct."

"They're not," Sarah said flatly. "George would never have an affair. He's not the type. Why do you think he's having an affair? Don't you think it might be wishful thinking on your part?"

"Of course it's not!" exclaimed Jennifer in a tone of injured innocence.

Sarah dropped onto the floor and sat back against the wall. "I'll tell you something else. Don't you think it's a little bit odd that you're thinking this now, just a little while after Andrew's left me? I have another friend who's voicing exactly the same doubts as you are about *her* husband. Now it may be that the whole world is having an affair at the moment but I think it's more likely that you're both paranoid. Not every man's like Andrew. In fact very few men are like Andrew."

"I am talking about some very interesting circumstantial evidence. For the last two Wednesday evenings, George has been out. The first time, he said he'd be working late. Last week he said he was working late and this morning at breakfast, I reminded him he had a parish council meeting tomorrow and he went bright red and said he had a meeting at work and *then* he said he didn't want any toast!"

"Well, perhaps he didn't want any toast."

"George always wants toast. He wanted to make a quick exit because he was telling a lie and he knows he's a hopeless liar."

"Perhaps he *is* working late. Perhaps he's fed up with parish council meetings. I don't blame him if he is, I must say. If that's all you've got, then . . ."

"There's more!" crowed Jennifer. "Listen to this. On Saturday morning we were in town, walking past the chemist, and a woman came out and said, 'Hello, George.' And George said"—Jennifer paused—"George said, 'Hello there.' "

"I see," said Sarah. "Sounds like a pretty dramatic meeting then."

"You don't understand," Jennifer said impatiently. "It was the way he said it: 'Hello there.' In all my life I have never heard two such bland little words spoken with such discomfort. As soon as he uttered them he dived into Boots and when I followed him in and asked him why we were in there, he grabbed a jar of moisturizer and said he had dry skin."

"Sounds plausible to me. . . ."

"Don't be ridiculous, Sarah. When has George ever worried about things like dry skin? And anyway he doesn't have dry skin. It could have been menopausal pills for all he cared. He dashed into Boots because he was desperate to get away from that woman or rather he was desperate to get *me* away from that woman."

"What did she look like?"

"A little like you actually: nondescript trousers and a sweatshirt, no makeup, untidy hair."

"Very like me," Sarah agreed.

"So all you have to do," concluded Jennifer, "is to ask him where he goes on Wednesday evenings and to watch him like a hawk as you do so. And then report back."

"If I do that," Sarah pointed out, "he'll know you're worried about him and anyway it's not very good manners for a guest to interrogate her host about his possible extramarital activities."

"It's not very good manners for a husband to *have* extra-marital activities. But I certainly don't want him to know I'm on to him. You'll just have to manage it with your usual tact. You could start talking idly about Wednesday evenings and what they mean to you and then—"

"They don't mean anything to me apart from the fact that I have to put the dustbins out."

"Well, pretend they do, for goodness's sake, Sarah. You're the creative one. And remember to act innocent."

"I'm rapidly going off this dinner party," Sarah said. "You know I'm no good at subterfuge."

"You're an actress, aren't you? How's the play going, by the way?"

"I have a rehearsal tonight. If it's as bad as the last one, I'll probably be an ex-actress."

"Nonsense," said Jennifer. "I'm sure you'll take to it like a duck to water!"

Some duck, Sarah thought bitterly, as Audrey interrupted her for the third time that evening to tell her to raise her voice.

"I'm trying to sound nervous and scared," Sarah protested feebly. "If I shout, I don't sound scared."

Audrey put a hand to her forehead. "You don't have to shout," she explained. "You have to *project*. Listen to Claire. She sounds cold and cool and menacing and you can hear every word."

"It's all about breathing," Claire added helpfully. "You have to talk from your diaphragm: here!" She put a huge hand over what was presumably her diaphragm.

"Quite right, Claire," said Audrey approvingly. "Now let's

try one more time. Claire, you enter stage left and see Sarah. Your lip curls with scorn. Very good, Claire, very convincing! Sarah, you shrink back . . . a little less obviously, dear . . . and off you go!"

Trying to remember her words while simultaneously trying to breathe from her diaphragm was not easy but at least this time the conversation proceeded without any more interruptions from Audrey. Ominously she made no comment at the end of the scene. Instead she beckoned to a gum-chewing boy who'd been drinking his beer in the corner of the room. "I want you all to meet Carl. Carl is my gardener's son and has kindly offered to take on the small but pivotal part of Robert." There was a silence while everyone tried to remember who Robert was. Carl himself put his hands in his pockets and raised his eyes to the ceiling and Sarah could tell that poor Carl had fallen victim to Audrey's unshakable will. "Robert," Audrey reminded her audience, "is the junior footman and appears on page thirty-nine in conversation with Frith, the butler. Now since Carl has a very important assignation with his young lady friend," (Carl's scrutiny of the ceiling became even more intense) "we will quickly rehearse his little bit so he can get away. The rest of you can sit down!"

With great relief, Sarah retreated to the bench by the window. As she watched the rehearsal from the sidelines, she thought about all the evenings Andrew had spent here in the autumn. Had Andrew been attracted to Hyacinth at the very first rehearsal? Had he been surprised by a sudden, passionate love for her or had the relationship begun as a little bit of adultery on the side? Surely there must have been at least one seminal moment when Andrew could have deliberately pulled himself back? Perhaps there was. Perhaps Andrew decided that given the choice between the familiarity of his wife and the possibilities of Hyacinth, the latter was far more attractive. In every sense. After all, who wouldn't trade in an old coat for a new one? In fact, Sarah thought, *she* wouldn't. She knew where she was with her old coat: it was comfortable and cozy. Who was to say that a new one would give such good service?

In all her years of marriage, Sarah had never been tempted by adultery. To be strictly accurate, she had not been exactly besieged by offers. The first had been made by the man who came to mend their roof and since he had suffered from a pretty hefty problem with body odor it had not been difficult to withstand his suggestion that they slip between the sheets. The only other would-be lover was the husband of the woman who used to run the boys' playgroup. At a drinks party one evening she had had a pleasant conversation with him about gardening and he had told her that it was essential to understand the type of soil one had. Would she, he had asked intently, like him to come round and test her soil? Sarah, who had drunk rather more than she should have, responded to the suggestion with great enthusiasm. When he came over the following afternoon she discovered that either she had misunderstood his offer or else he had misunderstood her enthusiasm. He had accepted her rebuff with stoicism but had rapidly lost interest in her garden and she never did find out whether her soil was too chalky or not. Over the next few years she met up with three other women whose soil he had tested and had had to suppress the urge to ask them for details of the analysis.

"Sarah!" Audrey's voice cut through her thoughts like a guillotine through a lady's neck.

"Yes!" said Sarah, springing to attention.

"I want you and Martin to do your last little bit at the end of scene one. The rest of you"—Audrey raised a benevolent hand—"can go."

Sarah moved to the center of the room with a pleasurable sense of anticipation. Thanks to the weekend walk, she knew these lines very well and she enjoyed acting with Martin. At least he didn't act as if she'd murdered Father Christmas every time she forgot her lines. Pausing only to wave good-bye to Margaret, she nodded at Martin, who launched into their dialogue.

Audrey leaned forward, watching the two of them intently, silently mouthing the words as they said them. Only when they finished did she sit back in her chair. Sarah and Martin stared at her expectantly.

"Sexual chemistry!" she said at last. "Sex! I want sex. Not from you, Martin."

"Right," Martin said, relaxing immediately.

"But from you, Sarah. I want it from *you!*"

"Why not from Martin?" Sarah asked.

Audrey rested her arms on her bosom. "Martin has to keep the audience guessing throughout the play. Why is he so moody and so difficult? Did he love Rebecca? Does he love his new young wife? The audience must know that you adore him, that you are desperate to reach out to him. Your audience must feel your pain and your passion when he rebuffs you and in order for this to happen you have to radiate thwarted passion."

"I do think Audrey's right." Martin nodded his head gravely. "You'd better start practicing your thwarted passion expression."

"Well, excuse me," said Sarah robustly, "but how can there

be any sexual chemistry if Martin doesn't reciprocate all my passion bits?"

"Ah!" Audrey's eyes lit up. "Martin's turn comes at the end of the play. Then, at last, he will provide us with a veritable explosion of sexual fireworks!"

Sarah smiled sweetly at her costar. "I can't wait," she said.

"It should be wonderful," Audrey agreed. "When Martin tells you he loves you, he will take you in his arms and the entire audience will erupt. He will kiss you with a passion and a tenderness that will electrify everyone who comes. The success of the production, Martin, will rest on your ability to consummate our hopes!"

"Will it?" asked Martin faintly.

"I'm sure you'll do it beautifully," Sarah said.

"Of course he will," said Audrey blithely. "But only with practice! Shall we try it?"

Sarah and Martin stared at each other in horror and then at Audrey. "Now?" they asked.

Audrey smiled. "No time like the present," she said.

"But, Audrey," Martin protested feebly. "We haven't learned the last scene yet. Shouldn't we wait until we know the lines?"

"No, no, no, you can read the words. It's the action I want. Page seventy. Off you go!" Sarah and Martin turned to page seventy and began, haltingly, to read their lines.

"Wait, wait!" bellowed Audrey, shaking her head violently, her double chins shivering as she did so. "We won't do this bit. The page seventy kiss is not the passionate one. Let us proceed straightaway to page eighty-five. I will play the part of Frith." She stood up and cleared her throat. "All right, Sarah, from the top. Spring into character!"

Never had an actress sprung with less conviction. As they proceeded further down the page, they said their lines slower and slower. At last, Audrey uttered Frith's closing line and made her exit from the stage. Martin and Sarah stood rooted to the spot like two particularly inexpressive blocks of wood.

"Now, Martin!" yelled Audrey. "Sweep Sarah into your arms, stride forward. . . . Stride forward, I said . . . that's right. . . . Now, take her in your arms. . . . No, that won't do, you look as if you're plucking at her sleeve. Put an arm round her waist and pull her to you. . . . Pull, I said, not twitch! That's better. Now, Sarah, stop looking at your feet. You've been waiting for this moment, you've been hungry for it, so raise your head proudly, throw it back with abandon. . . . Sarah, you look as if you have a cricked neck. Throw your head back and wait for Martin to kiss you!"

Martin lowered his face unhappily until his mouth was two centimeters away from Sarah's. She could feel her beating heart against his beating heart. At that moment, to her horror, she knew that more than anything in the world she wanted him to kiss her. Horrified by such a wanton, inexplicable urge, she shrank back and said, "Audrey, I think, I really think . . ."

"Kiss Sarah!" Audrey demanded.

Martin shut his eyes and pressed his mouth for a millisecond onto Sarah's.

Audrey rolled her eyes. "Well, really," she protested, "I have never seen such a miserable kiss in my life. If *that* is how the play is going to end we might as well stop rehearsing now. You don't even look as if you like each other!"

"We will," Martin promised. "We just need time to get into

our roles. We'll be better after a few rehearsals. . . . Going in cold like this . . . well, it's difficult."

"Oh for goodness's sake," said Audrey irritably, "I never had this trouble with Andrew and Hyacinth." She stopped, aware that she was guilty of a less than tactful comment. As Martin said to Sarah later, it was probably this that saved them from having to try again. "All right," she said quickly, "we'll leave it for now but sooner or later we are going to have to get this right. Perhaps, tonight, we'll call it a day. I'm feeling a little tired. Would you two mind clearing away the chairs?"

Sarah, embarrassed by Audrey's embarrassment, quickly agreed to her request.

"Thank you." Audrey put on her coat, picked up her bag, and walked slowly across the room. "I am sorry, Sarah. That remark was quite unnecessary." She lifted her chin and walked slowly down the stairs.

Martin waited until he heard the door at the bottom spring shut and then he whistled. "That's the first time I've ever heard her apologize for anything."

Sarah began to stack the chairs. "I almost feel sorry for her. She was mortified."

"So she should be. Are you all right?"

"Fine," said Sarah brightly. She tried to lift the pile of chairs and was stopped immediately by Martin.

"I'll do that," he said. "You stack, I'll put away. Do you fancy a drink afterward?"

"Better not," said Sarah. "I'm going to get an early night and learn scene two for next week. I made the mistake of assuring Audrey I knew it perfectly."

"In that case, let me finish up here and you get off home.

I'll look forward to seeing your word-perfect performance."

"If you're sure." Sarah picked up her coat and bag. She paused. "Are we still on for a calorie-crunching walk on the weekend?"

Martin grinned. "But of course. I'll be round at ten on Saturday, shall I?"

"Fine. Bye now!" Sarah ran lightly down the stairs and out of the pub into the cold night air. She was still shaken by her body's reaction to Martin. Perhaps she was going to be like her Aunty Mary, who went an unbecoming pink any time she was in the proximity of a halfway attractive male. If she was like this after a few months of abstinence, what would she be like after a year or five years or a decade? If she lived as long as her grandmother she might have to go through forty-two, no forty-three years without sex! Andrew Stagg, she thought grimly, I hope Hyacinth gives you herpes.

Nurture Your Friends

Taking Jacko for a walk was like waterskiing behind a boat with a dodgy driver. Sarah would swerve from one place to the next depending on which particular smell enticed Jacko's fickle nose. On the plus side it provided a calorie-reducing, if erratic, exercise. On the minus side, it made her look like an idiot.

Before Jacko, Sarah had used her walks to plan artistic compositions. Fresh air had always been a revitalizing antidote to a blank canvas. Post Jacko, she felt like a kaleidoscope in the hands of a bored child. She'd be thinking about a painting, Jacko would bark and *shake, shake,* all the many preoccupations inside her head would rattle around and then she'd find herself wondering when, or indeed if, James would let her know where in India he was presently residing. Jacko would lunge forward and *shake, shake,* she'd be trying to imagine how she'd cope the next time Audrey ordered Martin to kiss her.

At the moment, Jacko was walking beside Sarah with un-characteristic docility, leaving Sarah free to worry about the future. She had had a phone call from Andrew after breakfast. Could he take her out for a drink on Monday evening? He needed to "run a few things" by her. What a ridiculous turn of phrase that was. How could one *run* things by somebody? It conjured up a very unrelaxing meeting. Was it even slightly possible that he might be changing his mind about Hyacinth? "Now, Sarah, let me run this by you: should I come back to you, do you think?" It didn't sound very likely. Perhaps he wanted to stop putting money into their joint account. What would she do if he wanted to stop putting money into their joint account?

Jacko, quite suddenly, lunged with all the power of his great body away from Sarah. Sarah, taken by surprise, saw the leash fly from her grasp and her dog plunge through Clementine Delaney's hedge.

"Jacko!" Sarah yelled helplessly. "Come here! Jacko!! Come here at once!"

A bloodcurdling scream from the other side of the hedge made action, fast action, imperative. Sarah took a deep breath and pushed her way through the foliage, emerging on the other side with a beating heart and leaf-splattered hair. Before her was an appalling sight.

Jacko stood like a victorious prizefighter in the middle of a square section of grass framed by bricks. Sarah's horrified attention was focused exclusively on the small bundle of brown fur clamped between Jacko's evil teeth.

Sarah was not a brave woman but she did not hesitate. She plunged into the square, straddled Jacko's huge body, and gripped it between her legs while throwing her scarf over his eyes and round his neck and pulling it until he disgorged his tiny victim. "Sit, Jacko!" she bellowed with an authority she had not known she possessed. "Sit down this minute!"

Jacko surprised both himself and his mistress by sitting. At once Sarah put his leash on again while Clementine, who had watched the entire rescue from her patio, rushed up to the ball of fur, swept it into her arms, and began crooning gently, "Bruno! Bruno!"

For what seemed an interminable length of time, the brown blob didn't stir, and then at last, with a pitiful little shudder, it lifted its head, revealing itself to be a traumatized little guinea pig.

"He's alive," Clementine whispered. "Bruno's alive!"

Never had Sarah felt such relief. "Clementine," she breathed, "I am *so* sorry. I am so, so sorry. If there's anything I can do. . . ."

Clementine clutched the guinea pig to her chest. "Just go," she shuddered. "And take that . . . that animal away from my garden. I would be grateful"—she closed her eyes for a moment in an obvious effort to control her feelings—"if in the future you would avoid walking anywhere near my home."

"Yes," said Sarah quickly. "Yes, of course. I am so sorry. . . ."

"Please go!" Clementine's voice rose and teetered on the edge of hysteria.

Sarah, very sensibly, went.

*　　*　　*

The sky on Saturday morning was the color of porridge. It was one of those days when one couldn't imagine that spring would ever come. There were treacherous patches of black ice on the road and Sarah and Martin had to trudge carefully along Gassett Street, in a diametrically opposite direction to Clementine's house.

"I've been thinking and thinking," Sarah said, "and I have to face it. Jacko must go and if that means he'll be put down, then I'm sorry but there's no other answer. In the last few days I've rung anyone I can think of who might be sufficiently crazy to take him on and of course there is no one, no one at all!"

Martin grunted sympathetically. "What about Ruth?"

"She's asked me to hold on to him for another week while she tries to find a home for him. She says the rescue center won't rescue him anymore. I gather he nearly ate a poodle a few months ago."

Martin's mouth twitched. "Unforgivable," he said.

"Yes it is, and it's pretty unforgivable of Ruth to dump him on me in the first place. I can tell you I've gone off her in a big way. She seems to think it's my fault I can't handle him. How can anyone handle a dog who tries to kill a poodle?" She stared indignantly at Jacko, who was quietly padding beside Martin, looking as if he'd never even contemplate eating a poodle, let alone a guinea pig. "I don't suppose," she asked hopefully, "you've changed your mind about taking him on?"

"No," said Martin firmly, "I haven't. Besides, I'm off to Australia for a couple of months in the autumn and what would I do with him then?"

Sarah was conscious of a stab of dismay. In a very short space of time Martin had become a reassuring presence in her life. Australia was a long way from Ambercross and two months was a long time. "Australia?" she inquired. "Lucky old you!"

Martin released Jacko from his leash and ushered him under the stile. "I'm going to stay with my son," he said. "Tony's been out there for six years now. He and his wife had a baby in September. My first grandson!"

"You're a grandfather!" Sarah marveled. She had a vague recollection of Martin's son. Years ago, he had as a lanky, awkward teenager attended a couple of the after-play parties. It seemed extraordinary to think the shy young boy was now a father. "Will this be your first visit?" she asked.

"I went out there once . . . after Anthea left. I never seemed to have the time after that. And then in October I hit fifty. I thought I could either have a midlife crisis or I could take time off work to visit Tony. No contest really."

"Very sensible. I've always thought work was hugely overrated."

"I've worked out I can afford to pack it all in in five years time. And then I shall go backpacking."

"Sounds great," Sarah said dreamily. "I'd love to come with you."

"In five years," Martin said, "you'll be back with Andrew . . . or married again."

"Very unlikely. How long is it since Anthea left *you?*"

"That's different. You don't strike me as the sort of person who likes living alone."

"What has that to do with anything? Jennifer says once I stop waiting for Andrew to come home, I'll start to enjoy the solitary life. What do *you* like about it?"

"Well," Martin said, "it's a lot simpler than being married."

"That doesn't necessarily mean it's better."

"It is for me."

Sarah sighed. "I'm not sure I want a simple life if it means a life on my own. And anyway, my life has got far more complicated since Andrew left. I wouldn't have this dog, for a start." She sighed again. "I shall find it very difficult to forgive Andrew for this. Are you and Anthea friends now? Do you ever see her?"

Martin paused to let Jacko off the leash and push him through the gap under the fence. He climbed over the gate into the field. "I talk to her occasionally. She lives in Knutsford with her man. I think she's happy enough."

Sarah followed Martin over the gate. "I bet she isn't. Anthea always struck me as someone who wouldn't be happy with anyone for very long."

Martin picked up a stick and hit a frozen cow pat with it. "I don't know. When you knew her, she was a disappointed woman."

"Why should she be disappointed?"

"She would have liked more children and that didn't happen. She would have liked a husband with a glamorous occupation. She never liked the fact she was married to a plumber."

"I think plumbing is a very glamorous career. It sounds like something out of D. H. Lawrence, all masculine and earthy and powerful and basic."

"In that case," said Martin, "I should find it easy to provide all the sexual fireworks at the end of the play. I wonder what went wrong in rehearsal."

Sarah glanced at him uncertainly. "It was," she said tentatively, "very embarrassing. I found it embarrassing."

"I noticed," said Martin drily.

"You hated it too! I could see you did. It was so embarrassing."

"In that case," said Martin, "you were very lucky that Audrey shamed even herself by her remarkably spectacular gaffe. Otherwise she'd have kept us at it for hours."

"Martin," Sarah said hesitantly, "will you tell me something? Will you be absolutely honest?"

"That depends what it is."

"Do you think . . ." Sarah paused and bit her lip. "In your opinion did Andrew fall in love with Hyacinth as soon as he met her?"

"In my opinion," Martin said slowly, "Hyacinth fell for Andrew at the very first rehearsal and she never tried to hide her feelings. She flirted, he faltered and he fell."

"I see," said Sarah.

"Andrew did try to resist her," Martin said. "I'm sure he did. Hyacinth was a very determined woman."

"*You'd* have resisted her."

"Yes," said Martin, "but then I never found her attractive."

"Truthfully?" Sarah asked. "Why not?"

Martin frowned. "She has very odd ears."

"No, she doesn't," said Sarah, feeling suddenly better. "Why are they odd?"

"They are very big and whenever she was playing a particularly emotional bit they would go red. Quite extraordinary. I've never seen anything like it. I could never fall for a woman whose ears keep going red."

Sarah laughed. "I think you're making it all up."

"Not at all. Who did you say you were going to Majorca with?"

"Miriam. She's married to a very charming man called Clive. He's the sort of man who can't resist being charming to every woman he meets."

Martin raised an eyebrow. "Not easy for Miriam."

"No. She deserves better." Sarah stiffened suddenly. "Where is Jacko?"

Martin cupped his hands to his face and shouted. "Jacko! Here, boy!"

A terrible thought struck Sarah. "Do you suppose he's gone back for more guinea pig? He might have developed a taste for it."

"He'll be around here somewhere," Martin said. "If we go up to the edge of the wood we'll be able to see him." He strode ahead with a pace that Sarah could only feel belied his confident words. Panting hard, she tried to keep up with him. When she finally reached the top, he was scrutinizing the small copse. "I bet he's in there," he said grimly.

As if in answer, a cacophony of noise and feathers erupted from the trees as a cloud of pheasants flew up in the air. From somewhere within the trees, Jacko's rasping bark could be heard. "Stay there," said Martin. "I'll get him."

Sarah watched him stride toward the trees. Heaven knew what carnage awaited him. She turned her back on the wood and watched the cars driving through the village. From here, they looked like toys as they sped through Finn Street, past the village shop, past the pub, past the Norman church, and then on behind the hill.

No wonder she was tired; they had climbed a long way. At the bottom of the field, she could see two boys performing the most extraordinary maneuvers on their bicycles, flying in the air, and still, somehow being able to remain seated. She watched them for a while and then, remembering Jacko, turned and stared intently at the copse. Her feet and her hands were freezing. At last, she saw Martin emerge triumphant with Jacko on his leash.

"Martin," she said, running toward him, "you are my hero. I thought you'd never find him. And my hands feel like ice."

"Here," he said. "I'll rub them for you." At which moment, Luke Everseed appeared on the brow of the hill with his bicycle.

"Hello," said Sarah awkwardly. She saw him looking with unabashed interest at the two of them. "Martin's warming my hands," she explained quickly.

"Cool," said Luke Everseed.

Keep Away from Mirrors with Bright Lights

Andrew had suggested they meet at the new wine bar in Frome. Sarah would have preferred a cozy pub with a log fire, secluded alcoves, and comfortable seating. She presumed he'd chosen this place on the grounds that no one they knew would dream of coming here. Unless, of course, rejuvenated by his new, young girlfriend, he felt at home in this environment. It had not escaped Sarah's notice that he'd given up wearing ties and that he'd replaced his traditional floppy quiff with a new boy-band, shorter hairstyle.

Sarah perched precariously on a high stool in front of a mushroom-shaped table and tried to pull her skirt down and make herself comfortable. She had gone to considerable trouble over her appearance, which given the subdued lighting, seemed hardly necessary. She had washed her hair and blow-dried it according to her hairdresser's instructions, ironing out the usual tangle of curls so that a soft fringe fell tactfully over the burgeoning frown lines on her forehead. She had applied Red Fire lipstick and Charcoal eyeshadow, colors that would complement, she hoped, the short gray cardigan and little black skirt that she had finally chosen to wear.

If she'd known she'd be sitting on the equivalent of a baby's high chair, she'd have worn trousers like everyone else around her. At the neighboring mushroom table, a strangely androgynous couple sat drinking Special Brew, their mobile phones and packets of Marlboro set out in front of them. Their limbs were curled effortlessly round the legs of their high chairs and they talked earnestly in hushed voices. They mirrored each other's gestures, turning locks of their hair round their fingers, raising their bottles to their mouths in perfect unison.

Sarah shifted her bottom and wished she could relax in a proper chair. At least the music was good. James had introduced her to the Beta Band a few months ago and the sweet, wistful sound of "Dry the Rain" almost succeeded in relaxing her. But her back was beginning to ache and she felt far too old to be in a place like this. She wished Andrew would hurry up with the drinks.

A girl was standing at the bar, chatting in a desultory manner to a woman next to her. She was wearing a pair of low-slung trousers and a top that exposed a perfectly flat midriff. On the girl's other side, a man with a long red scarf sat sipping his beer, apparently immersed in his newspaper. The woman's companion finished her drink, looked at her watch, uttered her farewell, and left the bar. Sarah, looking at the clock above the bar, reckoned it would take the man a good five minutes to establish communication.

Thirty seconds! It took thirty seconds! That was impressive. The man said something, the girl responded briefly, he said something else, and the girl laughed. Bingo! Sarah, intrigued, wondered what it was he had said.

Andrew came back with the drinks and sat down opposite her. Sarah had asked for a white wine and was disconcerted by the size of the glass. At this rate she would end up agreeing to anything. Perhaps she should drink only half of it. She took a sip. It was very dry and very cold. Sarah decided it was important to be relaxed in any negotiations. She took another sip.

"So," said Andrew, "how are you?"

Sarah said she was very well and wondered how many polite questions Andrew would feel obliged to ask before he could approach the topic that really interested him.

"Have you heard from the boys recently?" he asked.

Sarah shook her head. "Not a word. I keep imagining James running round India with a girl in a tattered bridal gown but I suppose she's wearing something else by now. Ben promised me they'd keep in regular contact. I hope they're all right."

"They'll be fine. When I was their age I only got in touch with my mother when I wanted some money."

"You've only ever got in touch with your mother when you wanted some money."

"That's a bit harsh," said Andrew. "But you're probably right."

"In which case," said Sarah, "I can look forward to about eight conversations with my sons in the next twenty years."

Andrew grinned. "You'll get more than that. The boys are

much nicer than me and you are very much nicer than my mother."

"Thank you."

"It's the truth. How's the wine?"

"Lovely."

"Good. So . . ." Andrew clapped his hands together. Two polite questions, one compliment, and bingo! "I thought it was time we talked about practicalities."

He wanted to talk about money. In which case they would have to talk about solicitors and divorce and irrevocable decisions. Andrew was leaning forward and staring at her intently. An observer might have thought she was blessed indeed to have the full attention of such a good-looking man. And Andrew was looking particularly good in his dark suit and crisp white shirt. Sarah would have liked to ask if Hyacinth had ironed it for him. "That's a nice shirt," she said.

"What?" He frowned. "It's new," he said absently. So Hyacinth hadn't ironed it then. "The thing is," he said, "the last thing I want to do is rush you but I can't go on living in Hyacinth's flat forever. It's far too small and quite frankly it's not easy for either of us."

"Oh dear," said Sarah. "Poor you."

"I'm serious, Sarah. I've got nowhere to put anything. Now I know you love the cottage but I think we're going to have to bite the bullet—"

"*We're* going to have to bite the bullet?"

"I'm as fond of the house as you are but I can't afford to keep you in it indefinitely *and* buy a place for me and Hyacinth. Ideally, I'd like to put it on the market right away but the last thing I want is to make things difficult for you."

"That's very thoughtful of you."

"I've been talking to some chums and they reckon the house is worth about four hundred and fifty grand. We have a fifty-thousand-pound mortgage. If we sell the place and share the proceeds straight down the middle, then we could both get reasonable properties."

Sarah sat up very straight. "Don't you think all this is a little premature? You only left me in November and already you want to throw me out of my home."

Andrew gave a mirthless chuckle. "You do love to exaggerate! No one's throwing you out. I'm not even asking you to put the house on the market. Not yet. I'm simply asking you to consider the idea. I wouldn't dream of putting any pressure on you."

Sarah took a gulp of her wine. "That's reassuring."

"Well, of course I wouldn't. Funnily enough, I wasn't just thinking of myself here. Now that the boys have virtually left home, you must be rattling around in the place. You'd probably be far happier in somewhere smaller—"

"Excuse me," said Sarah, gathering her bag and standing up.

"Where are you going?"

"To the loo. Is that all right?"

"Do you want another drink?"

"No, thank you," said Sarah, "I haven't finished my first one." She stood up and Andrew took hold of her arm. An observer might think he couldn't bear to let her out of his sight. "Just tell me you'll agree to think about what I said."

"I'm going away in a few weeks," Sarah said. "I'm not going to think of any of this before I go away."

"You're going away?" Andrew asked. "Why?"

"Because," said Sarah, "I've been invited." Somewhere in a

parallel universe, a far prettier and far more confident Sarah was explaining to a suddenly distraught Andrew that she was being whisked away by her new lover. She raised her chin. "Miriam's been offered a free apartment in Majorca. So we're going out to get some sun and some sand."

Andrew laughed. "You won't get much sun in February. How is old Miriam? Is she still teaching?"

Teaching, like plumbing, was one of those professions that Andrew regarded with genial contempt. Miriam, unlike Martin, was not someone Andrew could patronize with impunity and he had always treated her choice of career as a bewildering aberration on her part.

"She's still teaching," Sarah said. "We're going away in her half-term. Now if you don't mind, I really do need to go to the loo." She edged her way between the tables and walked past Red Scarf and Flat Midriff. Red Scarf was saying, "How extraordinary! That's just what I've always thought!" Flat Midriff's eyes widened. "Really?" she asked. "I've always found . . ."

Sarah remembered the excitement of those early exploratory conversations and the joy she had felt when the object of her lust turned out by an extraordinary coincidence to share the same views on virtually everything of importance. She could remember Andrew listening to her with the same exclusive attention Red Scarf was giving to Flat Midriff.

Emerging from the loo a few minutes later, Sarah discovered that both Red Scarf and Flat Midriff had gone, presumably to explore other areas of common interest. Andrew was talking softly on his mobile phone. A tender smile played about his mouth. Sarah shut her eyes for a moment and swallowed. That he should ring Hyacinth *now* was almost unbearable. When he saw Sarah, he murmured a hurried good-bye and put the phone away.

Sarah wished she had a mobile phone. She wished someone would ring her right now and she could murmur lovingly, "I'll speak to you later." Instead, she could only sit down and say briskly, "I can't stay long," though she couldn't for the life of her think of a plausible reason as to *why* she couldn't stay long.

Andrew, of course, couldn't care less as to why she had to hurry off. "Listen," he said. "All of this can wait. I don't want to rush you. Let's meet when you get back. Do you have your diary with you? We could sort out a date now."

"Not that you want to rush me," said Sarah.

"Of course not." Andrew took out his diary.

Sarah finished her drink. It was amazing how such a big glass of wine had slipped down so easily. "I haven't got my diary on me. I get back at the beginning of March. Give me a ring then."

"That's fine," said Andrew graciously. "It will do you good to get away. Are you going to take your play script with you?"

Sarah, realizing with a sinking heart that she should indeed take her script with her, nodded enthusiastically. "Absolutely." She did not wish to talk about the play. She did not wish to stay talking to Andrew. Going to the loo had been a big mistake: the unforgiving light of the washroom had revealed, with relentless clarity, why Andrew had been so eager to ditch her and go off in the arms of the heavenly Hyacinth. His expression as he talked on the phone had only underlined the fact. He was not coming back. He was never coming back. The past meant nothing to him. He loved Hyacinth.

Don't Get Drunk at Dinner Parties

Sarah arrived home from her rehearsal, ignored Jacko's custom-
ary snarl of welcome, and put the kettle on the stove. She felt
scratchy, irritable, and above all cross with herself. It was bad
enough to be bad-tempered when one had reason to be, but
tonight had gone well. Her bit with Howard had gone so
smoothly that he had been unable to affect his usual I-am-trying-
hard-to-be-patient look. Her bit with Claire had gone so well that
Claire had congratulated her on her diaphragm control, which
was particularly satisfying since Sarah had in fact forgotten all
about her stupid diaphragm. She had met a charming neighbor of
Audrey who'd confessed to being wholly gripped by her scene with
Martin and who had joined her and Martin for a friendly drink
after the rehearsal. There was no reason why Sarah should feel as if
she were wearing an itchy hair shirt under her sweater.

Sarah fished out the tea bags and threw one into her "I am 39 and holding!" mug. The mug had been a birthday present from her sister-in-law on her fortieth birthday and Sarah hated it. She used it all the time in the hope that sooner or later it would break. Why did she feel like this? Why had the evening left her so restless, so dejected? There must be reasons.

REASONS FOR SARAH'S DEJECTION

A: Sarah was late for rehearsal, prompting a stinging rebuke from Audrey, who reminded her that since she had a large part to play in every single scene it was incumbent on her to at least make the effort not to keep the rest of the cast waiting. Sarah tried to explain she had been held up by a phone call from her mother, who had been worried about the disappearance of her cat. Audrey showed no interest in her mother's cat and, to be fair, Sarah didn't blame her.

B: Audrey introduced Sarah to her charming neighbor with the less-than-confidence-inspiring words, "This is Sarah Stagg, who has never acted before and is doing her best in the circumstances. Sarah, this is Sally-Anne Furlong, who will be here from the beginning of March in order to act as prompt. After the beginning of March, of course, there will be no more reliance on scripts." Which meant, Sarah thought, that the entire holiday in Majorca would be taken up with learning words.

C: Sally-Anne Furlong was not only charming and friendly but also stunning, with kohl-rimmed eyes, crimson lips, and hair that tumbled in carefully disorganized curls. She wore a tight red skirt and a black velvet top. Beside her, Sarah felt like a bag lady.

When Martin suggested a drink at the end of the rehearsal and Sarah said that would be lovely, Sally-Anne said she could murder a gin. For a terrible moment it looked as if Audrey might want one too but she decided it was time for her bed and Martin said he'd be happy to give Sally-Anne a lift home.

D: During a jolly drink together, Sally-Anne Furlong turned out not only to be stunning and charming but also extremely flirtatious. Having quickly established that Martin was available, she made it abundantly clear that she was too. Sarah had finished her drink quickly and made her excuses.

Sarah squeezed the last shreds of tea from her tea bag and threw it into the bin. She ought to be very happy for Martin. If anyone deserved a good time with an attractive and entertaining lady it was him. And even if he and Sally-Anne became an item there was no reason to think their own friendship would suffer. No reason at all.

Martin rang the following evening and said he wouldn't be able to make their walks that weekend. Sarah said quickly she quite understood and would have to go since Jacko was outside pulling up her herb garden. She rang off and looked at Jacko, who was asleep on his blanket. She didn't like lying to Martin but for some reason she really didn't want to know why he would be otherwise engaged.

AMBERCROSS DINNER PARTIES
FOLLOWED STRICT RULES

1: The hostess was duty bound to wear herself out over a hot stove for at least four hours beforehand and to leave it only when the dinner began.

2: The host was required to take coats, fill glasses, pass round canapés, and be ready at a moment's notice to kick-start a stalled conversation.

3: The guests were required to mingle comprehensively while enjoying their predinner drinks. Should they make the mistake of embarking on an interesting conversation with only one other guest, they should be prepared to end it the moment their antimingling behavior was spotted.

4: Guests were not supposed to get drunk and so if George Upton-Sadler was the host, they should never accept his martinis.

The reason why Sarah did just this was because she'd seen Clementine emerge from the kitchen and felt she needed Dutch courage. She smiled nervously at Clementine and complimented her on her appearance. Clementine thanked her frostily. Sarah prattled on for a bit about the problems of finding good clothes shops and then decided she could stall no longer. "Clementine," she asked earnestly, "how is the guinea pig?"

"Bruno died two days ago," Clementine said. "The vet thought it was delayed shock."

"Oh no!" Sarah spoke with genuine contrition. "I am desperately sorry."

Clementine responded with a sad little smile. "I'm sure you are. Unfortunately being sorry doesn't bring Bruno back."

"No," agreed Sarah humbly, "it doesn't."

"Here we are, ladies!" George arrived, bearing a tray of drinks. "A spritzer for you, Clementine, and a martini for you, Sarah. You'd better have a sip and tell me if it's to your taste."

Sarah, preoccupied by Bruno's tragic demise, took a huge gulp and was nearly knocked sideways. "Very good," she gasped.

"Excellent!" said George happily, and moved on to the rest of his guests, leaving Sarah to continue to struggle with Clementine. "I want you to know," she said, "I'm getting rid of Jacko. I would have taken him back to the rescue home this week but I've been waiting to hear from Ben's girlfriend. She's trying to find another home for him."

Clementine thawed slightly. "I think it's for the best. I hope you won't mind me saying this but I can't help thinking you have no control at all over your dog."

"I don't mind at all," Sarah assured her. "You are very perceptive. I have *no* control over Jacko, in fact I hate Jacko, I really, really hate him."

Clementine, a little discomfited by Sarah's vehemence, seemed relieved at the approach of the Reverend Michael Everseed. "Clementine," he murmured, "do you mind if I break up your little chat with Sarah? Your husband and my wife are having an argument about the new speed restriction humps and I think your calming influence is needed!"

Clementine gave a self-deprecatory smile. "I'll do my best," she promised, and left Sarah's side with visible relief. Sarah took the opportunity to tip George's martini into the vase of roses on the piano behind her.

"Shall we sit down?" asked the vicar, pointing to Jennifer's velvet-covered sofa.

George reappeared. "Is everything all right with you two? My goodness, Sarah, you downed your martini quickly! Let me get you another!" He disappeared before Sarah could call him back.

"Tell me," the vicar said gently, leading her to the sofa, "are you finding it difficult to cope?"

"Not at all," said Sarah, "I'm very well."

Jennifer flew in with a bowl of olives in one hand and a plate of cheese straws in the other. "Michael," she said, "I'll put you in charge of the olives. Would either of you like a cheese straw?"

"Thank you," said Michael, taking the bowl of olives in one hand and a cheese straw in the other.

"Yes, please," said Sarah, who was ravenous, having taken Jacko for a long walk in the afternoon. "They look brilliant. Are they homemade?"

"The day I buy my cheese straws," said Jennifer, "you can bury me in the ground." She glanced sharply at Sarah. "You don't have a drink! George isn't doing his job very well!"

"He's getting me one," began Sarah, "but . . ."

"Good!" said Jennifer, and rushed out, leaving Sarah to wonder, as she had done many times before, why people gave dinner parties when they were such terribly hard work.

The vicar bit into his cheese straw. "Delicious!" he exclaimed, and then dismayed by the volume of crumbs that were littering his clothes, added, "A bit difficult to eat however."

"Very," Sarah agreed. "I always eat them in one go!"

George returned with a new martini for Sarah. "There you are. One very dry martini. See if it's all right."

Sarah took a reluctant sip and nearly fell through the sofa. "Fine!" she whispered.

"Good show!" said George. "Do you like Jennifer's cheese straws?"

"By rights," Sarah told him, "you should be very fat. Jennifer's cooking is so scrummy. Why aren't you fat? What's your secret?"

"Exercise," said George. "I walk the dogs every morning before I go to work and every evening when I get home. Two brisk walks a day. That's all you need."

"Right," said Sarah. "I only do one and I don't seem to be shifting much weight."

"You don't need to lose weight," George protested. "Why is it always the most attractive women who worry about their weight? We men don't like walking skeletons, we like a bit of flesh to get between our fingers, don't we, vicar?"

"Yes, indeed," said the vicar, putting the bowl of olives on his lap and brushing bits of cheese straw from his knee.

"Women such as you," George continued benignly, "gladden the eye. How's your drink?"

Sarah took another sip. She was glad she was sitting down. "Very nice," she said.

"Good, good," said George. "Mine seems to be empty. I'd better fill it up. Won't be a minute." He beamed at them both and left the room.

"This is very strong!" Sarah said. "I tipped the last one down the flowers."

"Really?" The vicar smiled and passed the olives toward her. At the same time Sarah stretched out her arm and inadvertently knocked the bowl from his hand.

"Oh dear," said the vicar. "Oh dear, oh dear!"

"I am so sorry," Sarah stuttered, trying to rescue the olives from between his legs.

"Sarah!" said the vicar in a strangulated voice. "Please!"

"I'm so sorry," Sarah repeated weakly. She was horribly aware that the Delaneys and the vicar's wife had stopped talking about traffic humps.

At dinner, Sarah was placed between George and Simon Delaney. The sight of good food never failed to revive her spirits and as a bowl of *moules marinières* was placed in front of her, she began to relax. Simon passed her a plate of sliced baguette and murmured, "How's the demon hound?"

"I am so sorry," Sarah said earnestly, "about the guinea pig."

Simon's mouth twitched. "The word 'murder' was mentioned," he said drily.

"The dog," Sarah promised, "is going. He was a present, a very misguided present from my boys. They thought I'd be lonely when they went away."

"And were you?"

"The best thing about Jacko," said Sarah, "is that I will never, ever mind being on my own again. Being on my own is paradise compared to being with Jacko."

Simon laughed. He really was a very nice man.

By the time they had eaten the main course (roast monkfish and pumpkin puree) Sarah had forgotten all about the embarrassing incident with the olives. She had not, however, been able to forget her mission to find out about George's Wednesday evenings, since Jennifer kept raising her eyebrows at her. Cushioned by the very good Côtes du Rhône she'd been drinking, she turned to George at last. "How's work?" she asked hopefully.

"To tell the truth," George said, "it's a little slack at the moment. Always is at this time of year."

"It's good not to work too hard," said Sarah, preparing to take a synaptic leap toward her goal. "I find it's better to keep evenings free for more interesting things. I never work past six o'clock."

"Is that so?" asked George.

It wasn't actually but Sarah nodded vigorously. "I like to keep evenings free for seeing people I like."

"Do you?" asked George. "All I'm fit for at the end of the day is a bit of shut-eye in front of the telly!"

"Oh I'm sure that's not true," said Sarah, who was finding it very difficult to direct the conversation properly. She felt as if she were wading through treacle. "Take Wednesdays for example," she added desperately.

"Wednesdays?" George prompted politely.

"Yes. I mean, I find I get quite lonely on Wednesday evenings. For some reason."

"Do you?" George asked. "Dear, oh dear."

"What's this about Wednesdays?" Simon asked.

"Sarah says," George boomed, "she gets very lonely on Wednesday evenings."

The entire party stopped to look at Sarah, who finished her glass of Côtes du Rhône and tried to look as if she'd just made a very good joke.

"Who's for pudding?" Jennifer asked brightly.

Have a Good CD Collection

The telephone, never Sarah's favorite alarm clock, woke her at nine with the force of an electric drill. Sarah opened her eyes, wished she hadn't, closed them again, and reached for the handset, trying to ignore the listless hammer thudding mournfully inside her head. She mumbled a hello and fell back against her pillow.

"Sarah? It's Ruth." Sarah held the phone a few inches from her ear but the voice was still unnaturally loud. "I'm afraid I have bad news. I can't find anyone to take Jacko. I've tried all my contacts but no one wants him. You must do what you think best. I can't do any more."

Had Sarah been feeling stronger she might have questioned that last statement. Since she had a compelling urge to stick a pillow over her head, she merely mumbled, "All right. Thank you for ringing," and hoped Ruth would go.

Ruth didn't. "What *are* you going to do?" she asked.

Sarah put a hand to her aching head. "I'm thinking I might throw up," she said. She would never, ever again, she thought bitterly, drink anything stronger than an orange juice.

"Sorry?" asked Ruth.

"I'm not feeling very well," Sarah confessed. "Can I ring you later in the week? Oh, and Ruth, I don't suppose you've heard from Ben recently?"

"No," said Ruth. "I haven't. I wouldn't worry about him. He'll be far too busy partying to get in touch with you or me. You know what Goa's like!" There was a definite edge to her voice and Sarah, who had no idea what Goa was like but whose imagination was already whirring, said only, "I'll speak to you soon. Good-bye, Ruth." She put the phone back on its stand, pulled the duvet up to her chin, placed Andrew's pillow over her face, and waited for sleep to return.

It didn't. Ruth's phone call had effectively sabotaged all chances of blessed oblivion. Images of a dying Jacko chased images of a drug-crazed Ben, prompting the hammer in her head to redouble its efforts to open her skull. She threw back her bedclothes. There was no point in thinking about anything until she'd vanquished her hangover. It was time for strong measures.

An hour later, having bathed, washed her hair, made up her face so she looked at least half human, she was ready for her breakfast. She stared without enthusiasm at the scrambled eggs she had just made. It was her doctor who had told her of the healing properties of eggs and experience had proved him right. Now, with each mouthful, she could feel her head lose the semblance of a war zone.

Jacko stood in the middle of the kitchen, fixing her with an unnerving stare. If it wasn't for the fact that Jacko was always fixing her with unnerving stares she would have suspected he knew of her plan to subject him to the vet's lethal handiwork.

The phone rang just as Sarah finished her last piece of scrambled egg. This, Sarah decided, was a good omen. She picked up the handset and said hopefully, "Hello?"

"Sarah? I'm just off to church but I wanted to make sure you were all right." Jennifer sounded disgustingly healthy but then of course she hadn't been so mad as to drink one of George's martinis.

"That's kind of you," said Sarah. "I've been eating scrambled eggs."

"Very sensible," said Jennifer, who had the same doctor as Sarah.

"Tell me," said Sarah, only half sure she wanted to know the answer, "did I behave badly last night?"

"Of course you didn't," said Jennifer. "Though it did take us rather a long time to get you into the Everseeds' car."

"I didn't want to put them out," Sarah protested. "I could have walked home. I was *expecting* to walk home."

"I know, dear, but I'm not sure you would have found it. Anyway, I'm glad you're all right this morning."

"I didn't find anything out about George."

"I did gather that." Jennifer lowered her voice. "George thought you were making a pass at him."

Sarah sat bolt upright. "What!"

"Well, what do you expect? All that stuff you said about being lonely on Wednesday evenings!"

"You told me to say that! I cannot believe this. Jennifer, this is awful. He'll never speak to me again."

"Of course he will. I think he was rather flattered. I told him it was the alcohol talking."

"Thanks a lot!" said Sarah bitterly. "Now he'll think I'm a sad, old, sex-starved alcoholic. Which, Jennifer, I am not."

"Of course you're not," said Jennifer soothingly. "You're certainly not old!"

"I tell you something. This is the last time I try to find out what George is doing on Wednesday evenings especially since I don't think he *is* doing anything on Wednesday evenings."

"He is, Sarah, I know he is. . . . Yes, George, I'm coming. I'm talking to Sarah . . . Sarah, George sends his love."

"Well don't send him mine," responded Sarah crossly, "and you'd better ask God to forgive you for landing your friend in trouble. Oh and thank you for supper. It was delicious."

"It was good, wasn't it? I must go! Drink lots of water."

Drink lots of water! It wasn't water she needed, it was a public relations officer. Sarah stood up and began to clear away the breakfast things. Jacko sat down on his haunches and barked, reminding her that if she didn't want his blood on her hands she also needed a miracle.

"I'll take you for a walk in a minute," she said, "but first I shall wash the dishes." Jacko barked again, stirring the dormant hammer in her head. "All right," she conceded. "First, I shall take you for a walk." For someone who was supposed to be taking charge of her life, it was a little depressing that she could be bullied by a mere dog but then again Jacko could hardly be described as a mere dog.

As walks with Jacko went, it could have been worse. Yes, he splashed her newly washed jeans with very muddy water but he failed to lead her into the foul-smelling bog. Yes, he did trip her up and cause her to roll down the hill like a demented sausage but at least she managed to stop him from dashing across the road and being flattened by a passing milk lorry. Though actually, thought Sarah as she plodded back up Shooter's Lane, that might have been the miracle she'd been waiting for.

She noted with interest that there was a battered navy blue car sitting outside her gate. Unfortunately, Jacko noticed it too. When a huge man with a wild, gray beard climbed out from the driver's seat, Jacko gave a bloodthirsty roar. Giving one of his demonic leaps, he broke away from Sarah and zoomed toward his prey, his leash flailing uselessly behind him. Sarah yelled, "Jacko!" and ran after him. Killing the guinea pig was bad enough; killing an elderly man who looked like Moses was quite another.

Perhaps the man *was* Moses. She heard him say, "Down, Jacko!" and point his hand at the ground as if he were about to perform a miracle. Then he *did* perform a miracle. Jacko, who had certainly been on the verge of tearing the poor man into tiny pieces, came to a grinding halt in front of him, gave a tiny whimper, and lay down in front of the man's feet. Perhaps he'd had a heart attack? Sarah stopped running and paused to catch her breath. A second man emerged from the car and Sarah felt her heart return to its rightful place as she recognized Martin.

He looked quite calm. The man with the wild beard looked quite calm. And since Jacko's tail was wagging, he was clearly not dead. In fact as she went up to them all, he looked as if he were thinking of having a nap.

Sarah, still fighting for breath, felt dangerously close to tears. "I'm so sorry," she gasped at the stranger. "I thought he was going to kill you."

"No chance," said Martin cheerfully, "not with me here to protect him."

"You cheeky wee bastard," returned the man with the beard. "You couldn't protect a virgin in a monastery."

"You'll have to forgive him," Martin said. "He has the manners of a canary."

"What do *you* know about canaries?" the man asked. "Have you ever looked after a canary? I've known canaries with the sweetest natures imaginable. And talking about good manners, are you ever intending to introduce me to the young lady here or are we going to stand here all day listening to you going on about bloody canaries?"

"Sarah," Martin said, "allow me to introduce you to my brother, Jean-Pierre. . . ."

"Your brother!" Sarah exclaimed.

"I know," said Martin sympathetically. "He looks like he should be my father. . . ."

"You cheeky young whippersnapper!" interrupted his brother good-naturedly.

"But he is indeed my brother," continued Martin, "my very much older brother."

"Hello," said Sarah to Jean-Pierre. "It's very nice to meet you and I'm sorry about my dog. He's a monster. I can't do anything with him. He tries to kill everybody. To see him lie down for you like that . . . you have no idea how incredible that is. You're like Martin: you have the power. I don't know how you do it but I'm very glad you did."

Jean-Pierre waved a modest hand. "It's my natural authority. As to why the dog listens to my poor wee brother . . . now that *is* a mystery."

"I can't help noticing," Sarah said, "that you speak in a Scottish accent."

"Ah," said Jean-Pierre, "you noticed that, did you?"

"I did," said Sarah. "But Martin doesn't. And you have a French name."

Jean-Pierre shook his head at Martin. "You can't hide a thing from this woman, can you?"

Sarah looked from one man to the other. Jean-Pierre was an elderly giant with an aquiline nose whose only discernible resemblance to Martin was the very pronounced twinkle in his eye and the same spooky ability to manage Jacko. A happy thought occurred to her and she turned impulsively to Martin. "So this is why you couldn't walk with me this weekend!"

"Correct!" Martin said, taking a tissue from his pocket and carefully removing a smudge of dirt from Sarah's cheek. "I can see you've been having a great time without me."

Sarah laughed. She felt like a Christmas tree whose lights had been switched on. "It's so lovely to see you! Jacko's company does get a little oppressive after a while. Do you have to rush off? Can you stay for lunch? I have some sausages in the fridge. Organic," she added hopefully. "From the farm shop."

Martin hesitated. "I don't know. . . . We were on our way to the pub. . . . What do you want to do, Jean-Pierre?"

Jean-Pierre was stroking Jacko's tummy. Jacko, unbelievably, had now rolled over onto his back and was looking like he was in heaven. "Let's try the lady's sausages!" Jean-Pierre said. "But first, I need to stretch my legs. Can we borrow your wee dog for twenty minutes?"

"You can borrow my wee dog for as long as you like," Sarah said. She smiled at Martin. "I'm *so* glad you're here!"

"So'm I," said Martin. He picked up the end of Jacko's leash. "Come on, you horrible hound," he said. "Let's show Jean-Pierre how good you can be."

Funny, Sarah thought, how the right sort of company can revive both body and spirit. Her hangover gone, she tore round the kitchen like a tornado, clearing away breakfast things, peeling potatoes, making a salad, cooking the sausages. Since there was still no sign of the walkers, she went upstairs and changed into her three-quarter length brown skirt. It might be old but its low waistline flattered her hips. To complete the ensemble, she put on her multistriped sweater, a cheerful garment she had not felt like wearing for months.

Half an hour later she heard their voices at the gate. Through the window she saw Martin grinning broadly at something his brother was saying. Impossible to think Martin was the same man who held himself so stiffly and so awkwardly in the presence of Andrew. She went out to greet them and said, "Lunch is all ready!"

"It's a lovely place you live in," said Jean-Pierre. He walked into the kitchen and looked round the room with unabashed curiosity. "You must love living here."

"I do," said Sarah. "I shall hate to give it up."

Martin followed his brother in and took off his jacket. "Do you have to?" he asked.

"Sooner or later I will," Sarah said. "Andrew's already making noises." She smiled at Jean-Pierre. "Can I get you a drink? Would you like a beer or some orange juice?"

"An orange juice, if you please," said Jean-Pierre. "I have a long drive back to Cumbria this afternoon. . . ."

"I'd like a beer," said Martin. "Can I do anything to help?"

"Giving Jacko a good walk is quite enough," said Sarah. "You deserve a rest. Tell me, Jean-Pierre, you have a Scottish accent, a French name, and an English brother. Why?"

"It's a long story," said Jean-Pierre. "Can I use your lavatory first?"

"Of course," said Sarah. "Go up the stairs and it's first on the right. . . . Martin, you'll find some cans in the cupboard at the back." She reached into the fridge and brought out the orange juice.

Martin, casting an appreciative eye at the sausages on the stove, went to the sink to wash his hands. "It's very kind of you to make us lunch," he said.

"It's not kind at all, I'm delighted to have your company. Ruth rang this morning to tell me she can't find another home for Jacko. I don't want to have him put down but if I keep him here the whole village will rise up and stone me to death. I keep trying and trying to think of solutions and the only one I can think of is a lethal injection. Your company is a very welcome diversion. And besides"—she stopped to throw him a hand towel—"I've missed you this weekend. I like our walks."

"So do I," said Martin, drying his hands with studied concentration. He handed back the towel. "As far as the house goes you mustn't let Andrew bully you into moving. He can't make you move out."

"I know," said Sarah, "but—"

"Martin!" Jean-Pierre burst into the kitchen, radiating energy. "In Sarah's lavatory there is a very beautiful painting of a house and it is exactly like the house I've just made!"

"You're a builder?" Sarah asked.

"I am," said Jean-Pierre. "I have spent the last two years building the most perfect house you can imagine—in fact you *can* imagine it since it's in your lavatory."

"I painted that picture," said Sarah, trying to sound modest.

"Then you're a genius! It's a true work of art. Like my house."

Martin opened his can of beer and poured it into a glass. "Please," he begged Sarah, "don't get him started on his house."

"I'm very happy to hear all about it," Sarah retorted, giving Jean-Pierre his drink, "but first, I want you to tell me why you're Scottish. And why you have a French name."

"Our father," said Jean-Pierre, pulling out a chair, "was French."

Sarah studied Martin in amazement. "You're French!"

"Half," said Martin.

"Can you speak French?"

"Of course," said Martin nonchalantly. "Do you want me to say something?"

Sarah nodded and sat down between the brothers.

Martin thought for a moment and then said gravely, *"Mon hamster n'est pas sur l'armoire."*

Sarah was impressed. "What does that mean?"

"My hamster's not on the wardrobe."

"Wow," said Sarah. She frowned. "Chamberlain isn't a very French sounding name."

"Ah," said Jean-Pierre. "Our father's grandfather was English. He settled in France and married a French woman. Our father married a Scots lassie and came to live in Edinburgh. Then my mother left him and he moved to Leicester, where he married again."

"Martin's mother?" prompted Sarah.

"No, that was his third wife," said Jean-Pierre. "He was not an easy man to live with. Though Martin's mother never left him."

"My mother," Martin said, "was *very* easy to live with."

"Are they still alive?" Sarah asked.

"My mother is," said Martin. "She lives in Paris now with my sister, Agnetha."

"*Agnetha?*" protested Sarah.

"At the time my father was obsessed with the blonde singer from Abba," Martin explained.

"Your mother," Sarah said, "sounds a saint."

"His mother," Jean-Pierre agreed, "*is* a saint. Pappa was without doubt the most embarrassing man to be related to. He was the sort of man who could pick a fight with a plank of wood. If he didn't like you, he would not only have to tell you he didn't like you, he would have to tell you *why* he didn't like you. Fortunately," he added, "his English was so bad, most people couldn't understand what he was saying. Scotland was a much easier place once he left."

"But now you live in Cumbria?"

"I fell in love with a lass and followed her home. She died two years ago and I thought of going back to Edinburgh but I want to stay near my daughters and my grandchildren."

"Jean-Pierre has just finished making a house for his granddaughter," said Martin. "It's taken two years. Jean-Pierre will tell you if you let him why it's the best doll's house in the history of the world."

"I don't know much about doll's houses," said Sarah. "Mind you, I always wanted one. I asked Father Christmas for one every year but I never got one."

"The thing is," said Martin, "now Jean-Pierre's finished his house, he reckons he might have time to take on Jacko."

Sarah's eyes widened and her heart missed a beat. She looked at Jean-Pierre in the same way a drowning man might look at a lifeline. "You wouldn't . . . you couldn't think of taking him home with you?"

"He's a fine wee dog. I'd be happy to take him . . . that is . . ."

"Yes?" asked Sarah, hardly daring to breathe.

"If you're sure you don't want him."

"Has Martin told you what a terrible animal he is? Has he told you that the entire village lives in fear of him? I would love you to take him but you seem a nice man and I don't want you to ruin your life."

Jean-Pierre shrugged. "I'm happy to have him."

Sarah sat back in her chair and sighed deeply. "I don't think I have ever been happier," she said simply. She looked from one man to the other. "How can I repay you? What can I do?"

Martin smiled. "How about some sausages?" he asked.

*   *   *

That evening Sarah had a party. She might have been the only person there but it didn't dampen her spirits. There was wine in the fridge, pizza in the oven, and best of all, James's Christmas present to his mother, a compilation tape he had made for her, comprising all the greatest masterpieces of the twentieth century. Sarah put the music on and danced. She danced through Boney M's "Rasputin," stamping her feet and clapping her hands. She danced through the Clash's "Should I Stay or Should I Go," throwing back her head and singing to the chorus. She danced through Elvis Presley's "A Little Less Conversation," twirling her hips and skipping round the table. She danced through U2's "Elevation," jumping up and down on the spot where Jacko's blanket no longer rested. She danced through Dusty Springfield's "Son of a Preacher Man," through the Dandy Warhols' "Bohemian Like You," Ike and Tina Turner's "Nutbush City Limits," and finally Free's gloriously appropriate anthem, "Alright Now." She was all right, she was more than all right, she was on her own again and for tonight at least she was blissfully happy in her aloneness. She knew now there was life after Andrew and if it had taken the removal of a dog called Jacko to make her realize this, she was almost, if not completely, glad she had met him.

Never Turn Your Back on Miracles

Sarah woke in the middle of the night and went down to the kitchen just because she could. The house belonged to her again and the fact that it probably wouldn't for much longer was something she refused to worry about until after Majorca. In the morning she ran out to the postman and told him he was free to approach her door without risk to life or limb. In the afternoon she walked to the village shop and told Amy the news of her liberation, knowing it would be broadcast to the entire village within twenty-four hours. Amy wanted to know all about the madman who had volunteered to take over Jacko and when Sarah told her it was Martin Chamberlain's brother, Amy's volatile eyebrows almost jumped off her head and she said with barely suppressed curiosity, "Martin Chamberlain's brother? Now why would he do a thing like that?" Noting the speculative glint in Amy's eyes, Sarah deduced that Amy was probably concocting a romance between Sarah and Jean-Pierre or possibly even between Sarah and Martin. In Sarah's present mood this didn't seem too worrying. At least if Amy were to voice such fantasies, everyone at the dinner party would stop thinking she was trying to inveigle George or the vicar or Simon Delaney into a bit of Wednesday evening rumpy-pumpy.

A far more pressing problem than the state of her reputation was money or, to be more accurate, the lack of it. The health of Sarah's finances was at the best of times precarious and in the last few months, critical. This, Sarah knew, was partly her fault. Andrew's departure had precipitated a fatal hemorrhage of her confidence, exacerbating the discomfort she had always felt when touting for business.

In the seven years since Sarah had given up teaching at Trowbridge College, her income had been erratic. She still had her job at the summer school in Bath in July and August and her evening classes in the autumn. Her royalties from *Girl with a Flute* had never amounted to more than a few hundred per annum. The rest of her money came from modest commissions and group exhibitions.

Andrew had all the service bills on standing order and he continued to put money into their joint account. The boys would be going to university in the autumn. Could she really expect Andrew to support her while shelling out money for the boys? And then there was always the possibility that Hyacinth might want to start a family of her own.

The very thought made Sarah reach desperately for something happy to think about. Majorca! But that was another problem. At a time when she should be counting every penny she was about to swan off to Majorca! On the plus side, the apartment was free and since it was probably the last holiday she'd ever take, she was determined not to feel guilty about it. It wasn't *her* fault that the absence of money had suddenly become an issue. If Andrew hadn't allowed himself to fall in love with Hyacinth, if . . . if, if, if! *If* had to be the most pernicious word in the lexicon of smashed hopes, for it led in a straight line to frustration and fury.

The stark fact was that she had never made enough money to live comfortably on her own. If she went back to full-time teaching she would be all right but it would mean an end to any chance of artistic success and besides, good teaching jobs were thin on the ground. If she had the necessary computing skills she could at least widen her possibilities, but a computer course would take time and money.

She badly needed a miracle and since fate had already granted her one in the shape of Jean-Pierre, she was not expecting another. Fate, however, was obviously in a good mood: on Monday morning she had a phone call from Sophie King.

Of all her pupils at Trowbridge College, Sophie had been her most outstanding student. She was one of those people who is blessed by the gods with beauty, a sunny disposition, and a unique talent. Everything she created was suffused with sensuality; she could even make a high-street bank look erotic.

Sophie had gone on to prove she did indeed have star quality, producing artwork for music companies, illustrations for a book of fairy stories (Red Riding Hood's wolf was so gorgeous that had Sarah been Red Riding Hood she would happily have been eaten by him), and a number of successful exhibitions. She continued to keep in touch with Sarah though their roles had been speedily reversed. Sophie had been the one to encourage Sarah to leave the safety of the college and dive into the cold waters of a freelance career. She had a touching faith in Sarah's ability. Sarah, who knew her limitations, rather dreaded the day when Sophie found her out.

Sophie's phone calls were always carried out as if she were ringing while running a marathon. Today's was no exception. "Sarah? I can't talk for long but listen. Dave and I are moving to Tuscany. Did I tell you about Dave? I must have told you about Dave. He's perfect, we're in love, and we're going to Tuscany! Oh, and I'm pregnant. . . . I know, it's wonderful and I'm gloriously happy. Now listen, this is really important. A friend of mine is opening a nightclub in Bath in a few months. He's calling it the Fruit Basket and he wants to cover the walls in paintings of fruit and I mean seriously sexy fruit, suggestive bananas, oozing peaches, you know the sort of thing. I was all set to do it but I'm snowed under with work and I thought, who do I know who can produce sexy apples? What do you think, Sarah, are you interested?"

Sex, for Sarah, had now been relegated to the dim and distant past, along with bags of sherbet, Carnaby Street, and pop festivals. She was not at all sure she could produce a sexy smile let alone a sexy apple. On the other hand, Jacko was gone, which was good. She needed the money, which was bad, and Sarah knew one did not turn one's back on miracles. "Sophie," she said, "I would love to paint some sexy apples. What do I have to do? When do I start?"

"Good girl!" said Sophie, who was at least fifteen years

younger than Sarah. "First, you have to show Gordon, he's my friend, that you're up to it. You need to come up to London and show him your stuff. I've already told him how brilliant you are so he's ready to be impressed. It'll be easy."

"I'm coming up on February twenty-first," said Sarah. "I'm going to Majorca with a friend the next day. Could I see him then?"

"Leave it to me. I'll ring Gordon to see if that's all right. And when you come up, dress appropriately."

The miracle was beginning to sound distinctly dodgy. "When you say 'appropriately,' " Sarah queried, "what exactly do you mean?"

"Oh you know," Sophie said breezily, "dress like a woman who can produce sexy fruit. You know!"

"Right," said Sarah. Dressing like a woman who can produce sexy fruit should be no more difficult than acting the part of a child bride. Clearly, fate had a sense of humor.

In fact, Sarah positively enjoyed her rehearsal the following night. They were doing act 2, scene 1. Maxim and his household are preparing for the annual ball. He and his relatives indulge in jolly banter unaware that the child bride, under Mrs. Danvers's evil direction, is about to appear in the dress worn by Rebecca the year before.

It was a great scene and best of all there was no Jack Favell in it, which meant that Howard was not at rehearsal. In his absence, Claire was quite friendly to Sarah. Another plus was the presence of Audrey's gardener's son. He had only managed to memorize one of his lines. Audrey, possibly aware that he would relish any opportunity to get out of the play, was trying very hard not to lose her temper with him. Sarah had the pleasantly novel sensation of feeling superior. She was no longer the most useless member of the cast and was almost disappointed when Audrey let her go early. "You're coming along very nicely," she told Sarah. "We needn't do your bit again. Now Maxim, Beatrice, Giles, Frank, and Frith, let's go back to page forty-four. I want it fun, I want it frothy, I want it fast! We want laughter and gaiety, lots of gaiety! All right?"

Sarah caught Martin's eye. He mouthed, "Saturday?" and she nodded. She'd been worried he might have bad news about Jacko but presumably both Jacko and Jean-Pierre were still alive and Sarah felt able to look forward to hearing about them without fear of recrimination.

Outside, it was bitterly cold. Sarah was wearing Ben's old army greatcoat and she pushed up the collar and thrust her hands in its copious pockets. In less than a fortnight she'd be in Majorca and the sounds of Ambercross owls and the occasional screeching pheasant would be replaced by the rhythmic sway of the sea. I have things to look forward to, Sarah thought as she marched briskly away from the pub. I have things to look forward to and not just Majorca. Cleaning the house would be fun because it would be exorcising Jacko. Finishing her last two remaining commissions would be fun because she would be clearing the way for a new and exciting and best of all lucrative project. Walking with Martin at the weekend would be fun because walking with Martin was always fun. She would make him a thank you lunch to show him how grateful she was and that would be fun too.

It seemed that there was life after Andrew. There were still big question marks ahead, the most worrying of which was how long she'd be able to stay at Shooter's Cottage. Andrew's rejection still kept her awake at night but the pain no longer bludgeoned her senses or crippled her ability to function in other areas. Sophie thought she could paint sexy apples. Audrey thought she was coming along nicely. Martin had shown what a true friend he was. Sarah stared up into the thick dark sky enlivened by just two stars. My husband has left me, she thought, my husband has left me and I can still, on occasion, be happy. It was time to stop being and feeling a victim. The best riposte to Andrew's perfidy was not just to make him think she could be content without him. The best riposte was to prove to her sons, to her friends, and most importantly to herself that she could be content without him. And I can, she thought, I really, really can.

When Martin arrived on Saturday morning Sarah flung the door open before he had time to ring the bell. "Come in, come in!" she cried. "Come and see my kitchen! No messy water bowl, no manky old blanket, no nasty paw marks, and I've made us a fantastic lunch for after the walk. . . ." Her face suddenly fell. "You can stay for lunch, can't you? You don't have to rush off?"

"I'd be delighted to stay for lunch," Martin assured her. He glanced around him. "It looks different here."

"It looks *clean!*" Sarah said. "The whole house looks clean!" She reached for her coat and smiled. "Shall we go?"

It was a beautiful day, crisp and clear. A faint smattering of frost laced the hedgerows and the morning sun covered the landscape in a milky patina, denuding it of color.

"It's like a watercolor," Sarah said, hugging her arms to her chest, "or the beginning of the world."

"And we," Martin said portentously, "are Adam and Eve."

"I don't think Adam and Eve were around at the beginning of the world."

"Nor were fields or fences or trees."

"I sometimes think," Sarah said sternly, "you have no poetry in your soul."

"I know," said Martin humbly. "I'm sorry."

"I forgive you but only because you've saved my life. So tell me: how did you do it? Blackmail? Bribery? I can't believe your brother *wanted* to take Jacko."

"He did. In the end, he did. I have to tell you, I conducted a masterly campaign. It was funny because the very first time I met Jacko, he reminded me of someone and I couldn't think who."

"Beelzebub? Attila the Hun?"

"No, it was someone I knew. Jean-Pierre happened to ring me that evening and I realized who it was: his wife!"

"Jacko looked like Jean-Pierre's wife! Poor Jean-Pierre!"

"She didn't have yellow eyes or a slobbery mouth but she used to look at people . . . and treat people . . . like Jacko does. She was big and broad and scared everyone in the world except Jean-Pierre and their daughters. She snarled at people. She snarled a lot."

"But never at Jean-Pierre."

"Never. She loved him. And he loved her. She died a month after he retired. She had a brain hemorrhage while she was carving the chicken and dropped dead. Jean-Pierre was inconsolable. He wouldn't go anywhere, he wouldn't see anyone, he wouldn't eat. None of us knew how to help him. And then Kathleen found the answer."

"Who was Kathleen?"

"My niece. His younger daughter. She went round one morning with Annette, her youngest. She was going back to work, she said. It was her first day and her babysitter had let her down. Could she leave Annette with him for a few hours? He said he couldn't, he said he wasn't fit to look after anyone." Martin stopped by the stile. "Do you want to go on up the hill or into the wood?"

"Let's go up the hill. So what did Kathleen do then?"

"She left Annette anyway. She told Jean-Pierre he'd have to look after his granddaughter, there was no one else. And she walked away. When she came back in the afternoon she found the two of them playing Ludo."

"And then what? Did the babysitter come back?"

"No. I don't think there ever was a babysitter. In fact I'm pretty sure Kathleen only went back to work when she did in order to haul her father back from the brink. She knew Annette would save him. When Annette started school, she told him she wanted a doll's house. I saw it a couple of months ago; it's amazing. It's got electric lights, it's got everything. Anyway, that night, he told me he'd finally finished it and was taking it round to Annette the very next day. And so of course I thought of Jacko."

"Why?"

"It was obvious. Annette was at school, he'd finished the doll's house, he needed another project. So I told him all about you and your dog. I said you were going mad under the strain. . . ."

"Actually," Sarah said, pausing to catch her breath, for the hill was steep, "I probably was."

"I told him everyone was scared of Jacko, no one could control him except for me. I told him he'd be terrified if he ever went near him. . . ."

"I can't imagine Jean-Pierre being scared of anything."

"No, and neither can Jean-Pierre. Then I rang him and told him Jacko was going to be put down. No one, I told him, could train such a dog. When Jean-Pierre said he'd like to have a look at him, I knew I'd won. The only thing I was worried about was whether Jacko would take to him. When you let go of the leash, I made myself stay in the car but it wasn't easy. I was a little worried."

"You were worried? I was terrified! How's your brother coping with him now? Is he all right? Is Jacko behaving himself?"

"At the moment Jean-Pierre is wearing him out with ten-mile walks. And if you think I walk fast you should see Jean-Pierre. I suspect Jacko's too tired to raise even a hackle."

"Well, I'm eternally grateful. You will always be my hero!" She saw him make a face and she laughed. "Don't you want to be my hero?"

"In my experience," Martin said drily, "it doesn't pay to get too close to heroes. Not if you want to keep your illusions."

"Well, I'm close to you," Sarah said stoutly, "and in my book you're a hero."

Martin chuckled. "I think—" He stopped abruptly. "Never mind."

Sarah glanced at him suspiciously. "What? You can't say 'Never mind' in that patronizing way, as if I wouldn't understand. . . ."

"I would never dare to patronize you!"

"Well then! What were you going to say?"

Martin stopped to point at an odd-shaped mound in front of them. "Do you see that?" he asked. "Did you know there was once a Roman fort here?"

"Yes! Don't change the subject!"

"All right. It's nothing really. I was only remembering how the words, 'Andrew says' used to come up with great frequency in your conversation. And when you were with him, you would usually defer to his superior judgment."

"And that made you laugh?"

"No, but when you said I was your hero, I imagined you treating *me* like that and *that* made me laugh."

"Oh." Sarah wasn't sure what to make of this. "Would you like me to defer to your superior judgment?"

"The idea," said Martin drily, "is so improbable that I can't even consider it."

Pursue Career Possibilities

Sarah liked to describe her memory as wayward. Andrew always said it was nonexistent and was infuriated by her inability to remember names. Sarah would point out that she could *almost* remember them but Andrew remained unimpressed. An approximation, he said, was nearly as insulting as a complete blank. Now that she thought about it, perhaps Howard Smart had good reason to dislike her. In the first few months of their acquaintance she had persisted in calling him Henry.

In some areas her mind was razor sharp. She could remember the names of all Liz Taylor's husbands and could recount the entire history of Doctor Carter's intricate love life on *ER*. She might not be able to absorb road directions (she had given up asking passersby how to find obscure locations: her mind always shut down after the first "Turn left"), but she had an unerring aptitude for taking in the lyrics of the more irritating pop songs. This last was a skill she could have happily lost, especially at the moment when she found herself constantly regurgitating the remake of Cyndi Lauper's "Girls Just Want to Have Fun."

Furthermore, while much of her past had become a blank slate, there were certain incidents, sights, conversations that remained clear and intact, photographs that did not fade. Thirty-five years ago, basking in the temporary approval of the reigning Miss Popular, she had joined in the baiting of the resident Miss Social Outcast. Years later, those reproachful eyes could still inspire in Sarah regular bouts of self-disgust. Then there was the time at art school when she had stood in the shadows, gazing with masochistic misery at the gorgeous Barney Melton while he kissed his girlfriend. An even more painful memory was her angry reaction when a small, tearful James announced he'd lost the birthday watch he'd been given that morning. His birthday was ruined, his own mother had helped to ruin it, and she would always feel guilty. Sarah had no idea why her brain displayed such selective amnesia but there certainly seemed to be an element of sadism in the way it operated.

At the moment, the overwhelming presence of the Cyndi Lauper song was being driven out by Martin's comments on Saturday, which went round and round her brain like a wasp inside a jam jar. She *had* constantly deferred to Andrew and she *had* often repeated his opinions. Martin had implied that she'd put him on a pedestal and she had to admit she had always thought he was more glamorous, more interesting, and more connected with the world than she was. He knew how to make money, he knew how to meet the right people, and he knew the right things to say.

Living without Andrew was scary because living *with* Andrew had made her life so easy. She could enjoy the company of her sons, she could decorate the house, weed the garden, do her paintings, all in the knowledge that Andrew would see to the nuts and bolts of their life together. Now, for the first time, she was having to face what most people faced the whole time: the need to make a living and take charge of her own affairs.

Well, she would do it and she would do it without deferring to Andrew. She wanted Martin to know that she would never defer to Andrew again. She looked forward to telling him that on Tuesday, at her last rehearsal before Majorca.

In fact, she didn't get the chance to say anything much to Martin. They were doing act 2, scene 2. A distraught Maxim reveals the truth about Rebecca to his child bride. Horrified and fearful, she promises to stand by her man. It was a great scene and Sarah was enjoying herself. Then Audrey clapped her hands. "Perhaps, Martin," she said gravely, "you should kiss Sarah now: a sad kiss, born of desperation. No passion . . . we'll save the fireworks for the last scene but I think a sad little kiss would be rather poignant. Don't you think it would be rather poignant?"

"No," said Martin, "I don't."

Audrey's bosom arose along with her eyebrows. She was not used to such blatant contradiction, especially from Martin. "Don't you think," she boomed, "you should at least *try* it? I know you are not *happy* at the prospect of kissing Sarah but this is what drama is all about: doing things you would not in real life wish to do."

The statement, so gloriously rude, made Sarah's mouth quiver with appreciation. She glanced at Martin. His complexion had gone dark red, which in turn made Sarah blush. She could only be grateful the rest of the cast had gone home. Martin said, "This has nothing to do with personal feelings. Maxim is facing ruin and scandal. He doesn't want to kiss his wife, he wants to know how he can dig himself out of the hole he's in. Look at the words. Where does he mention love? The audience still doesn't know if he loves his child bride. If he kisses her now, you lose the surprise in the final scene."

Martin was right. Even Audrey had to agree he was right. They carried on with the scene and Sarah appeared to be the only one who thought it had lost its earlier spark. At the end of the rehearsal, Audrey instructed them to enjoy their week off from rehearsals and to come back refreshed and restored.

As soon as she'd gone, Martin began to clear the chairs with a speed and efficiency that precluded any chance of a post-mortem. A subdued Sarah pushed back the table and asked tentatively whether he'd like a drink.

"I can't tonight," Martin said. "I've loads of paperwork to do."

"Right." Sarah picked up her coat and scarf. "Well then. I'll see you after Majorca."

"I'll look forward to it," Martin said politely, adding as an afterthought, "I hope the weather's good for you. I'm sure you'll enjoy it." He switched out the light and they walked downstairs.

Someone at the bar called out, "Martin? Can I have a word about my boiler?"

Martin smiled apologetically at Sarah. "I'd better go. Have a great time now!"

Sarah walked home quickly. That Martin had been embarrassed rather than amused by Audrey's typically tactless remark was evident. The reason for his reaction was equally obvious. Sarah shivered as she walked and tried very hard not to be hurt by the fact that Martin dreaded the prospect of kissing her.

The good news was that Sarah was meeting Sophie at the National Portrait Gallery, just a stone's throw from the station. The bad news was that a walk across Waterloo Bridge, along the Embankment and up the road to Trafalgar Square, was more like a thousand stones' throws when one is carrying a suitcase and disabled by cripplingly uncomfortable ankle boots. Sarah had dug them out of the back of her wardrobe the night before and it was only now that she remembered why they'd been covered in cobwebs.

She felt better when she arrived at the gallery and was able to get rid of her suitcase. She was due to meet Sophie at half past three, which meant she had twenty-five minutes to repair her face and her composure. In the ladies room, Sarah studied her reflection. "Dress like a woman who can produce sexy fruit." Sarah had gone through her entire wardrobe. Her only smart outfit was a knee-length red dress she had worn with her gray jacket to a wedding two years ago. At the time she had received many compliments but when she forced herself into it last night she knew that her walks with Martin had failed to achieve the desired effect. She looked like an apple but not unfortunately a sexy one. In the end Sarah had gone for the safety of her black velvet trousers and a black V-neck of Ben's. The gray jacket and the boots completed the ensemble. At the last minute she threw her red dress into her Majorca suitcase. If she lost a few pounds in the next couple of days it would look fine.

Her one extravagance had been to buy a new lipstick. She had bought it for its name: Passion. According to the sales lady it had revolutionary lip-plumping properties. Sarah took it from her bag and applied it carefully to her mouth. She was rather pleased with the results. Her lips did indeed look a little plumper, a very, very little plumper, and the unaccustomed color made her feel sophisticated. She practiced an intelligent smile and said in a deep, throbbing voice, "Passion!" A moment later there was the sound of flushing water and an elderly lady emerged who gave Sarah a very peculiar look. Sarah, with a face the color of her lipstick, fled.

She went straight to the Tudor room and was grateful to be meeting Sophie here. History had been one of the few subjects in which she had excelled at school and the Tudors were particularly fascinating. The Stuarts had only produced one superstar in Charles II and the Hanoverians were fat and boorish. But the Tudors were a template for every soap opera in the world. There was Henry VII looking lean and mean and Henry VIII, who was fat and fickle. Looking at his huge portrait, Sarah felt a twinge of pity for the women who had had to share his bed.

She was studying a portrait of poor, plain Mary Tudor when Sophie appeared looking beautiful but very pale. "Sarah, I'm sorry I'm late. I keep being sick and I might have to disappear at any moment. Why do people call it morning sickness when it goes on all day? Now listen, we're meeting Gordon in the tearoom in five minutes. I told him you want a thousand pounds for each painting—"

"A thousand pounds! Sophie, that's crazy!"

"No, it isn't. Gordon is a man who doesn't think he's getting a bargain unless he pays through the nose. Did I tell you the club's going to be in Bath? That's good for you since he likes the idea of employing a local artist. You *do* live near Bath, don't you?"

"Twenty-five miles away."

"That's local. He's ready to be impressed. I told him you were my guru."

"Your *what?*"

Sophie grinned. "You're my guru! Right. We'd better go. Are you ready?"

Sarah straightened her jacket and pulled down her sweater. "I'm ready! Sophie, it is so kind of you to set this up. If I can ever do anything for you . . ."

"You can tell me how to stop being sick," Sophie said as they walked down the stairs.

Sarah gave her a sympathetic glance. "Digestive biscuits used to work for me." She could feel her own stomach contract as they reached the tearoom but there was no sign of Sophie's friend. Sophie sat down while Sarah went to the counter. As always when nervous, she felt ravenous and gazed longingly at the flapjacks and brownies. A woman who wears Passion on her mouth does not eat flapjacks or brownies and Sarah asked only for two teas and a packet of biscuits for Sophie.

Sophie's friend arrived just as she was unloading the teas, which was a pity because in her excitement her hands shook and a fair amount of liquid slurped onto the saucers. This meant that Sarah could no longer drink her tea since a woman who wears Passion does not drink from a cup that drips liquid from its bottom.

Gordon was far older than Sarah had imagined but in every other way he conformed to Sarah's idea of what a friend of Sophie's would look like. He was, like Sarah, dressed in black but she knew his well-cut trousers and jacket were twenty times more expensive than anything she was wearing. His gray hair was brushed back from his forehead and he had a dimple on his chin, like Michael Douglas. He was obviously enamoured of Sophie, Sarah thought a little wistfully.

"I love this place," Gordon said, talking ostensibly to both of them but actually to Sophie. "I come here every month to get my brain recharged. I've just been looking at the photo of W.H. Auden. Don't you think his face looks like a rumpled sheet?"

He eyed Sophie hopefully. Sophie, who'd been opening the packet of digestives, rose abruptly from her chair. "Will you excuse me? I think I feel rather ill. Please"—both Sarah and Gordon rose in alarm—"start without me. I won't be long."

Sarah watched Sophie run out and sat down again, feeling horribly guilty about the digestives.

"Poor girl," Gordon murmured. "Do you think she's all right?"

"I'm sure she'll be fine," Sarah said. "I remember when I—"

"She's so brave. Don't you think she's brave?"

"She is," Sarah agreed. "She's very brave. And she's very talented too."

"Very, very talented. I was so excited when she said she'd do my paintings for the Fruit Basket. However"—he looked at Sarah doubtfully—"she thinks the world of *you*. So let me tell you about the club. We're aiming it at the mature adult, the thirty to forty age group who want a good time in a civilized atmosphere. We'll have dancing downstairs and on the ground floor we'll have a large bar and a variety of big, comfy sofas where the punters can relax. I see it as a place where a man and a woman can check each other out, do a little verbal foreplay in a setting that's sexy, soft, and subtle. Now the paintings are important because they provide the signpost, the reference point, if you like. I want them big and bold, oozing sensuality. Now what I need to know is: can you deliver?"

No way, thought Sarah. "I'm sure I can," she said. "I've brought along some photos of my work. Would you like to see them?" She passed him the folder.

She saw his eyes flicker distastefully at *The Girl with the Flute* and thought he was right, he really was right. It was horribly twee and the girl with the flute looked asexual, anorexic even. She had the feeling her work was crumbling about her and the worst of it was she was letting poor Sophie down: first with the digestive biscuits and now with this.

Gordon turned to the last page on which Sarah had mounted a seven-by-ten photo of Raffles. "When did you do this?" he asked.

Sarah swallowed. "I finished it a few weeks ago."

He continued to look at Raffles and then stood up, with what Sarah took to be great relief as a wan-faced Sophie tottered back to the table. "Sophie," he said, "sit down. What can I get you?"

"I think," said Sophie faintly, "I'd just like some water."

"I'll get it." Sarah jumped up. She could not bear to be around while Gordon told Sophie what he thought of her guru's work. At the counter she asked for a bottle of water and looked again at the flapjacks. Sod it, she no longer needed to look like a woman who wore Passion. "I'd like a flapjack, please," she said.

Back at the table, Sophie was eating a digestive and looking better. "Thanks, Sarah," she said, taking the water and unscrewing the lid. She held the bottle up in the air and smiled. "Congratulations!"

Sarah looked at her blankly. "What for?"

Gordon leaned forward. "I was telling Sophie that if you can paint me some fruit like you painted that dog, then you're the artist for me. That is one sexy dog!"

Sarah stared in awe at Raffles. Mr. and Mrs. Doctor were absolutely right. Raffles was indeed one in a million.

Miriam and her husband lived on the ground floor of a Victorian house that sat on the border of the highly posh Blackheath and the definitely not posh Lewisham. The setting seemed highly appropriate for a woman who was happy to teach in an impoverished comprehensive while dressed in designer trousers.

Her home only underlined Miriam's protean nature. A coffee table from Ikea rested on an exquisite rug from Marrakesh; an ancient sofa, kept upright with the help of *The Shorter English Dictionary*, was bedecked with huge, hand-embroidered cushions. The bookshelves were an eclectic mix of teenage novels, travel books, Anthony Trollope, Agatha Christie, D. H. Lawrence, and P. G. Wodehouse. The CD collection was equally unpredictable, encompassing such unlikely bedfellows as Schubert, Eminem, Philip Glass, and Kylie Minogue.

"Kylie Minogue?" Sarah queried.

"That's mine," said Clive. "One of Miriam's little jokes."

He raised his glass in Sarah's direction. "Great champagne," he said. "It was very generous of you."

Sarah smiled. "It's not every day I get a nice fat job!" She returned Kylie's divine bottom to its place next to Guns N' Roses, collected her glass from the coffee table, and sat down on the sofa. "I'm feeling very pleased with myself!"

"So you should," said Clive. "I'm only sorry we're offering you nothing better than takeout."

"I love takeout," Sarah assured him. "I can't get them at home."

"Really?" said Clive. He laughed as if she'd made a great joke.

Sarah could see why Miriam had fallen in love with Clive. He was big and blond with blue eyes and extraordinarily thick eyelashes. He was also very good-mannered. Sarah was far too happy to mind that he could not quite conceal his irritation at being left to entertain her while Miriam did her packing. She was, however, very glad that she'd bought the champagne. There were little signs that all was not well here: a rather too enthusiastic welcome from both Miriam and Clive, the odd jokes the two of them made about each other, which weren't very funny at all. Champagne was clearly needed and Sarah had no hesitation in pouring herself and Clive another drink. Tonight, nothing, not even Clive's attempts at conversation, could daunt her spirits. She was going to put the Fruit Basket on the map! She was going to Majorca! She was, she was absolutely certain, going to have a wonderful time.

If You Want Sex and Sun,
Don't Visit Majorca in February

Majorca! A gleaming airport with staff who smiled; purple mountains, tree-lined promenades, smoke-colored sky, and an aquamarine sea; uncongested highways with not a roadworks sign in sight. Majorca! The Island of Calm, Miriam said, and Sarah could well believe it, particularly with Miriam as her traveling companion. Accustomed to Andrew's easily fueled impatience, it was a pleasure to be with someone who responded with such good humor to the forty-minute delay while they waited for their hired car.

They arrived in Puerto d'Andratx in midafternoon. Sarah, expecting to see English pubs and fat-bellied lager louts, was surprised by the litter-free pavement, the pretty harbor, and the near-deserted streets. The great, gleaming boats that bobbed sedately on the water, along with the large ornate villas dotted around the hillside, suggested a style and a wealth quite at odds with Sarah's previous perception of the island. The fact that the wind was bitingly cold presumably explained the emptiness of the place. Sarah, aware of the paucity of her holiday wardrobe, was rather relieved.

Their home for the week turned out to be just a few minutes from the waterfront, up a narrow side street, and above a mouth-watering clothes shop. Pressing her nose against the window, Sarah had a fleeting wish that she could possess both an income and a lifestyle to justify a close inspection of the garments on display. Ambercross, she felt, was not yet ready for the long, fluid wraparound dress that revealed so much of the dummy's pert, pointed breasts.

The apartment was at the top of a dark, creaky staircase. Miriam put down her bags, turned the key in the lock, and opened the door.

"Oh, wow!" said Sarah. White floors, white curtains, white walls, and white chairs dazzled her eyes. The only color was provided by the collection of wooden bowls on the vast marble table in the middle of the room. The bedrooms and bathroom were equally monastic in character and the small spotless kitchen had only a few honey-glazed cooking pots on display. "It's like a beautiful bubble," Sarah said. "Dare we cook in here?"

Miriam took off her coat and stretched her arms. "I haven't come here to cook," she said. "Not tonight anyway." She yawned. "I'm going to sleep for an hour. Which bedroom do you want?"

"You choose," said Sarah. "I'm far too excited to sleep. I shall study our guidebooks and work out our itinerary."

"Excellent." Miriam picked up her suitcase. "It's good to be away from home. Thanks for coming with me."

Sarah kicked off her shoes. "It is *wonderful* to be away from home and I am enormously happy to be here. Now go to bed!"

Miriam gave a sleepy wave and disappeared into her room. Sarah picked up her bag, settled herself in a large squashy armchair, pulled out her guidebook, and began to read. Majorca turned out to have a surprisingly exhausting history, with regular invasions by Romans, Vandals, Byzantines, Moorish Moslems, the Catholic Spanish, and the British tourists. It made Sarah feel quite tired just to think about it. Her eyelids began to droop. Outside, Roman soldiers looking like Richard Burton were fighting for control of the wraparound dress with members of the Spanish Inquisition.

One of them was tugging her arm. Sarah opened a startled eye and realized the sinister Spanish grandee was in fact Miriam, looking terrific in a long black dress with a wide brown belt that emphasized a waistline Sarah could only dream about. "Hello, Miriam," she said. "Have you had a good rest?"

"Very good. And I've been to the supermarket and had a shower. Are you intending to snooze all night or are you going to come out for a night of romantic adventure?"

Sarah blinked. "Give me ten minutes," she promised.

Forty minutes later, wearing her sexy fruit outfit and her Passion lipstick, she was ready. Thirty minutes later, having at last found a bar that was open, they sat drinking chilled sherry and picking at olives. Apart from two very old men sitting in the corner, they were the only customers. One of the men treated Sarah to a wide, toothless grin. Sarah smiled politely and hastily turned her attention to the olives.

"I have to admit," sighed Miriam, "that February is probably not the best time to be looking for Antonio Banderas. So much for a night of romantic adventure."

"It's too cold for sex," said Sarah. "And quite honestly, I think I can do without it."

"Given the local talent," said Miriam, trying to ignore the roguish wink directed at her by the toothless old man, "that's just as well."

"I'm serious," Sarah insisted. "I've been thinking about it a lot. Sex is like chocolate. It's very pleasant but it's not essential to one's well-being. When Andrew left me, I felt very sad that I might never have sex again, but now . . . If you told me I could never drink a bottle of wine or read a good book or see my boys or watch *ER* or paint a great picture or sleep in a comfortable bed, if I could never enjoy any of them again, *then* I'd be devastated. I think—and this is a momentous moment of self-discovery—I think I am at last a liberated woman."

Miriam drained her sherry. "I'd be pretty upset if I could never eat another chocolate caramel. And by the looks of things"—she nodded in the direction of the toothless man whose winks had become increasingly frenzied—"so would he. Shall we go and find somewhere to eat?"

Outside, the wind was cold and fierce. Worse, they could not find one restaurant along the seafront that was open. They plunged into the labyrinth of narrow streets and at last found a tiny place with bright, welcoming windows. The bored waiters and the empty tables did not augur well but it was warm and cozy and the smells emanating from the plates of the only two seated customers were enticing. There was one other customer at the bar chatting to a fat, jolly-faced man with an infectious laugh. The fat man was clearly the proprietor since he immediately called to one of the waiters, who ushered Sarah and Miriam to a table near the fire.

It was while Miriam was studying the menu that Sarah's attention was drawn to the man at the bar. She could only see his back view but there was something about the way he held his cigarette and the odd short growl of laughter that was familiar. She was only aware she was staring at him when he turned round suddenly and acknowledged his awareness of her interest with an ironic raising of his glass. He turned his back on her again and Sarah felt her bones disintegrate. "Miriam!" she said in an anguished whisper, "Miriam!"

Miriam looked up. "What is it? You look like you've just seen your worst nightmare."

Sarah shook her head violently. "The reverse! I've just seen Barney Melton!"

"Who's Barney Melton?"

"You must remember! He's the man who broke my heart at art school."

"You never went out with someone called Barney Melton."

"That's why he broke my heart. He was a five-star male and he only went out with five-star females. I can't believe that's him. It is him, I'm sure of it."

"Well ask him."

"I can't ask him. He hardly knew me. It would look so pathetic. Miriam! Don't turn round, he'll see you. . . . Miriam!"

"Excuse me!" Miriam called out. "Are you Barney Melton?"

The man at the bar turned round, exhaled a thin stream of

smoke, and said slowly, as if he were not quite sure, "Yes. I am Barney Melton."

Miriam nodded. "That's what my friend said." She turned back to Sarah. "He *is* Barney Melton."

Sarah, aware that her face must be the color of a particularly violent beetroot, could only muster a feeble smile as Barney Melton approached their table. "Have we met before?" he asked her. The same heavy lids, the same low, gravelly voice, the same whippet-thin body; he'd hardly changed.

Sarah nodded. "I was at art school with you." It seemed very important that she explain the state of her complexion. "I used to have a huge crush on you." She gave a little laugh, an indulgent sort of laugh, she hoped, a wasn't-I-absurd sort of laugh.

"Did you?" He smiled. "I wish I'd known." Then he walked back to the bar. Sarah, disturbed and deflated, proceeded to subject her menu to a detailed scrutiny.

"Sarah," Miriam murmured. "What's he doing?"

"I don't know and I'm not going to look," Sarah muttered through gritted teeth. "He obviously doesn't want to talk to me. I knew he wouldn't. This is *so* embarrassing." She lowered her head and looked desperately at the menu. The words seemed to be jumping about and she had lost her appetite anyway.

"Can we join you?" Barney had come back and this time he'd brought the jolly, fat man. "This is my friend, Antonio."

"Antonio?" Miriam's eyes met Sarah's for a second. "What a lovely name. I'm Miriam and this is Sarah."

"Hello, Sarah. Hello, Miriam." Antonio bowed gravely at each of them in turn. "This is my restaurant and you are Barney's friends. I will give you supper but first we will have some wine. . . . Raoul!" He motioned to one of the waiters, who came over with a bottle and four glasses. Antonio took the bottle and sat next to Miriam. "You like my name? I like your name. We have something in common already! You hear that, Barney? What do you think?"

"I think," said Barney, pulling up a chair beside Sarah, "you should open that wine."

"Of course I will open this wine. We will celebrate the arrival of two lovely ladies into my restaurant. Do we need more glasses? Do you have anxious husbands searching for you?"

"We have no husbands," said Miriam.

"We do have husbands," Sarah pointed out. "But mine has left me."

Barney gave a sympathetic nod. "My wife has left me."

"I'm pretty sure," said Miriam, "my husband is planning to leave me."

"Another thing we have in common!" said Antonio. "My wife has left *me!*"

Barney grinned. "Antonio, you don't have a wife."

"Of course I don't," said Antonio indignantly. "She left me."

Miriam raised a skeptical eyebrow. "*When* did she leave you?"

"Twenty years ago," Antonio said sadly, pouring out the wine. "I am a broken man."

"You hide your grief amazingly well," Miriam told him.

"When I sit next to a beautiful woman it is easy to forget. Now, take your glasses, we will drink a toast. Barney? You want to give the toast?"

Barney responded with the lazy half smile Sarah remembered of old. "To new beginnings," he said, "and old friends."

"We weren't exactly old friends," Sarah pointed out. "In fact I'm pretty sure you don't remember me at all."

Barney frowned. "Were you the girl who was sick over my shoes?"

"No I was not!"

"I didn't think you were. Were you the girl who wanted to teach art?"

"Most of the girls wanted to teach art. I knew you wouldn't remember me. In fact, I did teach art for a while."

"Teaching." Antonio nodded sagely. "It's a wonderful profession."

"Miriam's an English teacher," said Sarah.

Antonio clapped his hands together. "This is incredible! *I* was an English teacher!"

"Really?" said Miriam in a tone of deepest disbelief.

"I was a wonderful teacher in a terrible school. The boys were all crazy. The teachers were terrified. I go into the classroom and I smile"—he bared his teeth—"like that. I say, 'You treat me right, I treat you right. You treat me wrong'—I look at them all—'I treat you wrong.' They know I mean business. I was wonderful."

"In that case," asked Miriam, "why did you give it up?"

Antonio smiled. "I am wonderful at so many things."

Miriam raised her eyebrows. "Really?" she said again.

Sarah had no idea what they ate that night or how much she drank. She was aware of Antonio, continually finding amazing parallels between his life and Miriam's. Miriam had lived in New York: so had he! Miriam's first husband had been gay: Antonio's wife had shown definite sapphic tendencies; come to think of it, that was probably why she had left him. Barney said very little but there was not one moment in which Sarah was not conscious of his presence next to her. He was not a handsome man as was, for example, Andrew. He had small eyes that disappeared when he smiled and they had dark shadows underneath them. He had a small, almost puglike nose and his generous mouth was too big for his narrow face. His hair looked as if he had just got out of bed and he had the permanent demeanor of someone who was half asleep. Perhaps that was the secret of his undeniable sex appeal. He looked as if he belonged in bed and he looked at every woman as if she belonged there too.

Wine had a combative effect on Miriam and by the end of the meal it was clear she had had enough of Antonio's stories. Antonio asked her to name her favorite book.

"Easy," said Miriam. *"Middlemarch,* by George Eliot." She paused. "You're going to tell me it's your favorite book, aren't you?"

"How did you know? I have it upstairs by my bedside! This is a miracle!"

"This," said Miriam, "is untrue."

Antonio looked hurt. "You think I am making this up?"

"I do."

"I am not, I assure you."

"Prove it."

"You want me to go upstairs and get my copy?"

"You said it was by your bedside."

"It is!"

"Prove it! Show me!"

Antonio was clearly taken aback. "I can't take you upstairs. Your reputation would be ruined."

Miriam smiled sweetly. "I can live with that. If you're right, I'll buy us another bottle of wine. Are you going to take me upstairs?"

Antonio hesitated. "I may have moved it and—"

"Let's find out," said Miriam. She stood up. "Lead on, Antonio!"

Sarah laughed. Never did a man take a woman up to his room with such obvious reluctance. "Do you think he's telling the truth?" she asked Barney.

"I have no idea."

Sarah wrapped her fingers round her glass and drank a little self-consciously. She knew he was watching her. "Why are you watching me?" she asked.

"I'm trying to imagine what you looked like at art school." He took out a cigarette and lit it. "I suspect you haven't changed much."

"I haven't really," Sarah agreed. "I've got wider and older but I don't feel different. You imagine you'll change with age, grow wiser, acquire confidence. I'm forty-three: I still drink too much, I'm still getting my heart broken, I still feel an idiot most of the time. Nothing's changed. I look old, that's all."

"I've changed," Barney said. "For a start my memory's shot to pieces." He smoked his cigarette and reached for the ashtray. "When did your husband leave you?"

"In November. It's getting better. I've stopped expecting him to walk through the door and tell me he's made a big mistake. When did your wife go?"

"Before Christmas. I spent a month drinking and smoking

far too much and at the end of it I thought: I'm still alive. Human beings are so conservative. We don't like to be thrown out of our safe little ruts. At this particular moment I'm rather glad I have been."

"Are you?" Sarah swallowed. Her eyes were drawn inexorably to his.

He smiled, leaned forward, and kissed her gently on the mouth.

Sarah blinked. "You kissed me," she said, unable to think of anything sensible to say.

"You see," Barney said apologetically, "I wanted to see what it was like."

"Oh," Sarah said. With hands that were far from steady, she took her glass to her lips and then placed it carefully back on the table. "What *was* it like?"

He frowned. "I'm not sure." He leaned forward and kissed her again. "It was good."

"Thank you," Sarah said. She herself was in perfect agreement.

Barney smiled. "Will you have dinner with me tomorrow night?"

Sarah was spared the necessity of giving an answer. (Yes, she would love to have dinner with Barney Melton but she was aware she was well out of her depth. On the other hand, did it matter if she *were* out of her depth? Still, she was not about to leave Miriam all on her own.) Antonio and Miriam had come back and Antonio was looking very smug. "It was there!" Miriam said. "It was by his bed. He fixed it. I don't know how he fixed it but he fixed it."

Antonio smiled modestly. "Raoul is bringing another bottle," he said. "What have you two been talking about?" he asked. "I can tell you've been talking about something."

"I've invited Sarah to dinner tomorrow," Barney said. "I'm waiting for her answer."

Antonio beamed at Sarah. "You must go! I shall cook Miriam a meal here. The restaurant is closed tomorrow. I am a superb cook. Miriam? You will come?"

Miriam glanced briefly at Sarah, hesitated, and then smiled politely at Antonio. "How can I resist such an invitation?" she said.

"I don't know," Antonio said. "You are a very lucky woman."

"Really?" Miriam said.

Think Hard Before You Do Have Sex
in Majorca in February

Amazingly, neither Sarah nor Miriam had hangovers the next morning. Admittedly, they had spent most of the morning asleep and they had also taken the precaution of drinking an entire bottle of mineral water before they'd gone to bed. Even so, Sarah thought, their clear heads indicated the presence of a good angel hovering around them.

Better still, the weather, though cold, was at least dry, which meant they could enjoy the views of the pine-clad mountains as they drove toward Valldemossa. Sarah sighed contentedly. "This is a wonderful holiday," she said.

"I was just thinking," said Miriam, "that something's gone very badly wrong with it. It's all very well for you. You're going to be wined and dined by Mr. Sex-on-Legs while I'm spending an evening with a fat, balding man who never stops talking, who is almost certainly a compulsive liar, and who seems to think he's God's gift to women. How did I get into this?"

Sarah grinned. "He made you laugh. Admit it, he made you laugh."

"Politicians make me laugh. Some of my pupils make me laugh. My mother's dog makes me laugh. It doesn't mean I want to spend an evening with them."

"I thought he was lovely."

"You drank enough last night to make you think anyone was lovely. *I* drank enough last night to think anyone was lovely and I still didn't think Antonio was."

Sarah felt a twinge of guilt. She knew very well that Miriam had only agreed to go out with Antonio in order to make her feel free to accept Barney's invitation. "Would you rather not go?" she asked anxiously. "We could always make our excuses. . . ."

Miriam laughed. "You must be joking. I can't wait to find out if Barney turns out to be a prince or a frog. And if I'm absolutely honest, I do want to go out, if only to see what sort of a cook Antonio is. If he is half as good as he says he is I shall at least have a good meal and if he isn't I shall take great pleasure in telling him so."

Reassured, Sarah sat back in her seat and enjoyed the spectacular views. Valldemossa, Antonio had said, was a place of great romance, a small ancient town where Frédéric Chopin and his lover George Sand had enjoyed a romantic interlude. Barney had said it wasn't romantic at all. The lovers had hated the town and had split up soon afterward.

Barney was wrong. Valldemossa *was* romantic, with a breathtaking approach through narrow, woodland roads, up neat terraced fields, and into stately mountains. Antonio, however, proved to be equally unreliable, since the monastery he had told them to see and in which Chopin and Sand had stayed was closed. It was a huge, imposing building, brazenly opulent and quite unsuitable, Sarah thought, for a pair of lovers. She wasn't surprised George Sand had disliked it. Apparently the monks who lived there had only been allowed to talk to each other for half an hour a week. It was, Sarah felt, a place of great sadness and she was not sorry that they couldn't go inside.

After Valldemossa, they drove on toward Deià, past piney headlands and ancient olive trees whose contorted trunks made Sarah long for her paints. Deià itself was built on a hill, its sand-colored houses jostling for space around the church at the top. They parked the car and walked up the steep, narrow lane that led to the church.

"We must visit the cemetery," Miriam said. "Robert Graves is buried here. I want to pay my respects. He lived here with another poet, an American woman. She had a huge nose and she treated him very badly. She left him in the end."

"Poor Robert Graves," Sarah said. "Is this why we're paying our respects?"

"We're paying our respects," Miriam said severely, "because he was a great poet."

The light, airy cemetery was far more impressive than the dark, little church. Its stone paths and graves were neatly kept and its low walls revealed the majestic beauty of the landscape around them. Many of the tombstones incorporated photographs of the deceased incumbents. In contrast, Robert Graves's remains were marked by a simple stone slab on which had been scratched his name and occupation.

"*Sic transit gloria,*" murmured Miriam. "You wouldn't think this was the final resting place of the man who wrote one of the best books about World War One, two of the greatest novels of Imperial Rome, and who still found time to bed dozens of women."

Sarah gazed out at the mountains, their tops wreathed in mist. Evidence of man's attempt to subdue these mammoths was apparent in the neat terraces that traversed them, along with the sprinkling of green-shuttered houses. Presumably many of the bodies resting here had once helped to tame this area.

"I think," she mused, "that given the choice between being a famous poet with a raunchy sex life and being a valued and respected member of a village community like this, I'd go for the latter, I really would."

Miriam looked down at the maze of old peasant houses that covered the hill below. She gave a long sigh. "Sarah," she said at last, "I think you need some lunch."

They walked back down the hill and along the main street, past craft shops and tapas bars, all closed for the winter. They eventually found a restaurant that was open and were welcomed by the jolly proprietress as if they were long lost daughters. Ushered to a terrace with fantastic views overlooking a deep ravine, they were soon enjoying grilled fish with crusty bread.

"When you think about it," Miriam said, expertly filleting her fish, "famous love affairs don't seem to work out very well in Majorca. Chopin and George Sand fell out in Valldemossa and Robert Graves and his American poet broke up in Deià. Not a very promising track record."

"Oh I don't know," said Sarah. "Michael Douglas and Catherine Zeta Jones have a holiday home here, don't they?"

"Michael Douglas," said Miriam severely, "is not in the same category as Frédéric Chopin or Robert Graves."

"Michael Douglas," retorted Sarah, "is a god. I remember going to see *Fatal Attraction* with Andrew years ago. He was very shaken by it. The fact that our marriage lasted as long as it did is probably due to that film. If only I'd known what Hyacinth was planning I'd have made him watch it again."

Miriam rested her hands on her chin. "If it weren't for Hyacinth, you wouldn't be going out with Barney Melton tonight."

"I'm not really sure I am going out with him. We all drank so much. He might not even remember he asked me. He told me he had a terrible memory."

"If he doesn't turn up," said Miriam, "you can jolly well come out with me and Antonio."

"Antonio would love that!"

"He would do," retorted Miriam. "He loved the way you raved about his food."

"I shouldn't be eating so much," Sarah said. "I've been trying so hard to lose weight. Do you think I've lost any weight since Christmas?"

"You don't need to lose weight," said Miriam, meaning that Sarah had not.

By the time they got back to the apartment it was early evening. Sarah had convinced herself that Barney's invitation had been fueled by alcohol and almost certainly forgotten by alcohol. This conviction did not stop her from having a shower, washing her hair, making up her face, dousing her neck with perfume, and squeezing into the torture instrument that was her red dress. "It's too tight, isn't it?" she asked Miriam.

"It's nice," said Miriam. "It gives you a very flattering waistline."

A very flattering, tight waistline. Sarah had read once that Shirley Maclaine kept thin by wearing clothes that were too tight for her. Not a bad idea and since Sarah knew she would not feel like eating in the presence of Barney, the red dress would probably be all right.

At eight o'clock, Sarah and Miriam sat opposite each other in the white sitting room.

Sarah pulled at her dress. "You don't think I'm overdressed?" she asked.

"I told you. No."

"What about the brown eye shadow? I don't want to look as if I've tried too hard."

"You don't. You look like a sophisticated woman going out on the town."

"I feel like a thirteen-year-old on my first date. Suppose he doesn't turn up?"

"He will." There was a loud knock at the door and Miriam smiled smugly. "See? I'll let him in."

Sarah crossed her legs, picked up a book, and stared fixedly at the inside cover, only to close it with a mixture of relief and disappointment when she heard Antonio's ringing salutation. "Good evening, ladies! Have you had a good day?"

"We've had a lovely time," said Sarah. She noticed that Antonio had obviously dressed with as much care as she had. What remained of his hair was neatly combed back. He was wearing gray trousers that strained at the waist, a black shirt, a bright red tie, and a liberal dash of aftershave.

"I knew you would," he smiled. "Miriam, we should go at once. I have prepared you a feast and it is waiting for me to attend to it."

Sarah sprang up and collected Miriam's coat from behind the door. "Of course you must go! Have a good time!"

Miriam took the coat and cast a meaningful glance at Sarah. "You know where we are."

"Yes, of course. See you later." She gave a wave and shut the door on them. She tugged again at the red dress. Should she change? But then Barney might come and she wouldn't be ready for him. She went through to her room and found her copy of *Rebecca*. Better to spend her time learning lines than to keep checking her reflection.

Twenty minutes later, Sarah knew he wasn't coming. She had learned three lines. She sighed. At least she could take off the horrible red dress, which was slowly squeezing the life out of her and which she would give to the Oxfam shop as soon as she went home. She struggled with the zip at the back and let out a long, grateful breath, which suddenly doubled back to her lungs when the doorbell went. She grappled desperately for the zip, couldn't reach it, swore furiously, and ran to the door.

"Hello," said Barney. "I'm not late, am I?"

Sarah smiled brightly. "Not at all, I was just getting ready. . . . Would you mind zipping me up?" She turned her back on him and pulled in her tummy muscles in a frenzy of embarrassment.

"There!" Barney turned her round. "You look nice."

However nice she might look, she *was* overdressed: Barney looked cool and beautiful in old jeans, a blue sweater, and an antiquated leather jacket. "I should have realized," he said as they went down the stairs and out into the street, "there's nowhere open on a Sunday night. So you're going to have to endure my cooking. I hope you don't mind."

"Not at all," said Sarah politely. Barney opened the passenger door of his car and she got in, placing her feet rather gingerly on top of a greasy rag.

Barney got in and started up the car. "Sorry about the mess," he said. "Are you all right? You can throw the rubbish in the back."

"I'm fine. You should see my car. One of my New Year's resolutions was to clean it up. I've had the same New Year's resolution for years."

Barney checked his mirror and swung out into the seafront. "Now, Antonio would say that's an amazing coincidence. He would say we were obviously made for each other."

Sarah gave a slightly forced laugh. She was concerned that he might have regarded her unzipped presence on his arrival as a sort of come-on and she was also aware that in her inebriated state last night she had been acting like some fawning groupie. "How long have you lived in Majorca?" she asked, reaching for a politely conversational tone.

"I don't know." Barney scratched his head. "Six years? Seven? I'm not sure. It's a long time anyway. The house belonged to my dad. When he died, I moved in. I only meant to stay a few months and somehow I never left." He braked suddenly to let a couple of boys cross the road and Sarah flung a steadying hand onto the dashboard. They drove on past a huge yachting marina with large gin palaces and sleek sailing boats.

"Here we are." Barney turned sharply off the road, past a block of flats, round the corner, and into a small slipway that led back onto the road. On Sarah's left was the sea. On her right there were two houses. One was a big red villa with a huge wooden door and ornate white balconies at the upstairs windows. The other was a tiny whitewashed cottage with a blue door. Barney brought the car to an abrupt halt opposite the red villa and leapt out. Sarah opened her door and looked down at the small shingle beach. Across the bay, the lights of Puerto d'Andratx twinkled over the sea. She could understand why Barney had chosen to stay here.

"Come on in," Barney said. "It's freezing out here." He took a stack of keys from his pocket, walked across to the cottage, and unlocked the blue door. "Welcome to my home!"

Sarah stepped into a small open-plan area, whose walls were covered with black and white photographs. To the right, there were a couple of aged armchairs, a small table, a brown rug, and a fire. On the left, in front of the window seat, was a dining table with two chairs. Beyond these were winding stairs and a narrow passageway leading through to the kitchen.

"Barney!" Sarah exclaimed. "I love it!"

"Do you want me to show you round? There's not much to see."

"Please." Sarah took off her coat and draped it over one of the armchairs. Barney threw his keys onto the table and took Sarah's hand. "I'll show you the kitchen first."

It was tiny. Bottles of wine covered almost half of the work surface while the rest was strewn with peppers, onions, and sliced chorizo. "I'm not a great cook," Barney said, "but I can do a mean risotto. Are you all right with garlic?"

"I *love* garlic."

"Good. Now I'll show you upstairs."

Barney's bedroom, like the rest of the house, was simply furnished and tidy. There was one large window, with a thin gray curtain, overlooking the sea, a huge bed covered in a maroon blanket, and a chest of drawers on top of which stood a photo of Barney and a woman who looked very like Michelle Pfeiffer. Sarah glanced away quickly. "It's lovely. Did your father live here on his own?"

"He had the odd lady friend from time to time. There's another bedroom over here." He threw open a door to reveal a small chamber with a couple of single beds and a chair. "And that's about it. Shall we have a drink?"

They went downstairs again and while Barney retired to the kitchen, Sarah glanced at some of the photos. They were very good. One, a long, shimmering desert landscape, was outstanding.

Barney returned with a bottle and a couple of glasses. "What do you think of my gallery?"

"You seem to have been everywhere." She pointed to a picture of a dark, good-looking man, swathed in a torn blanket, grinning at the camera. "Who was he?"

Barney glanced at the photo and then opened the wine. "That was in Afghanistan. He was a mujahideen leader. He was a lovely bloke."

Sarah, observing the huge rifle in the man's hand, didn't

think he looked lovely at all. She pointed at another picture. Long ago she had seen a film called *The War Game,* which had given her sleepless nights for weeks afterward. It depicted a Britain devastated by nuclear war and the photo reminded her of that film. It looked like the end of the world but Sarah could see a couple of children playing in the rubble. Among the fallen buildings, looking absurdly out of place, sat a gleaming car, apparently unscathed. "Where's that?" she asked.

Barney handed her a glass and lit a cigarette. "A place called Suleimanieh, in Iraq. I was there after the Gulf War. It was a big town. Saddam's soldiers bulldozed it all." He sat down on one of the armchairs. "Not a pretty sight."

Sarah took a sip of her drink and sat down in the other chair. "What were you doing out there?"

"I was an agency photographer. I enjoyed it for a while. You see the world, you meet interesting people. You meet lots of pretty nasty people, too, and you try to show what they do. Eventually"—he shrugged—"I got fed up. One of my first jobs was in Northern Iraq, a Kurdish town bombed with poison gas. There were corpses everywhere. I was fine at the time. A few years later I started getting recurring nightmares about it and I lost my nerve. I didn't want to see any more." He looked up at Sarah and smiled. "Don't look so serious! I didn't ask you here to make you look serious."

"You were right to leave," Sarah said. "No one could go on witnessing things like that for long."

"Some do," Barney said. "I prefer to be here."

"What do you do now?"

"I look after people's holiday homes for them. I make sure their gardens are nice and tidy. I look after the electrics and the boilers. If there's a leaking roof, I'm onto it. It's very demanding."

"People like me," Sarah said slowly, "spend our whole lives unaware of anything outside our safe little worlds. You've earned your safety. You sound like you think you shouldn't be here. That's crazy."

"Thank you," Barney said. "You are a very nice woman." He stood up. "I'm going to get your supper. I'll give you some pretty pictures to look at. Over there. See the red folder? Photos of Majorca. Have a look."

"I will. Thank you." Sarah collected the folder and returned to her chair. She was glad Barney had left the room. She opened the folder and let the images of a beautiful island soothe away Barney's memories. No black and white here but a feast of color, fields with snow white carpets of almond blossom, olive trees with silvery green leaves, underground caves with stalactites and stalagmites, green-shuttered houses, and golden churches. Near the end was a picture of a vast golden cathedral. In front of it stood the Michelle Pfeiffer woman, laughing at her photographer. Was she the wife who had left him? She looked so happy. How could she have left Barney? Sarah closed the folder and drank her wine. Ambercross seemed a million miles away.

The risotto was good. Barney refused to accept her compliments since she ate so little and she felt compelled to confess that the red dress prevented her from enjoying too much of it. She was also, she told him, supposed to be losing weight. This prompted Barney into a long and passionate diatribe on the absurdity of modern ideas of beauty. Sarah assured him she was not a fashion victim but was suffering in the cause of drama.

Barney was a good listener. By the time they were on their second bottle she had told him all about Andrew and her unhappy initiation into the traumas of amateur dramatics. She said, suddenly self-conscious, "I've been talking too much."

Barney lit a cigarette. "I like listening to you." He smiled.

Sarah drank the rest of her wine. "You're looking at me," she said. "What's wrong?"

"I was thinking," Barney said, "that it's time we went to bed."

Sarah blinked. "Together?"

"Hey," said Barney, "that's an even better idea."

"We can't do that!" Sarah protested.

"Why not?"

Sarah frowned. Her husband had been bedding Hyacinth Harrington for months, her sons were bedding runaway brides. "At the moment," she confessed, "I can't think of a reason."

"Neither can I." He stubbed out his cigarette and stood up. "Come to the fire. Just for a moment."

She looked at him a little warily and then followed him to the rug. He turned her round and slowly unzipped the red dress.

Sarah swallowed. Things seemed to be happening very fast and she wasn't at all sure that she knew how to stop them, probably because she was even less sure that she *wanted* to stop them. Barney didn't appear to understand that she was still trying to think of a sensible reason as to why they shouldn't go to bed. She knew there *was* a sensible reason but it was very difficult to locate it while Barney was pulling her dress from her shoulders and she was trying to ensure that at least her slip didn't get pulled down at the same time.

Barney bent down and threw her dress onto the armchair. "I've wanted to do that all evening," he said.

Sarah had been looking forward to getting out of her red dress too but she had assumed she would be struggling out of it on her own. "Barney," she murmured, "I think . . ." She was finding it very difficult to say what she did think partly because she wasn't sure what she thought and partly because Barney was standing right behind her, kissing her shoulder and slipping his hands inside her bra. Sarah's head craned back involuntarily: rivulets of pleasure were seeping through her brain, flooding the few circuits of intelligent, rational thought that were still active. It was far easier to lean back against him and enjoy the sensation of his mouth on her neck, his body against her own. Inside her brain, one lone, dim light of sense struggled to be noticed and Sarah pulled away. "Barney, wait," she gasped, moving out of reach of his hands. "This is not what I do. I mean, I can count on the fingers of one hand the number of men I've slept with. And there'd still be a couple of fingers left. What are you doing?"

"I'm taking off my sweater," Barney said, taking off his sweater.

"Listen," Sarah said, "this is important. How many women have you slept with?"

Barney paused. "Actually," he said, "I can't remember."

"You can't remember! That's terrible! Barney, what are you doing?"

"I'm taking off my T-shirt," said Barney, taking off his T-shirt.

"Barney," said Sarah, "do you understand what I'm saying?"

"I think so," said Barney. "You're telling me you've slept

with too few men and I've slept with too many women. Antonio would tell you that's an amazing coincidence. He'd say we were definitely meant for each other."

"Barney, I think we . . ."

Barney put his hand to her lips. "I know what you're worried about. And by an amazing coincidence"—he reached into his trouser pocket and pulled out a box of condoms—"I have these with me."

"I hadn't actually got as far as thinking about that yet," Sarah admitted. She was a little taken aback by the condoms. "Do you always carry them around with you?"

"Only since I met you. Now if it's all right, I'd really like to kiss you."

Sarah had to admit, if only to herself, that it was very all right for him to kiss her and after he had kissed her, the one dim light of rational thought gave up and switched itself out. She followed him upstairs and smiled when he led her to his bed.

Now he was kissing her again and his hands were exploring her body with tantalizing slowness, now moving forward, now retreating, until she was just one mass of nerve endings, conscious only of his hands, his skin, his smell. Still he made her wait until she was desperate for him and then at last he entered her and she felt as if her body were exploding in a thousand bubbles of pleasure. She joined him in one final, crowning surge of satisfaction and then her body collapsed in a glorious wave of pure liquid bliss.

She was woken in the morning with a cup of tea. Barney, dressed and shaved, looked as if he'd been up for ages.

Sarah sat up and pushed her hair back. "You should have woken me," she said. "What's the time?"

"Half past nine." He put the tea on the floor beside her. "I have to go. Do you know how to find your way back? Just follow the sea back to town. Will you be all right?"

"Of course. Do I have to lock the door or anything?"

"Just bang it shut." He leant forward to kiss her. "It was fun last night." He smiled and left her. She could hear him go downstairs and slam the door behind him. Sarah bent down to pick up her mug and sat back against the wall. Her eyes met those of Michelle Pfeiffer on the other side of the room. She knew what those eyes were telling her. At the age of forty-three, Sarah had just had her very first one-night stand.

Do Not Sentimentalize the Motives
of Predatory Males

Sarah bought some sugared croissants on the way home. She had to ring the doorbell at least three times before she heard a very sleepy voice call out, "I'm coming!"

The transformation was instant. When Miriam opened the door her eyes were like slits and she was barely conscious. The moment she saw Sarah, her eyes widened and she was suddenly a sentient being again. "Sarah!" she breathed. "Tell me all! I'll make some coffee."

"Before I do anything," Sarah said, "I must get out of this dress. I won't be a moment." She went through to her room and shouted, "Can Antonio cook?"

She heard Miriam laugh. "I need some coffee before I answer that."

Sarah grinned and unzipped her dress. Funny how easy it was to take off when she wasn't in a hurry.

A few minutes later, after a lightning shower and dressed in her brown cords and sweater, she went through to the kitchen.

"Breakfast," said Miriam, "is ready!"

"Wonderful!" Sarah sat down at the small table and poured them both some coffee. "All right," she said. "Now tell me. Can he cook?"

"Yes," said Miriam. "I'm afraid he can. We had garlic mushrooms and tortilla and a terrific pork dish with pine nuts and raisins. So yes, the man can cook and I did tell him he could and then I wished I hadn't because he just smiled and said, 'But of course I can cook, I told you I could cook,' as if he never lies about anything."

"Perhaps he doesn't," Sarah suggested. "Perhaps he's been telling you the truth."

"Oh right, so he's the world's greatest teacher, his wife was a closet lesbian, his favorite book is also my favorite book and . . . oh yes, get this, last night he told me he'd been to Zelenograd."

"Where's Zelenograd?"

"It's a town outside Moscow. No one goes to Zelenograd. It's a boring town with great, concrete slabs of Soviet apartment blocks. The point is I've been there. I took a group of sixteen-year-olds out there years ago. We joined an arts camp there for a week. I was telling Antonio this and he said *he* had been to Zelenograd. He said he bought a coat in a supermarket there."

"I'm surprised you didn't ask to see it." Sarah eyed the piece of croissant lying on Miriam's plate. "Are you going to eat that?"

"No, you have it. Of course I asked to see it, and surprise, surprise, he forgot to bring it back from Russia. On the other hand, he described it to me and it sounded very like the coat one of my boys bought: gray tweed with a lining and deep inside pockets. They were really good coats and fantastic value, the equivalent of ten English pounds. In fact I often wish I'd bought one. So I still don't know what to think about Antonio. I'm beginning to wonder if . . . No, that's silly."

"What is?"

"I'm beginning to wonder if Antonio has telepathic powers. Don't laugh, it's not impossible. I mean, look at the facts. Every time I tell him about something I've seen or said or done, he's seen or said or done it too. I know it sounds farfetched but I can't think of any other explanation. Don't you think it's possible? Or do you think I'm crazy?"

"I think you're crazy."

"Sarah!"

"Well you are! Antonio does not look like a man with special, spooky powers. He doesn't. Why can't you accept he's just a well-traveled, well-read, brilliant cook who was once a brilliant teacher and who had a wife with lesbian tendencies? Sounds quite plausible to me."

"Well it doesn't to me," said Miriam darkly.

Sarah licked her fingers and stared regretfully at her empty plate. "I think you're very well-suited. In fact I was quite surprised to see you here this morning."

"That," said Miriam, "is not funny. I did wonder if I'd have to fight him off but he was surprisingly well-behaved."

"Well of course he was. Anyway you weren't exactly behaving like a woman besotted."

"I suppose. He's invited us both to supper on Thursday."

"That's kind of him. Are we going to go?"

"Since most of the restaurants are closed at this time of year, I think we should. At least we'll get a good meal. Unless of course you intend to spend all your time with Barney?"

"No."

"So? How did it go? Is he a prince or a frog?"

"A prince. Definitely a prince."

"Tell me everything. From the beginning."

Sarah sat back and put her hands behind her head. "We went to his house, which you'd have loved. It's a tiny little cottage, virtually on the seafront. Very pretty. He has photos all over the place. He used to be a news photographer. He was in Iraq and Afghanistan. . . ."

"Perfect. A man with a glamorous past."

"He cooked me a nice meal. We talked. Or rather," Sarah corrected herself, "I talked. I probably talked far too much. And then we went to bed."

"Good?"

"Very good."

"Lucky you. So when are you going to see him again?"

"I doubt if I will. He brought me a cup of tea this morning. He said it had been fun."

"That was nice of him."

"It *was* nice of him. I had a nice time."

Miriam folded her arms in front of her and looked at Sarah with a furrowed brow. "Don't you *want* to see him again?"

"Yes. Very much. But I don't expect to."

Miriam shook her head. "This doesn't sound like you at all."

"That's because I'm not me anymore. For twenty years I've been a very happy wife and mother who expected to go on being a wife and mother until the day I died. Well I'm not a wife anymore so there's nothing wrong in slipping into bed with the odd male from time to time."

"I agree. It's just that . . ."

"I admit, I readily admit I think Barney's amazing but I promise you I did not go out with him last night expecting or even hoping for some sort of relationship. Barney would never want me to be 'his woman' and I'm not into all that sort of caveman stuff anyway."

"I'm just saying . . ."

"We went to bed together. He didn't have to seduce me with promises of romance. I wanted him to make love to me and I enjoyed it very much. I never expected anything more: we have nothing in common. He's been all over the world, he's slept with hundreds of women, he lives a life where he's answerable to no one. I have two sons, I slept with just the one man for over twenty years, and until this week I've never been further than Brittany. Like I said to you, he's a five-star male."

"And you're a one-star woman?"

Sarah grinned. "Two-star perhaps!"

"Rubbish! Absolute rubbish! And if you're trying to tell me you have to travel widely and bed loads of people in order to be a fascinating person, then all I can say is you haven't met some of the deeply tedious bed-hopping travelers I've met. And if Barney doesn't want to see you again this week, then all I can say is he's not a five-star male at all, he's just a very stupid male. And now you can tell me to shut up."

"Did I ever tell you," said Sarah, "that I'm very glad you're my best friend?"

"So you should be. Now let's talk about today. Antonio said we should go and see Galilea and there's also a nature reserve he thinks we'll like. I'm hoping it will turn out to be a piece of old scrubland so I can tell him he was wrong. What do you think? Shall we try it?"

"Definitely. I bet you twenty euros Antonio's right."

Sarah won her twenty euros. Galilea was a beautiful village, high up in the mountains. Miriam, determined to find fault, complained that Antonio had neglected to warn them of the hair-raising bends on the narrow road up there. Even so, she was impressed by the pretty square and the small whitewashed farmsteads scattered around the tiny church. Better still was the tapas bar near the church, which was actually open, even if the waiter was surly. He clearly thought they were mad to want to sit outside but he did begin to thaw once Miriam spoke to him in Spanish.

"How many languages can you speak?" Sarah asked her, pulling her coat around her.

"Four," said Miriam, "but my Russian is very dodgy. Sometimes I think I might go traveling again if Clive does decide to leave me."

"You don't really think he will."

"My age is against me. It's not just the wrinkles. In term time I'd be happily in bed by ten and given the choice between a night out at the theater and a cozy evening in front of the telly, I'd probably choose the latter. Cozy is not a word Clive likes."

"You could always leave *him*."

"This is my second marriage, Sarah. I don't want to fail twice."

"Therein lies the curse of a successful woman. You won't accept failure."

"That's what makes one successful."

"In that case who wants to be successful? You're in a no-win situation. Failure is built in to us. No one can stay young and strong and beautiful for ever. Look what happens to all the beautiful people who won't accept that: plastic faces with people who can't smile any more. Most successful careers end in failure because successful people won't accept their minds aren't as sharp as they were. My marriage to Andrew has failed. I accept that now, and do you know something? It's not the end of the world!"

"Yes, but Andrew walked out on you. He made the marriage fail, you didn't. If Clive walks out on me I suppose I'll accept it. *I* can't leave *him*."

"I don't see why not. And anyway, why is it your fault if your marriages *do* fail? I don't see how you can blame yourself for the fact that your first husband preferred men to women. And as for Clive, if he makes you unhappy . . ."

"He makes me unhappy at the moment. Things will change, they always do. And while we're on the subject of boring, domestic problems, have you thought about seeing a solicitor yet?"

"No. Andrew hasn't insisted that I sell the house. He simply said that at some point we'd have to. He's actually being quite reasonable. We have a fifty-thousand-pound mortgage. If we sell the house for four hundred and fifty thousand, he says we can have two hundred thousand each."

Miriam shook her head. "You should hold out for two hundred and fifty. I presume you want to stay in Ambercross? Ben and James will still want to come home at vacations. I wouldn't think it was too easy to buy a three- or four-bedroom cottage in the country for two hundred thousand. Not a nice one anyway. And if I were you, I'd demand a big payout now rather than a monthly account. As Andrew's guilt wears off and Hyacinth's demands increase, he'll be less keen to give you anything."

Sarah grimaced. "I hate the idea of being beholden to him. . . ."

"For heaven's sake, Sarah, he owes you! Shooter's Cottage was a hovel when you moved in! You were the one who did all the work on it. You've supported Andrew through thick and thin and if he chooses to leave you now, he has to pay you back for that support. All right? Sermon over."

Sarah stared out at the breathtaking views in front of them. "There is nothing," she told Miriam, "as therapeutic as a mountain. It was here long before Clive or Andrew were born and it will be here long after they die." And Barney too, for that matter.

After lunch they drove along the windy road to Puigpunyent and then on to the nature reserve. With thirty waterfalls and three kilometers of mountain paths, it was a place for serious walking and the two women were both ready to accept the challenge. When they finally returned to the little car, Sarah said breathlessly, "The great thing . . . about doing this . . . is we can slob around for the rest of the holiday without feeling guilty."

Miriam was not a natural slobber but even she was happy to get home and look forward to a horizontal evening. They had omelets for supper and were in bed by ten. The long walk was every bit as successful as Sarah had hoped. Too tired to dwell on the disappointing fact that Barney did not wish to see her again, she fell asleep almost immediately.

18

Cherish Your Priorities in Life . . .

The weather did not improve in the next few days and there continued to be a distinct absence of Marcello Mastroianni Antonio Banderas look-alikes. Neither of these factors stopped Sarah and Miriam from enjoying themselves. On Tuesday they visited Sant Elm, a sleepy resort with a wide sandy beach. They did another marathon walk, this time to the abandoned Trappist monastery of Sa Trapa. On Wednesday, faced with aching muscles, they went only as far as the town of Andratx, four kilometers in from the port.

Wednesday was market day and most of the streets were lined with stalls. The variety of the produce on offer was extraordinary: artificial flowers, garden plants, carpets, cushions, nuts, sweets, spices, herbs, sausages, hams, cheese, wine, seeds, leather bags and wallets, ladies underwear, multicolored skirts, pots and pans, toys and jewelry. Miriam bought a sleek, smooth bowl made from olive wood and Sarah bought a strange wooden object from a cheerful lady who rolled it over her hips and told her it reduced cellulite. Sarah told Miriam she was buying it for its aesthetic value and Miriam said Sarah had an amazing ability to find beauty in the most unexpected things.

On Thursday they followed the twisting, coastal road up to Estellencs, a fairy-tale village with narrow, steep, cobbled streets and old stone houses. They had meant to drive on to Banyalbufar but sloth intervened and they went home for a siesta.

By now, Sarah felt she had put the Barney episode into its proper perspective. She might have bored him so much that he hadn't wanted to see her again but at least he had found her sufficiently attractive to woo her with risotto and since, in her unprejudiced opinion, Barney could attract any woman he wanted, this in itself was no mean achievement. She wondered if Barney had said anything to Antonio about her and hoped that he hadn't.

If Antonio did know anything, he was far too well-mannered to show it. That evening, he welcomed both women with equal displays of affection and ushered them into the restaurant. "Sit by the fire and get warm!" he commanded. "I will open the wine."

All the tables were bare except for one, which had napkins and cutlery set for three, with a long, flickering candle in the middle. "You haven't closed the restaurant for us, have you?" asked Sarah.

Antonio chuckled. "On a cold Thursday night in February there is no point in being open and even if there were, I would say, no, tonight I serve only two beautiful ladies!"

"Antonio," Miriam said, "you're such a liar."

Antonio turned to Sarah and put his hand on his heart. "You see how she treats me? I cook for her once, I cook for her twice, and still she scorns me! What can I do to make her be kind to me?"

"I don't know," said Sarah. "I told her I think you're made for each other."

"I tell her that too. I tell her to leave her boring husband who is no husband at all—"

"How," interrupted Miriam coldly, "can you possibly know that?"

"A good husband would not let his beautiful wife go to Majorca and fall in love with Antonio."

"His beautiful wife," Miriam pointed out, "hasn't fallen in love with Antonio."

"You see how she fights it?" Antonio sighed and bent his head close to Sarah's. "I think she loves me a little!" He picked up a bottle of wine from the ledge above the fire and opened it. "Tonight I made you a paella, a perfect paella. But first we will drink some wine and I will make you a suggestion."

"Really?" said Miriam.

"Really. I love the way you say 'really'! My sister lives in Esporles. Tomorrow my mother is eighty-seven and my sister is having a big party at lunch for her. It will be a wonderful feast as my sister cooks like an angel. It will be a wonderful party and you will both have a wonderful time. Then we will come back here and in the evening I will cook you a very simple meal and I will be very sad because you will be leaving the next day."

"But Antonio," Sarah protested, "we can't gate-crash your family party!"

"My sister wants you to come. Her son is going to London

next month and he can practice his English with you. You must come!"

"In that case," said Miriam, "we'd love to. It's very kind of you."

"It is very kind of me. You see how I think of you? I am a very kind person! Now your glasses are on the table so have some wine while I look at my paella. You will say it is the best paella in the world."

"That man," murmured Miriam as Antonio bustled away, "that man . . ."

"That man is very kind and we're lucky to have met him. Tomorrow will be fascinating." Sarah went over to the table and poured them both some wine. "This is a brilliant holiday."

"No regrets?"

"None at all." She raised her glass and said deliberately, "To Barney and Antonio!"

Miriam sniffed. "I'm not drinking to Barney and I'm certainly not drinking to Antonio. Let's drink a toast to the paella!"

The paella was every bit as good as Antonio had promised it would be and Sarah was glad she wasn't wearing her red dress. Antonio entertained them over dinner with tales of his family. There was his father, who at ninety-five was still being scolded by his wife for an affair he had had ten years earlier. ("She says he is disgusting, she says his girlfriend was far too young for him. She is quite right, the girlfriend was only sixty-two.") Antonio's older brother was flying in from Seville, where he had a flourishing textile business. "He has ten children, which is good because . . . just like Miriam, you see . . . I have no children." Antonio's sister was called Belen. According to Antonio she had been the most gorgeous girl on the island. She had been wooed by Antonio's best friend, Pedro, a man of great charm and beauty, but Belen had surprised everyone by marrying Nicolas, who was not beautiful at all.

"What happened to Pedro?" asked Miriam.

"His heart was broken," said Antonio. "He went to Barcelona." He made Barcelona sound like Siberia. "But now we are all very happy because Nicolas is dead."

Sarah blinked. "I'm sure Belen isn't very happy."

"Belen is happiest of all. Nicolas was a pig. He died ten years ago and Pedro left Barcelona at once. Now he is married to my sister and we are all very happy. You will see them tomorrow and also my little brother, who is—"

A loud knock at the door diverted Antonio's attention. He said politely, "Excuse me a moment," and crossed the room.

Sarah, sipping her wine, heard him cry, "Barney! You smelled my paella?" and nearly choked. She turned, caught Barney's eye, and saw his face break into a smile. He came over to her at once and cupped the back of her neck with his hand. "You didn't tell me you were having my woman to dinner, Antonio. Have you anything to give a starving man?"

Antonio shook his head. "You are always starving! Come through to the kitchen."

"I will." Barney kissed Sarah quickly but firmly on the mouth, smiled at Miriam, and followed Antonio out to the back.

Miriam looked across at Sarah. "Don't you dare cry," she hissed. "I will never talk to you again if you cry!"

Sarah shook her head, blinked furiously, and took a restorative gulp of wine. "I know," she murmured. "I know I'm utterly pathetic. I never thought I'd see him again and when he called me his woman just now I . . . the truth is I think I am a Stone Age sort of woman after all."

Miriam grinned. "You think I didn't know that? Only a woman with positively prehistoric views could have put up with Andrew all these years!"

Miriam was right. Sarah was prehistoric. She had forgotten how much she loved the proprietorial gestures of a confident lover. She loved the fact that Barney sat so close to her, that after he'd eaten, he threw his arm around her shoulders and played idly with her hair. When Barney smiled sleepily at her and asked if she'd come home with him it seemed perfectly natural for her to nod assent.

"Tomorrow," said Antonio, "we will leave at ten. . . ."

"I've been thinking," Barney said. "I want to take Sarah to Palma."

Sarah glanced uncertainly at Miriam. Miriam said in a tone of patient resignation, "I'll see you back here tomorrow evening."

"Is that all right?" Sarah asked Antonio. "Can I still have supper with you? I'd like to hear all about the party."

"Of course," Antonio said. "And I will look after your friend very well!"

Sarah smiled. "I know you will. Miriam's very lucky!"

"Really?" said Miriam and Antonio together. Miriam looked at Antonio.

Antonio smiled modestly. "I knew she was going to say that," he said.

*   *   *

Barney's car was perched drunkenly on the edge of the pavement. Barney started the ignition and turned it off. "It's no use," he said. "I have to kiss you first." He leaned forward and then moved back and started the ignition again. "On second thought," he said, "I won't."

Sarah, falling sharply against the window as the car careered off the pavement, was aggrieved. "Why not?" she asked.

"If I kiss you I'll want to make love to you and I'm too old to make love to women in cars. I put a note through your door this evening."

"Did you?"

"I did."

"What did it say?"

"It said: 'Please come and have some hot sex with me.' "

"It didn't."

"No, I think I phrased it more delicately." He glanced across at her. "We're not really going to spend your last evening with Antonio and Miriam, are we?"

Sarah moved a plastic bottle of water from under her feet. "You don't have to come."

"Well of course I'll come if you're going to be there. As long as we can leave early."

"Barney," Sarah said, "I'm not going to stay with you tomorrow night."

"But it's your last night."

"Until a few hours ago," Sarah said, "I assumed I wouldn't be seeing you again. You could have spent Monday night with me, you could have spent Tuesday night with me, you could have spent last night with me. But you didn't. So what's so special about tomorrow night?"

"It's your last night."

"Yes, and it's Miriam's last night, too, and she's not going to spend it on her own in the apartment."

They drove on in silence. Sarah gazed studiously out of the window. Barney, turning the car sharply into the slipway, brought it to a dramatic halt next to the red villa. He made no attempt to get out of the car. Sarah looked down at the small beach. The moon was dancing on a lone boot standing erect on the shingle. She wondered whom the boot belonged to.

"I think," Barney said, "I owe you an apology."

Sarah folded her arms. She said nothing.

"I had business on the other side of the island. I didn't have your phone number."

"I'm not on the phone. I didn't expect to hear from you anyway. . . ."

"I could have asked Antonio to tell you I wanted to see you. I did want to see you. Sarah? Sarah, will you look at me?"

Sarah kept her face resolutely fixed on the boot on the beach.

"Sarah?" Barney reached out and touched her face. "I'm a selfish bastard. I don't think things through, I never do, and I'm really, really sorry. Of course you must spend your last night with Miriam."

Sarah relaxed. "Apology accepted."

Barney pushed her hair back from her face. "You do realize," he said gently, "we have no time to lose. We must go in immediately."

Sarah picked up her bag from the floor. "Why?" she asked.

He smiled. "If this is our last night together," he said, "we'd better make the most of it."

217

. . . But Be Prepared to Ditch Everything Else

The next morning Barney brought her a cup of tea. Sarah eyed it warily. "Does this mean you're about to disappear again?" she asked.

Barney assumed an injured expression. "Oh, ye of little faith," he said. "It means I'm a very thoughtful man. I've been downstairs making you some scrambled eggs, so don't be long. Palma is waiting!"

They went to the cathedral first, a vast honey-colored building with strangely delicate features, like a bully in a tutu. The interior was forbidding, almost funereal, and the Gothic gloom was made greater by the presence of the sinister, spidery chandelier that hovered over the altar, ornate doorways, and flying buttresses.

Barney took her into a small anteroom containing grisly

relics, neatly displayed in shiny glass cases. "This is the best," he said, pointing to the supposed arm of Saint Sebastian, pickled in a glass tube and topped by a sickly blue plaster hand.

"Lovely," Sarah said faintly.

Afterward they walked hand in hand through the oldest part of the city, a warren of narrow corridors, dwarfed by the lofty Renaissance buildings. They peered through wrought iron gates at wide, elegant courtyards of almost ghostly serenity. Sarah was fascinated by the contrast between the cramped little shops and lanes and the glimpses of peaceful habitations with their vast stone pots and tinkling fountains. Palma seemed to be full of such contradictions: majestic architecture next to garish kiosks selling magazines full of film star scandal; elderly señoritas in dignified black, walking past girls in the tightest of trousers.

At last, foot-sore and tired, they wandered into a small bar and Barney ordered wine and a variety of tapas.

Sarah sat back in her chair and sighed. "I'm having a wonderful day. I wish I wasn't leaving tomorrow."

"You don't have to," Barney said. "You could come and live with me."

"Would you bring me tea every morning?"

Barney considered. "Probably not."

"Then it's out of the question."

The waiter arrived with the wine, opened it, and poured out two glasses. Sarah listened while Barney and the man chatted together in Spanish. The man flashed a wicked smile at Sarah before leaving.

Sarah leaned forward. "I wish I understood Spanish," she murmured.

Barney took out a cigarette and lit it. "He asked me if you were my wife. I said we were lovers and you had just refused to come and live with me."

Sarah smiled. "You shouldn't joke about things like that. I might just take you up on your offer."

"I never joke about things like that."

She stared at him uncertainly and took a sip of her wine. The conversation seemed to be drifting into very strange waters indeed and it seemed far safer to say nothing than to jump to conclusions that must surely be absurd.

"So?" Barney paused to exhale a thin stream of smoke. "Will you come and live with me?"

Sarah's eyes widened. "What?"

"I mean it. I think it would be very good. Don't you?"

Sarah felt as if her brain was exploding. She took another sip of wine to steady herself.

"Barney," she said weakly, "you hardly know me and I know nothing about you. I don't even know if you have children."

"I don't," he said. "No, actually, that's wrong. I do. Sort of."

"Sort of?"

"I was married for a few years in my twenties." Barney sounded as if he'd only just remembered this. "We had a son."

"You had a son! What happened to him?"

"He went to America. Well they both did. I was abroad at the time. She fell in love with an American and they all went to live in Seattle. I think it was Seattle."

"Are they still there? How old was your son when you last saw him?"

"Lord, I don't know. He couldn't walk or talk or anything so he must have been very young."

"What's his name?"

Barney frowned and scratched his head. "Sam! I'm sure it was Sam!"

"And you never see him? How can you bear it? Why haven't you kept in touch?"

"Don't look so shocked. It's not like I abandoned them to a life of poverty. The American was very rich. They're probably living in some vast mansion."

"But aren't you curious? Even a little?"

"Not really. I expect he's a great hulking quarterback now. I shouldn't think we'd have anything in common. As far as I can remember his mother and I certainly didn't."

"But, Barney! He's your son! He might be very like you."

"Do you think so?" Barney looked appalled. "I hope not."

"Barney, you're incredible. So you have a son. What else should I know? Tell me about your second wife."

"Odile? She's French. I met her five years ago. Very beautiful. Very young. Too young, I suppose. We were very happy for at least a year and then we weren't. She wanted children, a bigger house, more money. I didn't, so now she's left me. I don't have a very good track record, do I?"

"Well, I wouldn't want you to father my unborn children."

"Are you planning to have any more children?"

"Definitely not."

"In that case, there's no problem. When can you move in?"

Sarah laughed. She wished she could visit her younger self and tell her that one day Barney Melton would be trying to persuade her to move in with him. "Barney," she said, trying to be serious and fighting the irresistible bubbles of joy inside her head, "we hardly know each other."

"We will," he pointed out, "if you stay."

Sarah poured herself a glass of water and took three big gulps. "Life isn't that simple. And anyway, there's Andrew and the house and—"

"I thought Andrew wanted to sell the house? Fine. Let him sell it."

"And there are my boys . . ."

"They can come and see you out here. I bet they'd like it more than Ambercross. Your husband's left you, your boys are grown-up, and you've got to move anyway. So what's the problem?"

He made everything sound so blissfully simple, so straightforward, so reasonable. This was a man, Sarah reminded herself, who had made no effort to see her again after their first night together and who had fathered a son he couldn't be bothered to know. She rested her elbows on the table and put her chin on her hands.

"Speaking honestly," Barney said gravely, "I'd be surprised if you agreed to do something so risky because I suspect you're someone who never takes risks. Speaking honestly, I hope you might decide to change the habits of a lifetime."

Sarah opened her mouth and closed it again. Was she a natural-born coward? She tried hard to think of some serious risks she had taken. She had agreed to be in *Rebecca,* of course, but that was only because she had been bullied into it by Miriam and Audrey.

Barney grinned. "Sarah, I've completely thrown you, haven't I? Let's leave it for now. We'll go and look at the museum after lunch. We can talk about everything else later."

When Miriam asked Sarah later for her opinion of the museum, Sarah was unable to be very forthcoming. She knew she'd seen pots and paintings but she was unable to be much more specific. They went round all four floors and Sarah responded to Barney's comments with the appropriate words and gestures but all the time her brain was conducting an impassioned debate. Should she live with gorgeous, gorgeous Barney in the beautiful island of Majorca or should she return to her humiliating position as the Abandoned Wife of Ambercross and to an uncertain future in some bleak little flat? Or to put it another way, should she leave friends and a life that she knew in order to live with a man about whom she knew little except his ability to lose wives and son?

In the car going home, the cacophony of conflicting advice continued to bombard her head. She only stirred when she saw that they had driven past the turning off to the cottage. "Where are we going?" she asked.

"I want to show you something," Barney said. He parked the car on the side of the road and leaped out.

Sarah opened the door, followed him along the grassy mound, and stopped suddenly. "We're on the edge of a cliff!"

Barney stood behind her and put his arms round her waist. "I've got you!" he said. "Now look at that view!"

Sarah looked out at the sea. In the distance she could see a small island rearing up from the water like a sea monster's head. To the left were the hills around Puerto d'Andratx and to the right, endless sea.

"This is one of my favorite views," Barney said. "It's not particularly stunning or dramatic but I love it. Do you really want to leave all this?"

No, Sarah didn't. Standing there with Barney's arms around

her, his face next to her own, everything seemed to be quite clear. It wasn't as if she had a lot to go back to. Sooner or later, and knowing Andrew it would probably be sooner, she would have to give up her beloved cottage. The boys had effectively left home. Wasn't it time that she showed a little boldness? "Are you sure," she asked, "are you really sure you want me to come and live here?"

He turned her round to face him and traced her lips with his finger. "What do *you* think?"

He was looking at her as if she was the most desirable woman in the world. Standing up here, with the sound of the sea and the sun on her back, she really felt she *was* desirable. And sensual. And attractive. She laughed up at him with a new and wonderful confidence. "This is madness, you know that, don't you?"

"Total madness." Barney grinned. "When can you come?"

"A couple of months. I have to get this play out of the way. Ideally, I'd like to leave under cover of darkness as soon as it's finished so no one has to try to tell me it was all right."

Barney took her hand and led her back to the car. "I don't see why you can't leave at once," he said. "Surely they can find someone else to do your part?"

"They wouldn't have given me the part if there'd been anyone else. That's how desperate they were. I wouldn't feel right just abandoning them."

Barney opened the door for her and went round to his side. Two months without Barney did seem a very long time. She watched him climb into the car and put a hand on his knee. "I could come out at Easter for a few days."

"Too far away. Come out for my birthday." He leaned toward her and kissed her slowly, his fingers caressing the back of her neck. She felt her heart quicken. Her mind might be a mass of indecision but her body certainly wasn't. "I think," he murmured, "we should go home and celebrate."

Sarah tried very hard to collect herself. "We're meeting Miriam and Antonio in a couple of hours."

Barney put his keys in the ignition. "For the sort of celebration I have in mind," he said, "a couple of hours will do very nicely."

"So tell me," Sarah said, "what was Antonio's sister like? And the husband? Were they really the most beautiful people on the planet?"

They were sitting on their own in the restaurant. Antonio and Barney were busy in the kitchen. What lighting there was came from the log fire and the candles that Antonio had lit round the room. He had given both women large glasses of Rioja and in the candlelight, the dark red wine seemed to be possessed of an unearthly glow.

"No," Miriam said. She extracted an olive stone from her mouth and placed it carefully in the center of the ashtray. "But you knew they had been. Belen was very plump in a Rubens sort of way: lots of bosom, generous hips, big warm eyes. He wasn't thin either. He had a fantastic gray mane of hair. He reminded me of a noble stallion."

"That's very poetic," Sarah said. "I can imagine him pounding his feet on the floor. You obviously liked them."

"They were lovely to watch. They were so happy together. We had an amazing lunch and they sat at either end of this great, long trestle table. I saw him look at her once and they smiled at each other across the table. I can't remember the last time I saw a married couple smile at each other like that. I liked all the family. Antonio's mother asked me twice if I liked babies. She said it was her dying wish to see Antonio have a son!"

"Wasn't it her birthday? I hope you didn't destroy her hopes."

"Nothing I could have said would do that. I've never met a more besotted mother. I told her I didn't think she'd be dying for a very long time. Which I'm sure was true. Antonio says—"

"You are talking about me!" Antonio crowed, holding in front of him an enormous platter on which sat a huge, round tortilla. "We had a very good party," he told Sarah. "Miriam loved us all."

"I loved your *family*," Miriam corrected him pointedly. "And," she added in a more conciliatory tone, "I love your food."

"But of course you love my food!" Antonio turned back toward the kitchen. "Barney! What are you doing out there?"

"Working hard." Barney came over to the table. He was carrying a loaf of bread and a plate of sliced tomatoes sitting in a sea of olive oil.

"You cut a few tomatoes and call that working hard? No wonder you are so thin. You have never learned to cook!"

"He can make a great risotto," Sarah said.

"He made you a meal? Incredible! You must be a very special woman! Barney, on what are we supposed to eat?"

"Damn!" Barney said, and returned to the kitchen.

Antonio began to cut the tortilla. "Sarah?" he asked, "is that bit big enough for you?"

"Far too big," Sarah protested. "Half that size would be perfect."

"But that is nothing! You do not like my tortilla?"

"I love your tortilla. I'm not very hungry, that's all."

"Excuse me?" Miriam reached across and put a hand to Sarah's forehead. "You're not hungry? You're always hungry!" She waved a hand at Barney, who had returned with the plates. "Sarah's lost her appetite! What have you been doing to her?"

Barney regarded Miriam with a show of confusion that fooled no one. "Do you really want me to tell you?"

Miriam cast him a withering glance. "Sex has nothing to do with it. Sarah is always hungry."

"I think perhaps," Antonio suggested, "Sarah is too happy to be hungry."

"I think," Sarah agreed, "you're right."

"Never tell Antonio he's right," commanded Miriam, "even if he is. Why are you so happy? Our holiday is ending and you're happy?"

"I know why she's happy," Barney said. "Would you like me to tell you?"

"If you're going to tell me what I think you're going to say, then, no I wouldn't."

"If you think I'm going to say what I think you think I'm going to say, I'm shocked." Barney shook his head sorrowfully and helped himself to a huge chunk of bread. "Sarah is happy because, being a discerning woman, she has agreed to come and live with me in Majorca." He stared at Miriam's face with satisfaction. "Now you definitely didn't think I was going to say that."

"Sarah!" Antonio went round to Sarah and enveloped her

in his arms. "I am very happy! Now you can cook for him and he will stop eating all my food every day."

"That's a very good point," Barney said. "Can you cook, Sarah?"

"She's a brilliant cook," Miriam responded indignantly.

"In that case," Barney said, "the invitation still stands."

"We must have some champagne!" Antonio decreed. "Barney? Come with me! You can carry the glasses!"

"Boss, boss, boss," Barney muttered, but followed Antonio through to the kitchen.

Sarah picked up her glass and toyed with it gently, watching the liquid fall from one side to the other. "I know," she said awkwardly, "I'm mad."

"You are." Miriam shook her head in disbelief. "You are utterly mad. You know nothing about him. I can't believe you're going to do it! This is so unlike you! Are you sure this is what you want to do?"

Sarah nodded.

"You're not just living out your youthful dream?"

"Well," Sarah conceded, "I *am* doing that, of course."

"Sarah." Miriam shook her head again. "You've spent two nights and one day with Barney. On the strength of two nights and one day, you intend to give up your home and move in with him. Is this the act of a sensible woman?"

"No," Sarah agreed, "it isn't. I've been sensible all my life and look where it's got me. I'm in a state of limbo. I'm living on a question mark. Can you think of a better time for me to find out what it's like to do something that isn't sensible?"

Miriam threw up her hands in the air. "I don't know what to say!"

"That's not like you!"

"I know." Miriam appeared to be genuinely baffled. "I mean, I'm sure you're wrong but when you put it like that, it sounds sort of right." Her mouth twitched. "I wonder what Andrew will say."

Sarah gave a caustic laugh. "He'll be able to put the house on the market now. He'll be thrilled."

"Hmm," said Miriam. "I wouldn't bet on it."

A Happy Ex-Wife Is an Attractive Ex-Wife

Back in England, it was raining but Sarah didn't care. She was looking forward to broadcasting her news and lobbing back the suffocating sludge of pity that had been thrown at her in the last four months. No longer sad Sarah, she was Sarah the bold decision maker, about to move abroad to live with her lover in the sun. What a difference a week could make! As the train drew into Gillingham, she could hardly wait to get home.

She collected her car and drove straight to the supermarket. She spent far too long at the fruit counter, trying to decide whether bananas had more sex appeal than grapes. Pulverized by indecision, for in her present mood, everything looked sexy, she threw into her trolley bananas, apples, grapes, plums, mangoes, and peaches. For good measure, she added a bunch of white tulips, justifying the extravagance with the dubious logic that since the fruit was for her work, she could afford to buy flowers.

One of the pleasures of going away was collecting the mail and the phone messages. Sarah had never yet returned from a holiday to find anything more exciting than a letter from her mother, but she lived in hope. This time, there was the usual pile of possibilities waiting for her on the mat. She unloaded the shopping, made herself a cup of tea, and sat down at the table.

There was a photocopied letter from her sister-in-law inviting her to sponsor Tamzin's month-long sweet deprivation and an invitation from the arts center to exhibit a couple of her paintings.

There was a letter from an animal charity asking her to save donkeys and another from a clothes company suggesting she could change her life if only she sent off for its fabulous catalog. A garden catalog offered her a truly revolting dinner service with her first order. It dawned on her that she would never have to give or attend another dinner party in her life. Goodbye, Clementine Delaney, hello, Barney!

Finally, under the gardening catalog sat not one, but two letters from India. Sarah opened them both and laid them out. Despite being in different parts of the country, the boys had written to their mother on the very same day. The strangeness of twins never ceased to fascinate Sarah. Years ago, when the boys were only six, she and Andrew had taken them on a train journey up to York. Both boys had gone to the toilets at either end of the carriage at precisely the same moment. After about twenty minutes, Andrew had nudged Sarah, pointing out that queues were building up. Sarah had made her way to one end of the carriage to check on Ben, who had assured her from the other side of the door that he was fine. She had then struggled to the other end of the carriage and received the same sunny response from James. After another ten minutes, by which time Andrew was covering his face with his hands, both boys emerged at exactly the same moment. Sarah had been very impressed by this, the people in the queues rather less so.

Both letters were written in identical spidery handwriting. James, clearly smitten by the bride, was keen to let Sarah know that Andromeda . . . could she really be called Andromeda? . . . had shown great sense in leaving the bridegroom, who could apparently talk about nothing except the state of his bowels. Sarah felt a fleeting sense of sympathy for the bridegroom and could only hope that James would not fall ill while he was with the bride. Ben had fallen in with a group of Canadians. He mentioned one of them, a girl called Kate, at least four times. Both boys sounded very happy and neither of them gave any indication of nostalgia for Ambercross.

Sarah glanced around the kitchen. This had always been her favorite room. Dominating it was the old pine cupboard she and Andrew had bought for eighty pounds when they'd first moved here. At one end was the solid red stove they had bought from friends of friends in Eastbourne. It had been dismantled and brought up to Ambercross, where it had been painstakingly reassembled. Ten years ago they had bought the long trestle table on which the boys had sat for hours, building their intricate Lego contraptions. All these things Sarah loved. A week ago, the thought of their dispersal was painful but Andrew and the boys had moved on to the next stage and so should she. There was no point in trying to hang on to a past that no longer existed. Sarah hoped she would have achieved such understanding without the holiday in Majorca but had to admit it was far easier to embrace a new future when it included the chance to embrace Barney.

There were only three messages on the answering machine. The first was a sanctimonious one from Andrew. "I'm speaking to you on Tuesday evening. I went over to check on the house for you. Did you know you left the bedroom window open? Not very wise. I closed it. Hope you're having a good holiday."

The second was a breathy message from Jennifer. "Sarah! You'll never guess what I did last night. Ring me!"

The third was a far more diffident one from Martin. "Hi, Sarah, welcome back! I hope you've had a good holiday and that you're word perfect because I'm not. Anyway, I just wanted to say, well, I just wanted to say welcome back, really, but I've said that already, haven't I? I'm not very good at speaking into these things. So, I'll see you on Tuesday."

Dear Martin! Sarah couldn't wait to tell him her news. She wanted to spread her happiness like jam. But first, there was Andrew to ring.

Hyacinth answered the phone. A week ago, Sarah might have put the phone down. Now she said brightly, "Hyacinth! How are you? It's Sarah Stagg here."

"Oh. Hello, Sarah. I'm very well, thank you." Hyacinth sounded horribly embarrassed. "I'll get Andrew." Poor Hyacinth, Sarah thought indulgently, she couldn't wait to get off the phone. She settled down in her chair and put her feet up on the table.

"Sarah?" Andrew sounded wary. "Did you have a good time?"

"I have had," Sarah told him, "the best holiday of my life!"

"Did you?" Andrew sounded a little taken aback by such

fervor. He cleared his throat. "I'm so glad." He seemed to be searching for a suitable response. "I've never been to Majorca. Was the weather good?"

"The weather was not good but the island was beautiful. You and Hyacinth ought to go. You'd love it, you'd absolutely love it."

"Would we?"

"You would. It's perfect. It's absolutely perfect."

"Oh," said Andrew.

Sarah smiled. With every moment, she was enjoying this conversation more. "I wanted to tell you I'm leaving Amber-cross in May, so you can put the house on the market when-ever you like. Of course—"

"Wait a moment!" Andrew interrupted her sharply. "I don't understand what you're saying. You're leaving Ambercross in May? What do you mean? Where are you going? How long are you going for? I don't understand."

Sarah laughed. She had never heard Andrew sound so be-wildered. "I'm moving to Majorca as soon as the play is fin-ished. I've met a man, you see, a rather wonderful man, actually. He's asked me to live with him."

There was a stunned silence. "You met a man?" he said at last. "What sort of a man?"

"Oh, you know, the usual sort, two arms, two legs, that sort of thing."

"No, I mean, who is he? You spent a week in Majorca, you met a strange man, and now you're going to live with him?"

"Actually, he was at art school with me but we didn't really know each other. I used to worship him from afar. Miriam and I were sitting in a restaurant on our first night and there he was!"

"I see." There was another long pause. "Did you . . . when you . . . did you . . ."

"He lives in a little cottage on the seafront. It's beautiful."

There was a stunned silence, which Sarah saw no reason to interrupt. "So," Andrew said at last, "you're going to live in Majorca? What about the boys?"

"The boys are fine. I had letters from them today. They can come and see me in Majorca whenever they like."

"I'm very happy for you of course. . . ."

"Thank you," said Sarah. "I knew you would be."

"Well of course I am, but"—Sarah had been waiting for the "but"—"I have to say this all sounds a little absurd. If I'm honest, Sarah, and I know you'd want me to be honest, it sounds monumentally absurd. You go out to Majorca for a few days, you meet some man, and you decide to change your life. You must see it's absurd."

Sarah took her feet off the table. "You met a woman and you decided to change your life. A lot of people thought that was pretty absurd."

"There's no need to get defensive. I care about you, Sarah. I don't want you to get hurt."

"You didn't mind me getting hurt last year when you started sleeping with Hyacinth. The only difference between me and you, and it's a big one, is that you went off with Hyacinth, knowing it would break my heart, and I'm going off with Barney and I'm not hurting anyone."

"Barney? His name is Barney?"

"Yes, his name is Barney. What's wrong with Barney?"

"Nothing's wrong with Barney. Look, I don't want to have an argument with you. I'm very happy for you if this *will* make you happy, but I have to say it sounds like some crazy infatuation and I just hope you're not doing this while you're on the rebound."

Sarah took a deep breath. "It's sweet of you to be so concerned," she said, "but I was in love with Barney long before I knew you and he seems to think I can make him happy. And you should be happy too. Now you can get in touch with the realtors whenever you like."

"Sarah," Andrew sounded hurt, "I'm far more concerned about your well-being than I am about the realtors. And anyway," he paused, "I'm very busy. I thought you'd see to all that."

"I'm afraid I haven't got time. I'm inundated with work at the moment and after all, you're the one who's so eager to sell."

"Look," Andrew said heavily, "I need to think about this. I'll ring you in a few days."

"Fine," Sarah said. "Take care now!" She pressed the off button with a flourish and raised a hand in the air. "Yes!!"

Almost immediately, the phone rang.

"Good morning!" Sarah exclaimed.

"Sarah? It's Jennifer. You sound full of the joys!"

"I am. I've just had the most satisfactory conversation with Andrew."

"Really? Why?"

"I told him I'm going to live in Majorca with Barney Melton. He couldn't believe it!"

"No," said Jennifer after a small pause, "I don't understand."

Sarah grinned. "It's a long story."

"Hang on a moment. . . . What is it, George? They're in the sitting room. . . . What? . . . Well, they were in the sitting room! George, I'm speaking to Sarah. . . . What? . . . Sarah, George sends his love."

Sarah, remembering the dinner party, said with a smile, "Be sure to send him all of mine."

"Oh, for goodness's sake, George! Sarah, I have to go. We're about to go out and he's lost his glasses. Can you come to coffee tomorrow?"

"Can I come early, about nine? I have a load of painting to do."

"Come at seven if you like."

"Nine will be fine. I'll see you." Sarah put down the phone and went into the garden. The snowdrops were out and there were even a few brave daffodils. She stood, fizzing with excitement. She would have liked to ring Barney but Barney had warned her that he hated the telephone with a passion and used it only for business. She remembered Martin's message and smiled. She would ring Martin. She stretched her arms toward the sky and went back indoors.

Martin responded to her voice with flattering enthusiasm. "Sarah! It's lovely to have you back. How was it? Did your friend get her holiday romance?"

"Unfortunately not," said Sarah, "but I did!"

"Good for you! My father would say you should never trust a Spaniard."

"And your father would know, of course! Barney isn't Spanish, he's English."

"Barney?"

"My holiday romance. He lives in Puerto d'Andratx. He was at art school with me. I had a huge crush on him and he never noticed me. I couldn't believe it when I saw him out there."

"I take it he noticed you this time."

"Yes."

Martin laughed. "How very satisfactory. I bet you didn't want to come home."

"No, I didn't." She had been so eager to share her good news with Martin and she wasn't sure why she was finding it so difficult to tell him now. She said lightly, "Majorca's beautiful. You'd love it."

"I'm sure I would. So is the holiday romance over or will you see him again?"

"Actually . . ." Sarah hesitated. She felt increasingly embarrassed about telling him her plans. "Actually, I've decided to move there permanently. I'll go when the play's finished. Barney's asked me to live with him." Her revelation was greeted by a wall of silence. She said uncertainly, "Martin, are you still there?"

"Yes. I wasn't sure what to say. It's a bit of a surprise. I hope you'll be very happy."

"Thank you. I have some very important paintings to do first. Of course you don't know. I won the contract for the night club! A thousand pounds a painting! Can you believe it?"

"Knowing your talent, yes I can. I'm very pleased for you."

"Thank you."

"Well. I'd better go. I have things to do. I'll see you at rehearsal. Bye, now."

Sarah put down the phone. She felt quite deflated. Martin's response had been incredulous, bewildered, and cool. She felt as if a shadow had settled on her shoulder and spent the rest of the day trying to shake it off.

Try to Exceed Expectations

Jennifer opened the door before Sarah could ring the bell. "Sarah! You're five minutes late! I'm dying of curiosity! Come through to the kitchen, I've made the coffee, all you have to do is talk."

Sarah pushed Jennifer's Labrador gently from his position in front of her legs and followed Jennifer through. "I'm very happy to talk but *you* have to tell *me* what your message on the answering machine was all about: it sounded very mysterious."

"Tell me your news first. Tell me everything. From the beginning."

Jennifer was a very gratifying listener. Unlike Martin, who'd sounded almost uninterested by Sarah's earth-shaking announcement, Jennifer really did want to know every detail. So Sarah told her about the agonizing year she had spent at art school, watching Barney kissing girls who were far more beautiful and glamorous than she would ever be. She told Jennifer about the meeting in the restaurant, the subsequent dinner, and its consequences. ("Tell me he didn't snore," begged Jennifer, and on being assured that he didn't, said happily, "I knew he wouldn't. He sounds divine!") Sitting in Jennifer's kitchen, with the dogs gently padding about, the entire holiday seemed to take on a dreamlike quality.

"Oh, Sarah," Jennifer sighed, "it sounds too good to be true. You are a very lucky woman. What shall I do without you when you're gone?"

"You'll have to come and visit."

"Try and keep me away. I shall try very hard not to be jealous. I bet Andrew's cross."

"He has no right to be cross. He left me. I can do what I like."

"Yes, dear, but Andrew's ego is bottomless. You've fallen for a man who is not Andrew. He expected you to spend the rest of your life yearning politely for him."

"He wanted to sell the house. He still wants to sell the house. He should be over the moon. Everything's worked out perfectly for him. Now tell me about your news. What's happened?"

"Developments!" Jennifer pushed away her coffee cup. "On Wednesday I decided I had to know what was going on with George. So I drove to his office at five o'clock, made sure his car was still there, and settled down to wait. I tell you something, I'd never be a private detective, it's so boring. I had to wait for nearly an hour and then finally George came out. He got in his car and I followed him."

"Didn't he see you?"

"I was wearing my sunglasses and anyway I was very discreet—I didn't get too close. Twice, I nearly lost him. Anyway, he drove to Frome and parked on Somerset Road. I saw him get out and knock on the door of a house. It had a hanging basket with dead flowers in it. What does that tell you?"

"I suppose," considered Sarah, "it tells me the home owner is either an optimist who hopes the flowers will grow again or someone who has no time to change the hanging basket."

"The point is," Jennifer said impatiently, "George hates things like that. He can never pass a rosebush without deadheading it. But he knocked on the door quite happily, he didn't even look at the hanging basket, and then I saw her! The woman I'd seen in the drugstore. He kissed her on the cheek!"

"That doesn't sound very loverlike."

"You'd never get George kissing anyone in a public place. I had a good look at her. The woman is an absolute slob."

"This is the woman you said dressed like me?"

"Yes, but you're an artist and artists can get away with being slobs. What does he see in her? It makes me so cross."

"How long did he stay with her?"

"I have no idea. I drove straight off. He didn't come home until after ten."

"What did you say to him?"

"I said his meeting had gone on for a very long time and he agreed it had. I said he'd better be careful or I'd begin to think he was having an affair and he said . . . it was really very odd, it was such an un-George-like thing to say, he said, 'Would you mind if I were?'"

"That sounds pretty perceptive."

"Exactly. Not like George at all."

"What did you say?"

"I said I was going to make a cup of tea and go to bed."

"And what did George say?"

"He said he was going to watch *NewsNight*."

"Jennifer!" Sarah threw up her hands. "You had the perfect opportunity to get everything out into the open and you blew it! He threw the ball at you and you ducked! How could you duck?"

"I know! I know! I panicked! Until now, it's been a sort of a game and suddenly there was George being peculiar and I knew I was on the verge of this great big hole and I didn't want to jump because I didn't know what was at the bottom. Well, I do know I suppose. It's that slob of a woman who wasn't George's type at all. She was wearing combat trousers!"

"I like combat trousers."

"Well, George doesn't. At least, he didn't. I'm beginning to think I don't know George at all."

"Of course you do!" Sarah said stoutly. "And so do I! George is and always has been the perfect gentleman. I just can't picture him making furtive assignations with strange women. I honestly believe you're making a mountain out of a molehill. George is—"

The phone rang in the corner of the room and Jennifer rose to answer it. "Mummy! How are you? You what? You had a dream last night? Well, good for you. . . . No, Mummy, of course I want to hear but . . . No, I have no idea what a rocket means. It was a *black* rocket? Well I don't think *that's* very Freudian. There weren't any black rockets around when Freud was alive. . . . Hang on a moment, Mummy. I have a friend here and she wants to say something."

"Tell your mother," Sarah said, "that James has a book in his room that interprets dreams. I'll dig it out for her."

"Did you hear that, Mummy? Sarah has a book that interprets dreams. . . . Yes, that's very kind. . . . Look, let me ring you back in about twenty minutes. . . . Good-bye, Mummy." Jennifer put the phone down and saw Sarah reach for her bag. "Don't go yet. I can ring Mummy back anytime. She is obsessed about dreams at the moment. She has a notebook by her bed and writes them all down. Some of them are most peculiar."

"I'll drop the book in," Sarah promised, "though I can't remember if it says anything about black rockets." She stood up and kissed Jennifer lightly on the cheek. "I must go. I've loads of painting to do. Don't worry about George. Everything will be fine."

"You only say that," Jennifer said, leading Sarah toward the front door, "because everything is so very fine for you."

Sarah laughed. "That is not true. I genuinely refuse to believe George is interested in any other woman. I still think you should ask him straight out. He can only say yes or no." She eyed her friend curiously. "What would you do if he said yes?"

Jennifer frowned and for a moment her eyes drifted toward the silver birch at the end of the lawn. Then she gave a short laugh. "If I ever find the right moment to ask him," she said, "I'll let you know."

Sarah called in at the village shop on her way home. She needed some bread. Even if she hadn't, she still would have gone in. Amy was there on her own and wanted to hear about Majorca. "Our Jason's going to Magaluf in June," she said. "Do you think he'll like it?"

"I didn't go there," Sarah said, "but the island's gorgeous. There's a beautiful cathedral in Palma."

"I don't think Jason's interested in cathedrals. He's only interested in—"

Sarah never did find out what Jason was interested in. Clementine flew into the shop like a force of nature. "I can't stop . . . Oh, hello, Sarah, how are you? . . . I have so much to do, Amy, you wouldn't believe it. I have a list of errands as long as my arm, but I want you to put this notice up. We had our meeting on the Summer Fete last night and we're trying to sort out judges for all the competitions. I have to dash. Sarah, you will be able to judge the art entries as usual, won't you?"

"Fine," Sarah said automatically, then, remembering, she added, "No, I'm afraid I won't. I will have left Ambercross by then."

The force of nature, who had been hovering in the doorway, was suddenly rooted to the spot. It seemed she no longer had to dash. "You're leaving Ambercross? When are you leaving?"

"In May. I'm going to live in Majorca."

"You're going to live in Majorca? On your own?"

"Oh, no." Sarah, aware that she enjoyed the rapt attention of both women, took her time in checking her coins for the bread. "I've been seeing an old boyfriend from art school," she said, just as if she saw old boyfriends all the time. "He's a photographer. He has a wonderful house on the seafront."

"Well!" Clementine said, "how very exciting! Are you and he . . . ?" She looked for help to Amy, who was far too intent on studying Sarah to offer any clarification of the question.

"Yes," said Sarah, beaming happily, "we are! Now *I* must dash. I have paintings to do."

Oh it was wonderful to see the confusion and the consternation on Clementine Delaney's face! Sarah almost skipped back home. She did feel a little guilty about fudging the facts a little but it was worth it to see the look on Clementine's face. Good-bye, Sarah Stagg, object of pity and barely concealed contempt. Hello, Sarah, international woman of glamour and romance!

Do Not Monopolize Your Friends

Tuesday night's rehearsal was the first one Sarah attended without the usual fear of humiliation. Other events in her life had sidelined *Rebecca*. It was, after all, only a play for a village from which she would shortly be a willing exile.

She was far more concerned about seeing Martin again, if only to put to rest the irrational misgivings caused by their last conversation. She knew she was being paranoid. He had rung her with a charming message while she was in Majorca, he had welcomed her back on her return and had expressed his happiness at her good news. He had been about to go out and couldn't linger when she rang. End of story. Nevertheless, she sought him out as soon as she entered the rehearsal room and was reassured by the affectionate smile with which he greeted her.

"Have you come down to earth yet?"

Sarah laughed. "I expect this evening will do that! It's good to see you. Are you still up for our weekend walks?"

Was it her imagination or was there an infinitesimal pause before he said, "Of course."

Sally-Anne Furlong came over, looking outstandingly glamorous for an amateur dramatic rehearsal in a local pub. "I hope you two are word perfect," she said archly. "As the official prompt, I expect no less!"

Sarah smiled. "I have a horrible feeling you're going to be disappointed. By the way, I love your dress."

"Thank you! I like to dress up in the evening. It makes me feel good. I do wonder if this is too short for a woman of my age. Do you know what I mean?"

"If you have the legs," Sarah said sagely, "you should show them."

"I think you look marvelous," said Martin warmly.

"Thank you, Martin!" Sally-Anne cooed. "You're so sweet."

And so gullible, Sarah thought. Sally-Anne hadn't dressed up to make herself feel good; Sally-Anne had dressed up to make Martin feel Sally-Anne.

Audrey clapped her hands. "Gather round, everyone! I trust you've had a good break and are ready to give your all! Tonight we are rehearsing the all-important penultimate scene. This is absolutely crucial to the success of the production. By the end of act two, the audience knows the truth of Maxim's marriage to Rebecca. The audience knows that Mrs. de Winter loves Maxim more than ever but the audience does *not* know whether Maxim really loves *her*. The author teases the audience throughout the scene, apparently veering away from the marriage and toward the gentle interrogation by Colonel Julyan. And then, when Frank and Colonel Julyan leave, we have Maxim and his wife alone again and Maxim makes that wonderful little speech." Audrey paused to let her eyes travel round the faces of her cast. "And then they kiss. Now I agree we don't want any passion here since that would detract from our romantic, heart-stopping finale. What we want here is a sad, sweet kiss of two lonely people reaching out for support." Audrey took out a handkerchief from her cardigan pocket and blew her nose. "It should be a very touching little scene. So: let's get on with it! Let's create some dramatic tension!"

Sarah moved into position. She didn't have many lines in this scene since Colonel Julyan and Maxim did most of the talking. It was soon clear that Martin, for all his protestations, had learned his part well. The only person Sally-Anne had to prompt was Colonel Julyan.

It was at the end of the scene that everything went wrong. Martin made his speech and moved into position to kiss Sarah. Sarah raised her face to his. Martin froze. Audrey cried out, "Kiss her, Martin!"

Martin cast an agonized glance in Audrey's direction. The words seemed to be pulled slowly from his mouth: "I . . . don't . . . want . . . to kiss . . . Sarah!"

There was a stunned silence broken only by a nervous giggle from Sally-Anne. Sarah bit her lip and subjected the floorboards to an intense scrutiny.

"I'm sorry," Martin said. "I can't kiss Sarah like this. I can't do it."

"Martin!" Audrey said icily, "there are only six of us in here.

In less than eight weeks you will have to kiss Sarah in front of many more people than six!"

"I know," said Martin miserably. "But it will be on stage, it will be something I have to do." He made it sound as if kissing Sarah was an endurance test of the most extreme kind. "I've told you before and I promise you now, I will kiss her on the night. I won't let you down. But I can't kiss her now."

"I'm disappointed in you, Martin," Audrey said. "I am *very* disappointed. And I promise you, if you don't give Sarah a first-class kiss on the night, I shall never forgive you." She rose slowly from her chair and took off her glasses. "I think now would be a good time to end the rehearsal. Next week we will do the final scene. And let me remind you, Martin, that at the end of the final scene you have to produce a kiss to end all kisses. You might think about that. Sally-Anne, can I give you a lift?"

Sally-Anne hesitated. "No, thank you, Audrey. I'll make my own way back tonight."

"Very well." Audrey sighed. "I'm feeling rather tired. May I ask you all to tidy away the table and chairs?"

The cast, subdued and submissive, murmured assent. Audrey gathered up her coat and bag, wished everyone good night, and proceeded heavily down the stairs. Her disappointment continued to hang oppressively in the air. Only Sally-Anne seemed unaffected by the atmosphere. She chattered lightly about the weather while helping to stack chairs and then waltzed up to Martin. "I have a big favor to ask you," she said. "Could I possibly beg a lift home from you? There's something funny about my kitchen tap and I'd really like your opinion. I know you must be tired but it won't take a moment. Do you mind?"

Something funny about her kitchen tap! Really, Sarah thought, even she could have thought of a better excuse than that.

"No," said Martin, "I don't mind at all."

"Wonderful!" Sally-Anne said. "I'll get my coat."

Martin glanced at Sarah and walked over to her. "I want to apologize," he said, "for being such an idiot. I should never have agreed to do this part. I'm no good at acting all this romantic stuff. What I said . . . I know it sounded . . ." His eyes appealed to her for help. "You know what I meant, didn't you?"

"Of course I did." Sarah gave him a reassuring smile. "Don't worry. Audrey will get over it. Shall I see you on Saturday?"

"I'll ring you." He glanced in Sally-Anne's direction. "I'd better go and look at this tap."

Sarah waved and called out, "See you, Sally-Anne!" in order to make clear to Sally-Anne that she was quite happy to see Sally-Anne take Martin off for a little light seduction over the kitchen tap. Why it was so necessary to make this clear to Sally-Anne, she was not quite sure.

If You're Lying on the Ground, You Can't Fall Over. . . .

The day after the rehearsal, Sarah started work on the first of the fruit paintings. She had done preliminary sketches of all the relevant purchases from the supermarket. She had auditioned each of the specimens, looking out for style, sex appeal, and personality. She had almost been seduced by the roundness of the Gala melon and the sensuality of the plum but had finally chosen the apple for its iconic status, the banana as the ultimate phallic symbol, the peach because it was the juiciest of all the fruit she had bought, and the strawberry for its color.

The apple was to be the star of her first painting. In line with Adam's fall from grace, she had decided to paint the apple with a large bite taken out of it. She duly picked one from the fruit bowl and bit into it. She then wasted a good twenty minutes trying to imagine herself in Adam's shoes (except of course Adam wouldn't be wearing shoes; Adam wouldn't be wearing anything at all). When Eve tempted him with the apple, he knew God had forbidden him to eat it. It followed that in order to take that bite he must have been driven mad by desire for it and would therefore take one huge, crazed bite, leaving very little apple left to paint. Perhaps it was a mistake to empathize with Adam too much. Sarah sighed and discovered that while wrestling with Adam she had inadvertently eaten the whole apple apart from its very unattractive core.

She took another apple from the bowl, considered it carefully, took a medium-sized bite, and studied it again. That was it! Now she could begin!

Over the next few days, Sarah worked like a woman possessed. She played a selection of the sexiest music (Serge Gainsbourg, Donna Summer, and Prince proving the most effective) to keep her mind focused on the character of the picture. Barney remained her greatest inspiration. She had only to remember the expression in his eyes as he'd pushed her back against the pillows or the devastating slowness with which his hand had traveled up her inner thigh: at once, her paintbrush would work with renewed intensity. This painting, all of these paintings, would be a celebration of the joy, the excitement, and the fun of sex.

The disadvantage of recalling the sex she'd enjoyed with Barney was that it wasn't nearly as satisfying as actually *having* sex with Barney; in fact it wasn't satisfying at all. A mug of hot chocolate and a Georgette Heyer novel proved poor substitutes.

He rang on Sunday evening, his laconic tones reminding

her that the telephone was not a mode of communication he enjoyed. "How's the painting going?" he asked.

"Good, I think, but it's too early to say. How's everything with you?"

"Fine. Are you still coming out for my birthday?"

"I've booked my flight. I'm arriving at Palma on March twenty-first at 3:58."

"I'll be there at 3:57."

"Thanks. I can't wait to come out again. At the moment my entire life is devoted to the apple. It will be so good to have a break."

"The apple?"

"That's what I'm painting at the moment. I wish you could see what I've done. I wish I could see *you*."

"You will. On March twenty-first. At 3:58. Take care."

She could imagine him putting down the phone, lighting a cigarette. What would he do then? Perhaps he'd go and cadge a meal from Antonio or meet some friends in a bar. Sarah wished she were meeting friends in a bar. She had seen no one but the postman for nearly three days. She was glad she was seeing Martin in the morning.

At half past nine the next morning, Martin rang and she knew at once she would *not* be seeing him.

"Hi, Sarah," he said. "Do you mind very much if I don't walk with you today? Something's come up."

In the background, Sarah could hear a giggle and the giggle conjured up a picture that Sarah didn't like at all.

"That's fine," she said. "I've masses of painting to do." She added quickly, "I'll see you on Tuesday," to show that she wasn't expecting a walk on Sunday.

Martin said, "Good luck with the work," and rang off.

So Martin did not want a walk on Sunday. He did not want a walk on Sunday because he would be pursuing a far more enjoyable form of exercise.

It was wonderful that Martin was having fun. He deserved to be happy. Sarah was very happy for him.

The truth was Sarah wasn't happy for him, she wasn't happy at all. In a mood of self-disgust, she put on her boots and her anorak and stomped out of the house. She was a self-ish cow. In a few weeks she'd be going out for a blissful week-end with Barney and she had no right to begrudge Martin his own shot at happy cohabitation. He'd been a good friend to her and she should not resent the fact that he no longer had time for the odd walk. As for her irrational dislike of Sally-Anne, it was, well, it was irrational. Sally-Anne was an attrac-tive, vivacious, friendly woman.

A phone call from Andrew in the afternoon put her in a better mood. He made a stiff apology for his intemperate reac-tion to her news and he even agreed that it was only fair that he took charge of the house sale. "I've rung a couple of real-tors," he said, "but I don't want to rush you into this. If you have any doubts, any doubts at all about the Majorca idea, you have only to let me know and I'll put the whole thing on hold. I suggested to Hyacinth that we could always move into the cottage after you leave but she says it would be too isolated for her. If you really are going in May, I don't like the idea of leav-ing the house empty when people come round to see it."

"Of course not," said Sarah. "It's far better to show poten-tial buyers round when I'm here to keep the place nice."

"In that case," Andrew said, "I'll get the agents to ring you next week. Do you mind showing them round the house or do you want me to arrange to be there?"

Sarah, mollified by such unaccustomed consideration, said she would be perfectly happy to receive them.

"Thank you. I want you to know I hope you'll be very happy in Majorca. I wasn't really thinking last time we spoke. The truth is, I shall miss you."

Sarah gave a short little laugh. "I doubt that."

"I mean it. Your friend, Barney, is a lucky man. Has he been in touch with you since you got back?"

"Yes, of course he has."

"Good. Well, I'm glad you're so happy."

Sarah, unsure how to respond to this new, improved Andrew, decided it was better to terminate the conversation. "Andrew, I'd better go. I'm in the middle of a painting."

"Your painting! I knew I had something else to tell you. I've been asked to handle the publicity for a new nightclub in Bath. I was talking to the chap who's opening it and he asked me if I was related to Sarah Stagg. I asked him why and he started raving on about some dog picture you'd done. He said you were doing a series of paintings for the club. Is that true? Why didn't you tell me?"

"I suppose I've got out of the habit of telling you things."

"I know. I wish you hadn't. Anyway, I'm very proud of you. It's funny that we're both working for the same man."

"Very funny," Sarah agreed. "Now I'd better get on. Good-bye, Andrew." She put the phone down and went back to her studio. She owed Barney so much. If it weren't for Barney, she would now be wasting precious time, analyzing Andrew's words, digging away fruitlessly for signs of a change of heart.

As it was, she was pleased that Andrew was impressed with her success and encouraged to work even harder.

Over the next two weeks, she was increasingly aware of her good luck in meeting Barney. Without Barney, she would have found Martin's new preoccupation with Sally-Anne difficult to take. At rehearsals, Sally-Anne stuck to Martin like glue. Gone were the after-rehearsal drinks, gone were the weekend walks. Sarah couldn't wait for the play to be over. March 21, shone like a beacon, keeping her going throughout the days of solitude.

On the evening of March 20, she stood in her studio pleased with the work she had done. The apple was finished. The banana was beginning to take shape. Just looking at the banana made Sarah yearn for Barney. On Thursday night she went to bed with an extra big mug of hot chocolate.

The plane was delayed by half an hour. Sarah, imagining Barney's impatience, almost ran out to meet him, looking for him eagerly. She set her red suitcase on the floor and perched on top of it. The pretty young girl who'd sat in front of her on the plane was greeted with rapture by an intense Spaniard with the baggiest pair of trousers Sarah had ever seen. The elderly lady who'd sat next to Sarah was taken off by a middle-aged couple with matching spectacles. Sarah checked her watch. There was still no sign of Barney so she repaired to the washroom and reapplied her makeup and her perfume.

Half an hour later there was still no sign of Barney. Sarah located a telephone and rang his number. Barney, as always, sounded as if he'd just woken up. "I'm not here. Please leave a message."

Sarah, striving to sound calm and unworried, said, "Hi, Barney. It's five. I'll wait until six and then I'll get a taxi. Bye now."

At six o'clock, Sarah rang again. She heard the same voice saying the same words: "I'm not here. Please leave a message."

Sarah, trying not to panic, swallowed and said, "Barney! It's me again. I'll get a taxi!"

At twenty past seven, Sarah paid the taxi driver, who'd chattered to her cheerfully in Spanish throughout the entire journey, undeterred by the fact that she could only nod uncomprehendingly. She walked across to the familiar blue door and noticed it was slightly ajar. Inside, her throat constricted from the smell of stale tobacco and whiskey. She put down her suitcase and her bag. An overflowing ashtray and an almost empty bottle stood on the table. Barney's leather jacket lay sprawled across the floor. She picked it up and put it over one of the armchairs. She walked through to the kitchen. In the sink, looking like a big pale slug, lay the remains of a joint. She went back through to the front room and glanced at the staircase. Then she went upstairs.

At first she thought Barney was dead. He lay diagonally across the bed on his tummy, his limbs splayed out like a semaphore man. She heard a small, unmistakeable groan and rushed over to him. "Barney?"

He raised his head slightly; bloodshot eyes looked dully at her. "Fuck!" he said. He rolled off the bed and made for the bathroom, whence she heard a noise that sounded as if his insides were being extracted. She ran after him. What looked very like his insides were bubbling all over the bathroom floor. She helped him back to his bedroom, pulled his sweater over his head, and pushed back the duvet. After what seemed an eternity she managed to get him into bed. She ran downstairs to the kitchen, found a bucket from under the sink and a bottle of water from the fridge.

Back upstairs, Barney was lying as she had left him. His head had lolled forward, giving him the semblance of a double chin. She took the lid off the bottle and said, "Barney, try and drink a little water."

"Fuck off," he said, drank a few sips, and murmured, "Fuck off," again.

"Have a little more," she said, "just a little more." She put the bottle to his lips and then removed it swiftly. A sound like the approach of an underground train was emanating from his throat. Sarah whipped the bucket out. It caught most of the vomit; the rest landed on Sarah's arm.

Sarah, who had never been able to endure the smell of sick, swallowed hard. "All right . . ." she said, "it's all right now."

"Fuck off," said Barney again. He lay back against the pillows, closed his eyes, and began to snore. Jennifer would not have been pleased. There was a small dribble of sick on the side of his mouth, which Sarah dared not remove in case he woke up.

She went to the bathroom, stepped round the foul-smelling quagmire, and emptied the contents of the bucket into the toilet. She took off her sweater and caught sight of her reflection in the mirror over the basin. She was wearing her very best black bra. She felt a lump form in the back of her throat, took a deep breath, and went back to Barney's room to find something to wear.

An hour later, she had cleaned the bathroom floor and the

rug by Barney's bed. She had washed Barney's sweater and rinsed out the sleeve of her own. Downstairs, she emptied the ashtray and threw away the remains of the bottle of whiskey. She went into the kitchen, found a clean dishcloth, doused it with water, and wrung it out. She went back upstairs. Barney was now snoring loudly and there was a glistening film of sweat on his forehead. She cleaned his face with the cloth, removing the bit of vomit that had moved down to his chin. Then she went downstairs.

In the kitchen, she washed her hands and opened a bottle of wine. She poured herself a glass and went through to sit on one of the armchairs by the fireplace. The Michelle Pfeiffer picture was lying in the grate, the beautiful face defiled by a long gash down the middle of the glass. Sarah sat back in her chair and took a long gulp of wine. She was too tired to think. She sat up and sipped the rest of her drink as if it were medicine. Then, she put the glass down, sat back in her chair, and closed her eyes.

She woke to the unlovely sound of further retching upstairs in the bathroom. She shivered, stood up, and put on Barney's jacket. She ought to go upstairs but she had had enough of being Florence Nightingale. She went back to the armchair. Why had she not noticed before how uncomfortable it was? She was so cold. She thought of the beds in the spare room but couldn't face the thought of meeting Barney on the landing. Then she heard the sound of footsteps on the stairs and felt her heart beat wildly.

Barney said, "What the fuck are you doing here?" He looked dreadful. His eyes were red, his face was white, and his hair stood up as if it had been electrocuted.

Sarah tried to meet his hostile gaze. "Actually," she said, "you invited me."

"The fuck I did." He came down and almost fell into the armchair. "You're right," he said, "I did. You're Sarah." He caught sight of the picture in the grate. "Bloody bitch!" he yelled. He reached out for it and hurled it at the wall on the other side of the room. Shards of glass fell onto the table. He looked at Sarah. "Where are *you* going?"

Sarah had stood up when he threw the picture. She backed away from him. "I thought I'd make some coffee."

"You thought you'd make some coffee! I don't want any fucking coffee!" He stood up quite suddenly and lunged toward Sarah. Sarah tried to avoid him, tripped, and missed her footing. She felt an agonizing pain as the right side of her face hit the table. Her legs gave way and she crumpled on to the floor. Barney came toward her and she shrunk away, holding her hands to the side of her face.

He knelt down beside her, scared into sobriety. "Sarah, I'm sorry. Look, I'm not going to hurt you. I'm sorry, I'm sorry. I'll get something for your face. Stay there, stay there." He went away and Sarah sat, keening backward and forward in an effort to control the pain.

Barney returned with a wet cloth and made her press it to her eye. "I'm sorry," he said. "I'm so sorry. I'll make us some coffee. Would you like some coffee?"

Sarah nodded but kept her face turned away from him. He was beginning to sound like the Barney she had flown out to see but she couldn't bring herself to look at him. He went away again and she stumbled over to the window seat and sat huddled in the corner.

When he returned he had put on a black T-shirt and combed his hair. He put down two mugs on the table and passed one to Sarah before sitting down opposite her. Sarah took a sip of the hot coffee and coughed as the liquid hit her lungs. Barney looked at her for a moment, stood up, and disappeared to the kitchen. He came back a few moments later with his cigarettes and an ashtray. He lit one and inhaled deeply.

"You smoke too much," Sarah said.

"I know." He turned his face away to exhale the smoke. "I was supposed to meet you at the airport today."

Sarah looked at her watch. "Yesterday," she said. "It's yesterday now."

"I wish you hadn't come," said Barney.

Sarah sniffed. "So do I," she said.

Barney took another drag of his cigarette. "It's my birthday."

"I know." Sarah stood up and went over to her suitcase. She pulled out a parcel and brought it over to him. "Happy birthday."

Barney unwrapped it. Sarah had bought a book of photos of Somerset. "I like Don McCullin's work," he said.

"I thought," Sarah said, "you could do the same sort of thing with your Majorca photos."

Barney put the book on the table. "Thanks," he said. He took a gulp of his coffee. "I owe you an explanation."

"You still love Odile."

"Sarah." He stopped and rubbed his forehead. "I do care about you."

"That doesn't matter anymore."

"Yes it does." He raised the coffee to his lips and proceeded to drink it all. "I'll get some more. What about you?"

"I'm fine."

She watched him go to the kitchen and then glanced at the broken picture on the floor. Sarah shivered and wrapped Barney's jacket tightly round her. How could she have thought she could ever take the place of a woman who looked like that?

Barney came back with his coffee and lit another cigarette. "I saw Odile on Thursday night," he said. "She had always been a jealous woman. She couldn't bear it if I looked at anyone else. I told her about you and me. I told her . . ." He bit his lip, raised his eyes to the ceiling, and shook his head. "Oh, fuck," he said. He put his hands over his face and began to sob. Sarah didn't move. Eventually he stopped and wiped his eyes. "I thought," he said, "I thought she'd be furious. Do you know what she said?"

Sarah shook her head.

"She said, 'I hope you'll be happy,' that's what she said. 'I hope you'll be happy.' She had only come to see me in order to tell me she'd met someone else. She's going to have a baby, so she hasn't wasted any time. I'd have given her a fucking baby. But no. 'I hope you'll be very happy.' That's what she said." He looked at Sarah but she didn't say anything. "What do you think of that?"

Sarah pushed her hair back from her face. Her hair felt sticky, either from blood or from vomit. "What do you expect me to think?" she asked wearily. "Are you asking me to feel sorry for you? You asked me to live with you. I didn't expect you to ask me but you did ask me. You asked me to live with you so you could make Odile want you again. That's what you're telling me."

"It wasn't like that. I think you're a lovely woman. . . ."

"Please! Spare me that! There is nothing more humiliating than being told you're a lovely woman by a man who's in love with someone else."

"I didn't know what I was doing. It was only when I saw Odile . . ." His voice trailed away as he lifted his hands helplessly.

"It was only when you saw Odile that you knew why you'd asked me to live with you." Sarah stood up. "I'm cold and I'm tired and my face hurts. I'm going to sleep in the spare room. I'll go tomorrow. I mean, today."

"You don't have to. How long were you staying for?"

"I was going back on Monday."

"Well, stay until Monday."

"No. I'll get a taxi to Palma in the morning."

"Don't be silly, I'll drive you. There might not be any flights. Go on Monday."

"I don't want to go on Monday. If necessary, I'll sleep at the airport until Monday."

"I never meant to hurt you, Sarah."

"I don't think you ever thought about me at all." She picked up her suitcase and went upstairs. In the spare room, she stripped off to her underclothes and got into one of the beds. She could hear Barney coughing downstairs and a little later she heard him go to bed. She lay, open-eyed, looking out at the black sky. Finally, as pale streaks of light began to slice through the darkness, she fell asleep.

When she went downstairs the next morning, Barney was dressed and making breakfast. "I've rung the airport," he said. "And . . . my god, Sarah, your eye's horrible. You look as if you've been beaten up!"

"I feel as if I've been beaten up. What did the airport say?"

"You're in luck. There's been a cancellation. There's a flight to Bristol at six this evening."

"Would you ring for a taxi? I want to go now."

"For heaven's sake, Sarah! Look, I know how you feel—"

"You have no idea how I feel."

"At least eat your breakfast and then I'll drive you to Palma. I am not going to ring for a taxi. You don't have to talk to me, I'll just drive you. Shouldn't you . . . shouldn't you put something on that eye?"

"Like what? A paper bag?"

"I've made you some scrambled eggs."

"I don't want any scrambled eggs."

"Then you can sit and look at them while I get your coffee."

The truth was she was ravenous, having eaten nothing since the cheese and pickle sandwich she'd had on the plane. When Barney retired to the kitchen, she took a mouthful of food and then quickly ate the rest. When Barney came back with the coffee, he noted the empty plate but didn't say anything.

She did let him drive her to Palma since she had no wish to inflict her messed-up face on a taxi driver. They drove in silence and when they arrived at the airport, she got out without saying a word.

"Look," Barney said, "your plane doesn't leave for hours.

Won't you let me take you to Palma? We can find a place and have some lunch. We ought to talk."

"What on earth would we talk about?" Sarah struggled to rescue her suitcase from the backseat.

"I'll get it," Barney said. He pulled it out and gave it to her. "I feel terrible."

"I'm sure you do. You drank an awful lot of whiskey."

"You know what I mean. I hate seeing you like this."

"That's all right, you don't have to see me any longer. Good-bye, Barney." She walked toward the airport without looking back. She made straight for the washroom and regarded her face stonily. Her right eye looked as if it had been squashed and then stamped with blue and yellow paint.

She went out to the concourse, found a seat, and settled down to wait for the plane.

... But It Might Take a While to Get Up Again

Sarah arrived back late on Saturday night. After dropping her bags on the kitchen floor, she got herself a glass of water and crawled up to bed.

She awoke in the morning, sweating profusely and shivering fiercely. Which was good, because that meant she was ill and could therefore stay in bed without having to think or do anything at all. She spent most of the day slipping in and out of sleep. Once, she heard the telephone go but that was all right. The answer machine was on and she was ill. She didn't have to speak to anyone.

On Monday, she felt wobbly but well enough to go downstairs in her pajamas and dressing gown and make a cup of tea. She wandered through to the studio. She looked at the apple canvas resting against the wall and then at the banana on her easel.

They were appalling: clichéd travesties of sexual innuendo painted by a frustrated, sad, middle-aged has-been who was all the sadder for never having been anything in the first place. She couldn't bear to look at them. She couldn't charge a hundred pounds for these, let alone a thousand.

Sarah went through to the sitting room, switched on the television, and settled down on the sofa. A man told her how to make wedding bouquets, a woman told her how to improve her body, and a chef called Phil told her how to make something that looked like the vomit on Barney's bathroom floor. Then she watched the news, which made her realize that she was a very lucky woman because she was living in a country without locusts or earthquakes or drought. Knowing that she was a very lucky woman made her want to cry but now there was another program in which an actress, a comedian, and a singer were guests on a chat show and spent the whole time trying to wrest the spotlight from each other. Sarah switched off the television. Watching daytime television was like being force-fed a very big bag of marshmallows. The telephone rang again but she was ill, she didn't have to answer it. She went back to bed.

On Tuesday she woke up and knew she was no longer ill. She got up and went to the bathroom. The yellow rings around her right eye had gone purple. She had a shower, washed her hair, and dressed quickly.

Downstairs, there was nothing to eat or drink. There was no bread, the milk had gone bad, and Sarah, predictably, was starving. She spent a long time looking for her sunglasses and finally found them in her dressing table drawer.

She was halfway down the garden path when she realized

there was no way she could face the village shop. She went back into the house, collected her car keys, and drove to the supermarket in Gillingham, where she met Clementine Delaney wheeling a very full trolley back to her car. Thank you, God, she thought, thank you very much. Is it any wonder that I don't believe in you?

"Sarah?" asked Clementine. "I hardly recognized you in those glasses!" (Translation: "Why are you wearing those glasses?")

"Hello, Clementine," said Sarah.

"How are you? Haven't you just been out to Majorca?"

"Yes," said Sarah, "I have."

"You are *so* lucky! At this time of year, I'd happily go and live somewhere else. Although, actually, this last week, the weather has been lovely. I spent three hours in the garden yesterday, sorting out the vegetable patch. It was heaven!"

"Really?"

"Absolute heaven! So tell me: when are you moving away? We ought to throw a farewell party for you. Did you say it was May or June?"

"May." Sarah glanced at Clementine. She might as well tell her now. Clementine would tell everyone and then she wouldn't have to. "Actually, the move is off. My friend and I decided it wouldn't work out."

"Oh Sarah! I *am* sorry! You were *so* excited! I've never seen you look so happy. (Translation: "Is that why you are wearing those glasses?")

"I've had time to think about it," said Sarah. "It wouldn't work." She checked her watch a little ostentatiously. "I must get on. Good-bye." Sarah moved away quickly, praying she wouldn't meet anyone else she knew.

She spent the afternoon doing what she should have done ages ago: sorting out everything that belonged to Andrew, including his books and those pieces of holiday pottery he had particularly liked. After she'd packed them into boxes, she went to the boys' bedrooms and sorted through their drawers, putting out for Oxfam all those clothes she knew they'd never want to wear again.

In the evening, she made herself some cheese on toast and left it too long in the Aga. When she took it out, the cheese had become a brown, curled crust. She threw it away and opened a bottle of wine instead. It was time to think about what she was going to do. Was it even worth trying to start the pictures again in the hope that she could actually produce an original painting? Sarah searched her brain for an original thought but her brain remained achingly empty.

One bottle later, Sarah had considered and discarded various options: she could tell Gordon she'd broken her arm and was unable to finish the paintings. She could give him the apple canvas and insist he pay her for it or she could confess that she simply couldn't deliver.

The truth was, she couldn't deliver anything. She'd thought she was a good wife and Andrew left her. She'd thought she and Martin were good friends and he lost all interest in her as soon as Sally-Anne appeared. She'd thought she could become a successful artist and she couldn't even manage a sexy apple. She'd thought Barney wanted to start a new life with her and she meant so little to him that he'd forgotten she was coming out to see him. She'd got everything wrong; nothing was real. The truth was, she was an unqualified, untalented, unattractive, uninteresting piece of flotsam. She'd produced two beautiful boys and they no longer needed her. She was good for nothing now. She was a waste of space.

A heavy knock on the front door made her freeze. The burglars had come for her at last! Jacko had kept them away but Jacko had gone. Andrew had gone. Ben and James had gone. Barney had gone. Sarah began to cry. Why did everyone go? She stopped midsob. There were footsteps in the garden. The burglars were in the garden! Sarah looked round frantically and grabbed a weapon. There was a burglar outside the back door! She could see his silhouette! Oh, God, he was opening the door, she could see the handle move! She raised her weapon above her head and prepared to strike.

"Sarah?" Martin said. "What are you doing with that milk pan?"

Sarah took one look at him, dropped the pan, and burst into tears.

"Shush now," said Martin, putting an arm round her. "It's all right, you're all right. Shush, Sarah, come and sit down." He led her to her chair and sat down beside her. "I didn't mean to frighten you. I'm sorry. I could see you were in the kitchen and when you didn't answer the door—" He stopped abruptly. "What happened to your face?"

"It's an ugly face!" Sarah wept. "And I'm an ugly woman!"

"No you're not!"

"I am! I'm an ugly woman! You think I'm an ugly woman! And you don't want to kiss me!"

"Of course I want to kiss you! Now tell me how you got that black eye?"

"I got it in Majorca! I'd been so happy and I'd got Barney a birthday present and still he didn't come to the airport so I had to get a taxi and I went to his house and he was drunk and he kept being sick and I had to clear it all up and when he stopped being sick he came downstairs and he told me . . . he told me he loved his wife and he thought she'd come back to him if she thought I was going to live with him. But she still didn't want to go back to him and so he got angry and I thought he was going to hit me and I fell down and I hurt myself on the stupid table and it really hurt. And I've been so stupid, I've been so stupid, silly, stupid, and I told everyone I was going to live in Majorca with a wonderful man and I was so thrilled they wouldn't feel sorry for me anymore and now they'll all laugh at me when I tell them I'm not going to live in Majorca and I think I'm about to be sick!"

"Hang on, Sarah!" Martin grabbed her arm and rushed her to the sink, where Sarah proceeded to make noises very similar to those made by Barney a few nights earlier. "Good girl!" said Martin, "Good girl!" He took a piece of kitchen paper from the roll on the side and wiped her mouth. "Now come and sit down." She could hear him sluicing out the sink and then he was putting a coat round her shoulders. "Here," he said, "I've got you some water."

Sarah drank some more water. "My head hurts," she said.

"I imagine it does."

She looked up suddenly. "Don't tell Sally-Anne about me and Barney."

"I won't tell anyone about you and Barney."

"They'll all guess anyway. Clementine guessed at the supermarket. They probably guessed all along. And now there's my painting too!"

"What about your painting?"

"They're stupid paintings! I'm supposed to be painting sexy fruit! I can't paint sexy fruit! They're stupid fruit. Do you want to see my stupid fruit?"

"I think you should go to bed. I'll go and have a look at your fruit in a minute."

"They're in the studio. They're stupid."

"I promise I'll look at them. Do you think you're going to be sick again or can I get you up to bed?"

Sarah gave a deep sigh. "You can get me up to bed."

He guided her up the stairs and into her room. He took the pajamas from her pillow. "Can you put these on yourself or do you want me to . . . ?" He looked relieved when Sarah shook her head. "I'll go and get your water."

Left on her own, Sarah struggled with her sweater and eventually got it off. She put her pajama top over her bra and climbed into bed. Martin reappeared with her glass and set it down on the bedside table. "Lie down," he told her, and pulled her duvet up to her chin.

Sarah looked at him. "Everyone will laugh at me."

"No one you care about will laugh at you. No one else matters."

Sarah frowned. "Why did you come here tonight?"

"You weren't at rehearsal. We tried to ring you. I was worried."

"I forgot the stupid rehearsal," Sarah said. "What was it like?"

"Very stupid."

Sarah smiled. "I do like you, Martin!"

"I like you too. Now go to sleep."

"I'm sorry I was sick."

"Never mind that. Go to sleep."

"Martin?"

"What?"

"I thought you were a burglar. I was going to hit you with my milk pan."

"I'm very glad you didn't."

"So am I," said Sarah, and closed her eyes.

Look Outward, Not Inward

Sarah woke up at six with a throbbing head. She drank the rest of the water and decided the only sensible course of action was to go back to sleep. She slept until eleven, raised herself cautiously from her pillow, and was relieved to find that her headache had gone. After a long bath, she was left with only a slight feeling of nausea, which was less, she told herself severely, than she deserved. She put her dressing gown on and walked slowly downstairs. There was a note on the kitchen table from Martin. "I'll drop by this evening. Please keep away from the milk pan. I had a look at the paintings. I don't like apples but your apple made me want to eat it. I'm not sure what that says about me but I know what it says about your painting."

Sarah took the box of tissues from its place by the bread bin and put it on the table. She took one out and blew her nose fiercely. Then she squared her shoulders and went through to the studio. She positioned her chair a few feet from the apple canvas, sat down, and looked long and hard at it. It was all right. It really was all right. So the man who'd inspired it had turned out to have a less than inspirational character. That didn't affect the painting. The painting, after all, was about sex, and whatever his other failings, Barney had been a great lover. Sarah swallowed hard and made herself concentrate on the banana. She could paint it. She would paint them all.

She heard the doorbell and left the studio quickly. Jennifer stood outside the front door, car keys in hand, her body poised for flight. "I don't have to come in," she said quickly. "I'll go if you're busy." Her eyes registered Sarah's black eye and then swerved away quickly.

"Come in." Sarah smiled. "I was about to make coffee. It's good to see you."

Jennifer's face relaxed. She followed Sarah into the kitchen and removed her Barbour. "Before I sit down," she said, "you can tell me to mind my own business and I won't be offended if you do. But how on earth did you get that black eye?"

Jennifer listened to Sarah's story in shocked silence. "And I thought it was all so romantic!" she said mournfully. "The Barney man sounded such a hero!"

Sarah brought the coffee pot to the table and smiled ruefully. "I know. I thought so too. I was so naive. I suppose if you believe in heroes at forty-three, you deserve everything you get. I should have known he was just an ordinary man who—"

"Excuse me, Sarah, he was not an ordinary man at all. An ordinary man doesn't invite a woman to fly across Europe and then neglect to pick her up from the airport. An ordinary man doesn't get disgustingly drunk before his guest arrives. He doesn't sound ordinary at all. He sounds like a self-pitying, self-indulgent, inadequate wreck."

"But apart from all that, he's very nice!" Sarah gave a rueful laugh. "I don't know. I'm not completely blameless either. I suppose I was ready to have a fling with anyone who could make me feel I was still attractive. Barney was a great lover. He made me an offer that was obviously absurd and in any other circumstances I'd have turned it down without a thought. I wanted to believe in it because it seemed to give me an easy escape from all the problems in my life. I ought to know by now that there is no such thing as an easy escape." She sighed and poured out the coffee. "In the meantime, I have to break it to Andrew that I will no longer be leaving Shooter's Cottage in May. He'll think I'm so pathetic! I can't face ringing him yet. Do you realize I told him he could definitely go ahead and put the house on the market? He's going to be so cross!"

"Don't be silly, Sarah. The man has no right to be cross with you about anything. You have every right to stay here as long as you like."

"I'm not sure I do want to stay here. I'm not sure about anything." Sarah bit her lip. "Tell me about you and George. What's going on? Don't tell me you still don't know what's going on."

"No," said Jennifer slowly. "I do." Her eyes drifted out toward the garden. "Look!" she cried. "That little bird on the lawn! He's trying to pull that worm from the grass. He's shaking his little head with such determination."

Sarah rested her chin on her hands. "I love this time of year. Look at the sun on the trees over there. This time next week they'll be completely green again."

"I'm sure spring's come early this year."

"I think it has. Have you thought about bedding plants yet?"

Jennifer caught Sarah's eye and laughed. "I wasn't stalling, I promise. I do want to talk about George, only don't expect me to make any sense because I don't understand anything anymore, especially after what you just told me. Nobody seems to be what they're supposed to be anymore."

"Jennifer, what has George been doing on Wednesday nights?"

Jennifer sighed heavily. "He's been going to cookery classes."

"Cookery classes? *George?*"

"I know, I know! I was speechless when he told me."

"Really? For how long?"

"Don't be naughty, Sarah. For at least a minute. And do you know *why* he's been going to cookery classes?"

"I very much hope you're going to tell me."

"He thought I was going to leave him! So he decided he'd better learn to cook. Sarah, if you're going to laugh, I'm not going to say another word!"

"I'm sorry!" Sarah covered her face with her hands for a few moments before revealing a suitably composed expression. "It's only that it's such a gloriously practical reaction!"

"It's a very humiliating reaction. I mean, I know you've had a bad time with Barney but George is my husband of many years! You'd think he might be a little upset at the thought of losing his nearest and dearest. But no, he decides he'd better learn to cook!"

"What about the slob woman?"

"She's also taking the course. Her car was stolen a few weeks ago and he's been giving her lifts."

"So what," asked Sarah curiously, "are you going to do now?"

"What do you mean?"

"Well, *are* you going to leave George?"

Jennifer raised her eyes to the ceiling as if seeking an answer from a higher power. "That's what George asked me. He even offered to move out and let me have the house."

"That's what you wanted."

"Yes, well I don't want it now. I wanted to break up with George because he never surprised me. And now he has surprised me. He made a steak and kidney pie last night."

Sarah's mouth twitched again. "I always said George had hidden depths."

"Yes." Jennifer glanced at Sarah with new respect. "You always did. You're right, he has. You should have tasted his pastry: it was light as a feather." She stood up and collected her Barbour cost. "I must go. The girls break up tomorrow. I swear their terms get shorter and shorter." She kissed Sarah lightly on the cheek. "I'm very sorry that your Barney turned out to be so sad but I can't help being glad you're not going to leave Ambercross. It wouldn't be the same without you."

"Thank you," Sarah said, "and I'm glad about you and George. You've made me feel a lot better."

"We're having a small dinner party on Saturday. Do you want to come?"

"No," said Sarah, "Thank you. I'm not feeling *that* much better."

It seemed to be a day of surprises. In the afternoon, Sarah had a call from Andrew. "I've decided to go with Cramptons," he said. "They've produced a very impressive brochure of the house. I've asked them to send you a copy. I said they could start pushing it next week. Is that all right?"

Sarah took a deep breath. "The thing is," she murmured, "I . . ."

"Have you a date yet for Majorca? When exactly do you want to move out?"

Sarah had a sudden picture of Barney taking her hand as they came out of the cathedral at Palma. "I'm not going to Majorca," she said.

"What? Why not?"

Sarah shut her eyes and then opened them again. "I went out there this weekend. It turned out . . ." She swallowed hard. She was *not* going to break down. "It turned out Barney wasn't . . . we weren't . . . Basically, we both made a mistake. We're not going to see each other anymore."

There was a long silence and then, "Sarah," Andrew said gently, "I'm so sorry."

"Aren't you going to tell me you told me so?"

"I know you have a very low opinion of me and you have every right to have a low opinion but even I wouldn't be that crass."

Sarah wished he would be. It would have been much easier to receive than this unexpected sympathy.

"Look," he said, "I'll ring Cramptons and tell them we've changed our minds."

Sarah hesitated. "Are you sure?"

"Of course I'm sure. Are you all right? Would you like me to come round?"

"No, I'm fine. And I have masses to do. I've only finished one painting so far."

"You'd better get a move on. The club's opening in three weeks."

Sarah smiled. That was more like the old Andrew. "Thank you for reminding me. I already have my invitation."

"Me too. I'll leave you to your work. Sarah, I'm so sorry. I'm sorry about everything."

"Me too." Sarah put the phone down quickly. It was bad enough that Andrew could still make her cry. At least he was not going to know that he could.

Martin came by at six and found Sarah pruning roses in the front garden. "I thought you'd be painting," he said.

"Don't worry, I'm not giving up on them," Sarah assured him. "Thank you for your note. It was just what I needed. In fact, thank you for last night. I feel thoroughly ashamed of myself. I shall never touch alcohol again."

Martin laughed. "That's what I always say."

"I mean it. I'm really sorry. You must have found me utterly repellent."

"I did. I do. I can hardly bear to look at you."

"I wouldn't blame you. Do you want a cup of tea?"

"I'd love one but I have another call to make. I only wanted to make sure you were all right."

"I am. And I've had some good news today. I told Andrew I wasn't going to Majorca anymore and he said he'd cancel the realtor."

"That's big of him."

"He was actually very kind. It rather threw me. I wasn't expecting him to be kind."

"No," said Martin grimly. "I imagine you weren't."

Sarah took off her gardening gloves. "I wanted to say," she said carefully, "I can't remember a lot about last night but I probably said some very embarrassing things. . . ."

"You didn't," said Martin. "You didn't say anything you shouldn't have." He bent down to pick up a rose cutting and threw it into the wheelbarrow. "We ought to go for a walk on the weekend. The weather forecast is good. How about Saturday?"

"Great," said Sarah.

"Good. I'll get Sally-Anne to come too."

"Great," said Sarah.

Be Prepared for Setbacks

Sarah was pulling on her boots when Martin arrived. "No Sally-Anne?" she asked.

"No, I'm afraid it's just me."

"Never mind!" said Sarah, guiltily aware that her Saturday had become a hundred times better. "Isn't it a perfect day for a walk?"

It was. The sun was not only shining, it was warm. The lambs were out in the fields, there was blossom on the trees and a sweet, fresh smell in the air that only a springtime in England could produce. Sarah said politely, if untruthfully, "I'm sorry Sally-Anne couldn't come. How is she?"

Martin thrust his hands in his pockets and neatly side-stepped a dog turd on the edge of the lane. "I don't know," he said. "We're not seeing each other anymore."

"Martin!" Sarah stopped in surprise and then hurried after him. "I'm so sorry. I thought everything was fine. When did this happen?"

Martin sighed. "Last night."

"Last night? But I don't understand! Anyone could see she was nuts about you."

"Apparently not," said Martin sorrowfully.

"But she was! I could tell she was. What did she say?"

"She thinks we're not compatible," Martin said. "Do you mind if we don't talk about it?"

"Of course. But I'm so sorry." She took his arm and searched his face. "Are you sure you want to walk today?"

Martin gave a brave smile. "It's what I need," he said. "It will take my mind off it. Tell me about the banana. Have you made any headway?"

Sarah, impressed by his stoicism, launched into a description of her latest creation. Then she remembered she'd never told him about her meeting with Gordon at the National Portrait Gallery and after that she told him about Miriam and Antonio and the walks she'd had in Majorca. She had just finished telling him about the monastery at Valldemossa when they arrived at the pub. "Do you want to find a table?" Martin suggested. "I'll order lunch."

"I'll order lunch," Sarah said firmly, remembering what he'd ordered last time. She went to the bar and asked for two fish and chips and two orange juices. She glanced back at Martin. He had picked up a paper and was doing the crossword. He was being very composed, Sarah thought. In fact he was giving a very convincing impression of someone who had not had his heart broken at all. But then that was typical of Martin. He was never someone who liked to display his emotions.

She brought the drinks to the table and sat down opposite him. "Tell me about Jean-Pierre," she said. "Is Jacko behaving himself? Or am I better not knowing?"

Martin put aside his paper. "I knew there was something I had to tell you. Jean-Pierre is seeing someone and it's all thanks to your dog. I can't imagine a more unlikely Cupid."

"Don't tell me, I can guess! He attacked some helpless young woman and Jean-Pierre rescued her!"

"Quite the reverse. It was Jacko who needed rescuing. Jean-Pierre had taken him for a walk in the hills. It was early in the morning, no one else was up, so Jean-Pierre let Jacko roam. Then he heard this howl and found Jacko cowering in fear while some dragon was bashing him with her leash."

"Jacko never cowers!"

"That was the word Jean-Pierre used. He said Jacko was cowering. Jacko had gone for the woman's spaniel and . . ."

"I can imagine!" Sarah shuddered. "I saw what he did to Clementine's guinea pig."

"Well, he wasn't allowed to get near the spaniel. And then she tore into Jean-Pierre."

"With the leash?"

"With her tongue. By the end of it, she had him humbly apologizing. He invited her to tea."

"I wouldn't have thought Jean-Pierre was the sort of man to take tea."

"He said he went to the shops and bought a Swiss roll. It turned out the woman was a dog trainer and an expert in self-defense. Jean-Pierre says she's lovely. Mind you," Martin mused, "he said his wife was lovely so he's not very reliable. Now they go walking together every day. He says Jacko even likes the spaniel now."

"If I were that spaniel," Sarah said darkly, "I'd watch my back. Will you send my regards to your brother next time you speak to him?"

"I will. He liked you very much."

"Did he?" Sarah asked. "How very nice!" She felt ridiculously pleased. It occurred to her that this time last week she had been sitting in the airport, feeling like she'd never laugh again. "You know," she mused aloud, "I wonder if I might actually be a shallow person?"

"Sometimes," Martin said, "it's very difficult to follow your train of thought."

"I was just thinking: I'm having such a lovely morning and yet this time last week I was completely miserable."

"It shows you have remarkable powers of recovery. It's very commendable." He looked disapprovingly at the fish and chips that were being brought toward them. "Why are we eating these?"

"It's my treat," said Sarah. "I've been eating my way through rotting fruit for the last few days. Also the banana is proving difficult and I need proper sustenance. I'll eat yours if you don't want it."

"I'll eat it," said Martin, "under protest." He took a chip and put it into his mouth. "Very good," he said, and took another one. He was aware that Sarah was looking at him. "What?" he demanded. "Why are you smiling?"

"I was thinking," she said, "how very adaptable you are, making yourself eat those chips. It's very commendable."

"Sarah," Martin said suspiciously, "are you laughing at me?"

"Yes," said Sarah with great affection, "but in a very nice way."

Sally-Anne Furlong was not at the rehearsal on Tuesday and for some reason Audrey was determined to blame Martin. "Unfortunately," she said ponderously, "for personal reasons, Sally-Anne has decided to vacate the position of prompt." Her eyes fell on Martin. "I am sorry that at a time when we are only three weeks . . . three weeks! . . . from the production date, certain people have chosen to act in a manner toward Sally-Anne that can only be described as irresponsible. Fortunately, we do have some people in the play who understand the vital importance of a prompt." Her eyes traveled to Howard, who responded with a modest little smile. "I believe you are going to visit Sally-Anne to try and persuade her to change her mind?"

"I am," said Howard, "I'm taking her out for a drink tomorrow."

"Thank you, Howard. You go with the good wishes of us all. At least," she added grimly, "I *hope* you go with the good wishes of us all. And now, because Sarah unaccountably failed to appear last week . . ."

"I'm sorry." Sarah raised her arm. "I was ill. I'm sorry."

"If you could let us know when you are going to be ill," Audrey said with heavy sarcasm, "we would be grateful. So, because as I say, Sarah failed to appear last week, we were unable to do the last scene properly. We shall therefore do it now. I take it, Martin, that you still find yourself unable to kiss Sarah?"

"Sorry," said Martin cheerfully. "I'll be all right on the night!"

"I can't wait," said Audrey with dreadful sarcasm. "I suppose I shall just have to hope for a miracle. In light of your recent behavior I no longer know what to expect of you. Now, let us get into positions!"

"It's so unfair!" Sarah whispered to Martin. "It's not your fault that Sally-Anne can't face you. It's not right to have a go at you like that. I jolly well feel like saying something."

"Don't," murmured Martin. "We'd just get another lecture and I would like to get home before midnight."

Martin, Sarah thought, was an object lesson in how to behave. The fact that he could not talk about Sally-Anne showed how much he'd been affected by her rejection of him and yet he'd been terrific company on Saturday. He retained a dignified silence in the face of Audrey's outrageously unfair assault, and he was even able to put in a great performance at the rehearsal. If Martin could be such a stoic, then so could she. She would banish all thoughts of the Barney debacle from her mind.

Throughout the next day, Sarah worked hard on the banana. At ten past six on Wednesday evening, she put the final dab of color on the canvas and rubbed her aching back.

The banana was good. The color, a milky yellow with threadlike glimmers of green, was perfect, and the dark charcoal background showed it off to perfection. Sarah smiled and set about washing her paintbrushes. There was, after all, something to be said for living alone. If Andrew had not left her, he would be coming home about this time, demanding to know what was for supper. She smiled again, took off her painting apron, and went upstairs to have a bath.

Later, she came down in her dressing gown and returned to her studio to have another look at her canvas. She had been considering signing up as a substitute teacher but for the first time she let herself imagine an alternative possibility. Perhaps her fruit paintings might lead to further well-paying commissions. Perhaps she might be able to make at least a modest living out of her art alone. Perhaps, just perhaps, Sarah Stagg might be able to make a name for herself as someone other than the wife of Andrew or the mother of Ben and James. It was an exhilarating idea.

She went through to the kitchen, opened the back door, and sat on the step, enjoying the sound of birdsong and the scent of blossom in the air. Andrew had left her. Barney had used her. So be it. Now she was anticipating a future without a man in her life and it didn't bother her. "Sarah Stagg," she said out loud, "I think you're growing up at last."

Offer Advice. It's More Fun Than Receiving It.

Sarah hadn't spoken to Miriam in weeks. She had rung twice in order to tell her about Barney but had got Clive both times and he had been hurried and uncommunicative.

When she finally got hold of Miriam, it was a relief to be able to tell her. "I should have known," Sarah said. "It made no sense for him to suddenly ask me to move in with him. I suppose I was just ready to believe anything."

"Barney's a very attractive man," Miriam said. "If someone like that asks you to come and share his bed you're not likely to want to question his motives."

"Yes but the whole thing was so unreal. And in my heart I knew it was. Neither of us ever mentioned the word 'love,' for instance. I knew Barney didn't love me and I certainly didn't love him. How could I? I hardly knew him! I fancied him like mad and I thought he was the coolest man on the planet but I didn't love him. He didn't make me laugh, he didn't make me feel comfortable; I was never relaxed with him because I was always so much in awe of him. Apart from lust, gratitude was what he most inspired in me. I was grateful that he noticed me. That's no basis for a relationship."

"Of course it isn't."

"The stupid thing was I kept saying how unreal it was! And when it all went wrong I was completely gutted, of course, but I think that was because I felt such an idiot. It was humiliating having to tell everyone back home that my great romance was not a romance, but apart from all that, I think I miss the idea of Barney rather than Barney himself. Do you know what I mean?"

"Yes," said Miriam. "I know exactly what you mean."

"So anyway," Sarah sighed, "I hope I am now older and wiser!" She was beginning to feel alarmed. She had been talking about herself for at least ten minutes and the prime reason for her doing so was that Miriam was hardly saying anything. "Miriam," she said, "you're being fairly quiet. Is everything all right?"

"I'm pregnant," Miriam said.

"What?"

"I'm pregnant."

"Miriam!" Sarah was stunned. In all the years she had known her friend, Miriam had never once expressed any desire to have children. She had no idea what Miriam expected her to say. "That's wonderful!" she said, adding cautiously, "Do you think it's wonderful?"

"Yes, I do. It's early days. I only did the test on Saturday."

"Oh, heavens, this is so exciting! I can't believe it! I have two beautiful cribs in the attic. You're welcome to either of them and I still have the boys' blankets. Oh, Miriam, I'm so thrilled for you!" Sarah paused suddenly. "Is Clive pleased? What does Clive say?"

"Clive says very little. In fact, Clive is hardly talking to me."

"He's probably in shock! He'll come round. You wait until he holds his baby in his arms and then—"

"The thing is," said Miriam, "it isn't Clive's baby."

"It isn't?" Sarah gulped. "Whose baby is it?"

"Well," said Miriam, "it's Antonio's."

"What do you mean? How could it be Antonio's?"

Miriam said a little testily, "Well, I haven't slept with anyone else in the last few weeks."

"I don't understand. You slept with Antonio? You never gave the slightest hint of anything like that! I had no idea you and Antonio got so friendly! When *did* you get so friendly?"

"Do you remember when you went back with Barney the second time? After we'd all had dinner together?"

"And we left you two in the restaurant. Are you telling me you got together with Antonio that night?"

"I'm afraid so."

"I had no idea." Sarah reached for a chair, kicked off her shoes, and sat down. "Now that I think about it, I should have known. You were always going on about Antonio's failings. Any woman who complains about a man as often as you did is obviously attracted to him. This is so extraordinary. What are you going to do now? Will Clive accept the baby? Is he very angry?"

"He has no right to be angry. He's admitted he's been having an affair since Christmas."

"Oh." It all sounded a terrible mess. "I'm sure," Sarah said in a spirit of hope rather than conviction, "you'll sort something out."

"I have done," said Miriam. "I'm going to live with Antonio."

"Now, Miriam," Sarah said, "just because Antonio is the father of your baby does not mean you have to give up everything to go and live with him. You need to think carefully and calmly. . . ."

"I have been thinking very carefully and calmly. Antonio has asked me to marry him."

"That's very honorable of him but it doesn't mean you have to accept."

"I want to accept. I love Antonio."

"You love Antonio? Miriam, you knew him for a week. . . ."

"I know and I had more fun with Antonio in one week than I did with Clive in the whole of our married life! He was funny, he was kind, he was interesting, he made me feel good."

"Why didn't you tell me any of this?"

"I thought Antonio was behaving in exactly the way people expect Spanish men to behave to gullible, vulnerable English women. I knew I was vulnerable and I was prepared to suspend reality for a few days and be gullible as well. And then when I came home, I felt so ashamed of myself."

"Because you'd slept with him?"

"Because I missed him! And then I started getting the postcards."

"What postcards?"

"From Antonio. They worked a treat with Clive. He didn't like them at all. They were lovely cards and they kept on coming. Then we started talking to each other on the phone. I wanted to tell you all about it but then Antonio told me about you and Barney. . . ."

"You knew about that?"

"Yes." Miriam hesitated. "I didn't know what to do. I didn't feel I could tell you how happy I felt about Antonio when you were getting your heart broken by Barney. I should have known that you're far too sensible to have your heart broken by someone like that."

"Has Antonio seen Barney lately? How is he?"

"Drinking too much. Antonio says he always drinks too much. That's why his wife left him. You're well out of it."

"I suppose I am. Tell me, what did Antonio say about the baby?"

"I wasn't going to tell him. I mean I'm only a few weeks pregnant and at my age anything can happen."

"But obviously you did tell him."

Miriam laughed. "Pathetic, aren't I? He was over the moon. He wanted me to give up work at once and fly out. I've told him I have to stay at school until the end of the school year. I don't want to plan ahead at the moment. I'm just enjoying being happy again."

"Who would have thought it?" sighed Sarah. "We both go out for a holiday of sex and romance and we actually get a holiday of sex and romance! You'll have to call your baby Marcello."

"Since I already have Antonio. Very funny."

"I suppose," Sarah said, "after what's happened to me and Barney, I should be telling you you're crazy."

"It doesn't feel crazy."

"I don't think it is. Now you've told me, I can't think how I missed it. You and Antonio are so good together."

"Thank you. And what about you? Are you really all right?"

"I am," said Sarah. "I know people think I've made a complete mess of things. Well, I *have* made a complete mess of things but I'm working too hard to worry about that. I think work is the answer. I just need to keep working. And no more romantic adventures."

Miriam laughed. "You never know!"

"Yes I do," said Sarah. "They're far too expensive for a start. No more weekend jaunts abroad for me! And I'll tell you something Barney's taught me: there's a lot to be said for being single!"

Keep Busy

For the next few days, Sarah did nothing but paint. She was supposed to be taking the finished canvases up to the nightclub premises on April 17, and as the day of reckoning approached, she became increasingly nervous. The apple was good. Sarah thought it was as good as the Raffles picture. The banana was also pretty good but she was beginning to panic about the peach and the strawberry. She had left herself too little time to do them justice. The peach was as mouth-watering as a soggy cornflake and the color of the strawberry was wrong. The fact that in this all-important week, Audrey had decreed an extra rehearsal on Wednesday did not bother her. After the hours of standing at an easel she was happy to go anywhere in the evening, even to rehearsals run by an increasingly bad-tempered director.

The play, Audrey said, was not going well. Mrs. Danvers needed to inject more menace into her performance, Colonel Julyan needed to be less histrionic in showing his doubts about Maxim's probity. Mrs. de Winter still had a tendency to speak too quietly and Maxim was very good at being stiff and stern but: "You're no good at showing passion, Martin! Where is the passion? When you tell Sarah you hated Rebecca, you sound as if you have a mild bout of indigestion. You are a tormented soul! Be tormented! In fact we need more oomph from everyone. I have to tell you I am getting sleepless nights about this play!"

"I'm having sleepless nights about my paintings," Sarah told Martin as they sat in the pub after Wednesday's rehearsal. "I'm taking them to Bath tomorrow and they're nowhere near ready. And what if Gordon doesn't like them? What do I say?"

"You tell him he knows nothing about art. Then you take your money, you go home, and you enjoy your Easter weekend."

"That's another thing," said Sarah gloomily. "On Friday, I'm driving up to my parents. My mother will spend the whole weekend lamenting the loss of Andrew and my father will spend the whole weekend telling me I should have married Gerald Hodge."

"Who is he?"

"I knew Gerald Hodge when I was a teenager. Whenever I was at a party without a boyfriend . . . which was most of the time . . . Gerald would come and stand next to me. Then he'd spend the entire evening delivering a running commentary on what was going on around us. If I tried to get away he'd just follow me and keep talking. When I was at art school, he visited my father and asked for my hand in marriage. He said he knew we were very young and he was therefore planning a long engagement. I came home for the weekend and my mother had bought champagne and salmon and was very cross with me when I said I'd never go out with Gerald Hodge much less marry him. Anyway, a few weeks ago my father saw a picture of him in the paper. Apparently he's a filthy rich financier or something, so now Dad keeps telling me I could have married him."

"Well obviously you could have."

"Thank you, Martin. That's what my father will be saying throughout the weekend. What are *you* doing for Easter?"

"I'm going to Paris. I'm off on Thursday."

"You're going to Paris!" Sarah finished her drink in one gulp. "Here I am driveling on about my exciting weekend in Swindon and you're going to Paris!"

"I'm going to stay with my mother and sister. I always go to Paris at Easter."

"I've never been to Paris. I wish I could come with you. Paris at Easter! It sounds so romantic!" She shot a concerned glance at Martin. "I'm sorry. That was tactless."

"Was it?" asked Martin. "Why?"

"You know. You and Sally-Anne."

"Oh," said Martin. "Yes, I see." He looked as if he were about to say something but concentrated instead on smoothing the empty peanut packet.

"I must go," Sarah said. "I have a long day tomorrow." She stood up and put her bag over her shoulder. "Martin, I just want to say I really appreciate . . . what I mean is, ever since I got back from Majorca you've been really kind, going for walks with me and things. Sometimes I think the only good thing that's happened to me since Andrew left me is the fact that you and I became friends." She kissed him quickly on the cheek. "I just wanted you to know I'm grateful." She smiled awkwardly. "I'll see you tomorrow."

"Sarah?" Martin threw the peanut paper into the ashtray and stood up.

"Yes?"

He hesitated. "Good luck with the strawberry," he said.

Sarah finished the strawberry at ten past one on Thursday morning. She was too tired to care if it was any good or not. All she knew was that she would never be able to eat strawberries again.

A few hours later she woke up with a sick feeling in her stomach and a presentiment of doom. She tried to imagine herself arguing her case with a furious Gordon. "I'm sorry, Gordon, you know nothing about art. This strawberry has caught the very essence of what it means to be a strawberry and I'm sorry if you don't like it and I'd like my money now." Pigs might fly.

She washed her hair and spent a long time riffling through her wardrobe. She wanted to look businesslike, sensible, and intelligent. None of her clothes seemed to fit these categories. In the end she wore her black trousers and one of Ben's white school shirts.

On the drive up to Bath she rehearsed her defense. She must betray no doubts. If she gave the impression that she thought the fruit were brilliant, then Gordon might just accept her judgment. Sarah switched on the radio. Gloria Gaynor was singing, "I Will Survive."

At twelve she stood amid a maelstrom of builders and decorators in the nightclub premises. She couldn't imagine what the place would look like when it was finished. She stiffened as Gordon came toward her.

"Sarah!" he said, "thank you for being so prompt. Let me introduce you to my partner, Jeremy Strickland." Sarah shook hands with Jeremy, who was wearing black trousers and a white shirt, like Sarah. On Jeremy, they looked glamorous. She hoped she radiated the same air of svelte sophistication.

"So!" said Gordon. "Can we see them?"

Sarah swallowed hard. She felt like throwing up and was quite unable to say any of the things she had thought about saying. In silence, she took the blanket off the canvases and set them out in front of the two men. They stood silently, with their arms folded. Sarah looked at them with a face determinedly devoid of expression. At least they weren't squirming with horror. They weren't dancing for joy either. Sarah felt like jumping up and down and shouting, "Say something!" Perhaps Gordon was telepathic because he glanced at her and said, "Thank you, Sarah. These will do very nicely. Let me give you your check."

"Thank you," Sarah stood uncomfortably while Gordon wrote his check out. Jeremy had walked over to the strawberry. Gordon gave her a wintry smile. "You will be coming to the opening party next Thursday, won't you? The local press will be there. They might want to take some photos so get yourself something glamorous to wear!"

"I will." Sarah took the check, wished both men a happy

Easter, and walked up the stairs and out onto the pavement. She had been in the nightclub for less than fifteen minutes. She felt a deadening sense of anticlimax. All that worry and all that work and what was the result? The pictures would do nicely! She stared down at the check. She was holding a check for four thousand pounds! She had been told to buy something glamorous to wear. She was in Bath, a city with shops full of glamorous things to wear! She grinned and set out to spend some money.

Sarah drove up to her parents on Good Friday. She arrived in a mood of infectious enthusiasm, bearing champagne and Easter eggs. Her parents, pleased with the champagne, refrained from dwelling on either Andrew or Gerald Hodge and even allowed themselves to express optimism about Sarah's future.

On Easter Sunday the phone rang. Sarah's mother picked up the receiver and was soon chatting animatedly. It had to be Andrew since he alone elicited the particular flirtatious giggle coming from the hall. A few minutes later, her mother put her face round the door. "It's Andrew! I've had such a lovely chat with him! He wants to wish you a happy Easter!"

Sarah raised her eyebrows and went through to the hall. "Andrew," she said, "happy Easter!"

"And to you! And congratulations, Sarah, about the paintings."

"You heard." Sarah sat down on the bottom stair and put the phone on her lap. "The important thing is they gave me the money. They didn't seem to be that impressed by the pictures but I got the money."

"Don't you believe it, they loved them!" Sarah hadn't heard

Andrew sound so excited in a long time. "I've been liaising with Abby. Did you meet her when you went to the club? She said Gordon and Jeremy Strickland were very enthusiastic."

"That's very kind of her to say so," said Sarah doubtfully. "They didn't *look* very enthusiastic."

"They wouldn't. Abby says they're talking about getting you to do some work for their place in London. If they appear too keen they'll expect you to up your fee. Sarah, this is very exciting. Jeremy Strickland has all sorts of connections in the art world. You could be on the verge of something big. I always knew you could make it."

This was news to Sarah but she was too pleased by his enthusiasm to tell him so. "I'm looking forward to seeing them up on the walls. The place looked like a building site. I can't believe it's going to be ready by next week."

"You are coming to the opening party, aren't you?"

"I've bought a new dress for it."

"Good. It's important you look right. I'll be there from late afternoon. Why don't you come up by train? I'll give you a lift home."

"Are you sure? That would be great."

"We can conduct a postmortem in the car. And we need to talk."

"I know. I'm ready to sort things out now. I've packed up everything at home that I think is yours. And as far as the house is concerned . . ."

"Don't worry about the house," Andrew said. "We don't need to do anything just yet. We don't want to rush into things. I seem to have made rather a mess by rushing into things. Do you know what I mean?"

"Not really, no."

"Well. We'll talk on Thursday. How are the rehearsals going?"

"Audrey says she's having sleepless nights."

"I've never been in a play that hasn't given Audrey sleepless nights." Andrew laughed. "I'd better go. Sarah?"

"Yes?"

"I'm very proud of you."

Sarah put the receiver back on the phone. She had received too many setbacks in her artistic career to let herself be carried away by Andrew's assurances of future stardom. She took a lock of hair and wrapped it slowly round her finger. It was going to be far less easy to remain unaffected by Andrew's other comments. Was it possible that he was beginning to regret leaving her? Could the hyacinth be losing its bloom?

29

Enjoy the Moment

The dress rehearsal was a disaster. Mrs. Danvers's skirt was too tight and could only be worn with the help of a giant safety pin. Claire pointed out (quite reasonably, Sarah thought) that Mrs. Danvers was not the sort of woman who'd wear a skirt held up by a giant safety pin. Audrey launched into the first of many eruptions, declaring that she could hardly be expected to spend time worrying about safety pins when faced with a lighting man who knew nothing about lighting and that Claire, as an experienced actress, should surely be able to rise above such trivial problems. Claire muttered sulkily that the only way she could rise above this particular problem was to keep one hand fixed over the offending pin and that it was difficult to project the requisite aura of sinister evil with a hand clamped permanently to her waist. Audrey responded that if she didn't sort out the lighting man, no one would be able to see Claire's safety pin anyway. Sarah felt that this point was also a reasonable one since the lighting man was indeed proving very volatile with his equipment, pointing lights at empty areas of the stage while the actors were left to emote their lines in darkness.

There was also the problem of the stage. This was the first time they had acted in the village hall. The set designer and his team had created a terrific set with a real staircase. Unfortunately, the terrific set left little room for the actors. Accustomed to the generous area of the rehearsal room above the pub, they found their ability to move was seriously circumscribed and they kept bumping into each other, which did nothing to create the requisite dramatic tension. These problems came to a head in the scene between Mrs. Danvers and Mrs. de Winter at the top of the stairs. There was Claire, softly suggesting with serpentlike venom that the other woman should fling herself over the banister when there was no way that Sarah, wedged between the stair rail on the one hand and Claire's enormous bulk on the other, could move a finger, let alone her entire body. Sarah began to giggle, which roused Audrey to new heights of fury, not helped by the fact that the spotlight was darting round the stage like a drunken firefly.

By the time they got to The Kiss, Audrey was almost prostrate on a chair in front of the stage. Martin took Sarah in his arms and kissed her with all the passion of a man who has a train to catch. Audrey gave vent to the frustrations of the evening. "This play," she yelled, "is a travesty! I have devoted the last three months to producing a work of art and you reward me with the sort of acting that would not be out of place in a primary school! I have, I think you will all agree, shown exemplary patience but there comes a point when I can take no more. I have to tell you that I wash my hands. My reputation lies on the verge of extinction. And Martin, if you don't know how to kiss a woman at your age, then I can't help you. I will only say that the villagers of Ambercross will be paying their money on Friday in the belief that the Ambercross Players will be giving them their usual professional entertainment and instead they will be getting this farce of a performance. I tell you all that if it weren't for the fact that the set team has worked so selflessly in the last few weeks, I would contemplate canceling the play. I will say no more." She took a breath. "I will only say that I ask you all to think long and hard about your commitment to this project. We have one more rehearsal tomorrow night and then on Friday we perform. I am in your hands! You can either leave me to end what I think you will agree is a long and illustrious career in the theater or you can try to salvage something from this disaster. Now we will finish this play and then we will all go home and attempt to get some sleep!"

They finished the play at half past ten and left the village hall, subdued and silent. No one dared speak to Audrey.

"I'll give you a lift home," Martin murmured to Sarah. He opened the car door for her and she gave him a quick glance. He looked tired and dejected.

She watched him climb into the car and start up the engine. She gave his arm a consoling pat. "Andrew says that Audrey always gets hysterical before a play goes on."

Martin sighed. "She's not usually this bad. I wish I'd never agreed to do it."

"Well I don't," said Sarah bracingly. "You're terrific in the part and I couldn't have done it without you as Maxim."

"Thank you." Martin gave a short laugh. "I can't bear all these tantrums at the best of times but they're not usually directed at me. This is the last time I take the main part." He stopped to brake abruptly as a huge, ungainly badger loped across the road.

"There!" Sarah said, "That's a sign of good luck!"

"Since when was a badger a sign of good luck?"

"Since tonight!"

He smiled. "You're in a very positive mood. I take it they liked your paintings?"

"They did. Andrew rang over the weekend. He's doing the publicity for the club. He seems to think I'm on the verge of being a successful artist."

"Perhaps he's right." Martin turned into Shooter's Lane. "Will Andrew be at the opening night?"

"Very much so. He's organizing it."

"He must be very pleased for you." Martin pulled up outside Sarah's gate.

"Andrew has been very nice lately. In fact . . ." Sarah hesitated and picked up her bag from the floor of the car.

"In fact, what?"

"It's nothing. I'm probably being silly. It was just something he said that made me wonder if he might be having second thoughts about leaving me."

"Oh?" Martin turned off the ignition. "Do you think he wants to come back to you?"

Sarah shook her head. "I've probably got it wrong."

"But if you haven't? What would you do?"

Sarah shrugged. "I don't know what I think about anything anymore. I've had enough ups and downs for a lifetime these last few months and I'm finally starting to appreciate life on my own." She laughed. "I never thought I'd be able to say that."

Martin reached across Sarah to open the door for her. "I hope you have a wonderful party," he said. "And I'm sure you'll do whatever you think is right. But I hope . . ."

Sarah had climbed out of the car and now she lowered her head and stared quizzically at him. "What do you hope?"

"I suppose I hope," Martin said slowly, "that you won't rush into anything too quickly."

Sarah chuckled. "You are speaking to a reformed character. I will never rush into anything again, I promise you."

"That's good." Martin cleared his throat and his face reddened slightly. "You've changed so much in the last few months. You've been through so much and you've refused to be beaten. I think you're very impressive." He stopped abruptly and turned on the ignition. "Anyway, none of this is any of my business."

"It certainly is," said Sarah warmly. "You've had to listen to me moaning and groaning ever since I joined the Players. You won't disappear once *Rebecca*'s finished, will you? I should miss you very much."

Martin jerked his head slightly. "Thank you," he said. "Good night, Sarah."

Sarah watched him drive off. It was only after he'd disappeared from view that she realized he hadn't answered her question.

*　　　*　　　*

Sarah arrived at the nightclub at half past eight. She was pleased with her appearance. The dress was long, black, and severely cut with a dramatic red motif zigzagging diagonally from neckline to hem. It was the sort of outfit she would never have dreamed of wearing before a week ago but it was precisely the sort of outfit that a woman who's been paid four thousand pounds for four pictures was entitled to wear and Sarah knew that it suited her. She was Cinderella, wearing a smashing frock and going to the ball at last.

Sarah stood at the top of the stairs and looked down. She would never have believed this was the same place she'd visited a week ago. The walls were now dark olive, providing a perfect backdrop to her paintings. Three enormous red velvet sofas sat on the polished wooden floors and there was a vast glassy bar behind which a beautiful young man was serving champagne and cocktails.

The place was packed with people, all shouting to be heard above the noise. Sarah stood uncertainly for a moment and decided to make her way to the bar. As she walked downstairs she could see her husband, handsome as a prince in his dinner jacket, talking earnestly to a ponytailed man in a white suit. Andrew saw her and shouted, "Sarah!" He made his way through the melee to get to her. "Sarah!" he said. "You look incredible. I was beginning to think you'd got lost. We need to do the photographs now. Come with me."

Sarah had to stand between Gordon and Jeremy under the apple painting. The three of them were told to smile at the camera; then they had to appear to be in animated conversation; then they had to gaze up admiringly at the apple, a pose that Sarah fervently hoped would not reach the papers since it was unbelievably cheesy and it made her look smug. Finally, the photographer announced himself satisfied.

"Thank heavens for that," said Gordon testily. "There is something about being told to smile for the camera that always makes me want to stick my tongue out. Sarah, you look lovely." He sounded faintly surprised. "How do you think your paintings look? Don't they look good?" He nodded at Andrew. "You have a very talented wife."

Andrew put his arm round Sarah. "I know. I'm very proud of her."

He hasn't told them, Sarah thought. They think we're a couple. She was unsettled by Andrew's conjugal manner and stood a little stiffly with a vague smile on her face.

"Sarah!" said Jeremy, "you don't have a drink. Why don't we go to the bar? There aren't going to be any more photos, are there, Andrew?"

Andrew checked his watch. "No, but Mary Moss is here from the *Chronicle* and wants a few words."

"Gordon, you'll do that, won't you? You're much better at that sort of thing. You come with me, Sarah."

After a few sips of champagne she began to relax with Jeremy. He might be terrifying but he was also inviting her to submit a couple of her paintings to a gallery he had at St. James's in London. Sarah could feel her confidence growing by the minute and when she discovered that they both shared a love of the first *Star Trek* series and of William Shatner in particular, she forgot that she'd ever felt intimidated by him.

She was telling him that her best ever *Star Trek* episode was the one in which Captain Kirk has to let Joan Collins, the latest love of his life, die in order to avoid Hitler winning the war, when Andrew came up to join them. "Sarah," he said, "Mary Moss wants to have a word with you."

Jeremy took her hand. "It's been a pleasure talking to you, Sarah. I'm already looking forward to our next meeting."

"Me too!" said Sarah cheerfully, and allowed herself to be led away by Andrew.

Andrew smiled. "Were you flirting with him, Mrs. Stagg?"

Sarah laughed. "Certainly not. We were bonding over *Star Trek*." She was aware of Andrew's hand on her back, guiding her in a proprietorial manner toward the journalist.

Sarah had never been someone who enjoyed parties very much. She always found the bite-size conversations that such occasions demanded difficult to manage. There seemed to be a very difficult balance to be made between hogging one person's company for too long and thinking of enough interesting things to say within the space of a few minutes in order to validate one's invitation.

Tonight was different. Tonight, people went out of their way to talk to her. She had the heady experience of being interviewed by a charming reporter who appeared to find her views fascinating; she lost count of the number of people who wanted to ring her about possible commissions. And throughout the evening, she was aware of Andrew's eyes following her movements, seeking her out. The voice of reason, an irritating but permanent resident in Sarah's brain, kept reminding her that people always gush at parties, she'd done it herself countless times, praising to the skies pictures that she found either banal or incomprehensible. The voice of reason also told her that Andrew was only looking at her so much because he'd never seen her as a focus of attention before. Sarah didn't care. She was just intent on having a good time tonight.

At the end of the evening she climbed into Andrew's car, feeling a little light-headed and pleasantly sleepy. Andrew watched her stretch her arms in front of her and grinned. "You look like the cat who's eaten all the cream," he said.

Sarah yawned. "It's been a wonderful, wonderful evening! Everone's been so nice to me. Jeremy's offered me some more work, loads of people asked for my number. Life suddenly seems very exciting. A few months ago I thought my life was finished and now . . ." She stopped, embarrassed by what she had just said. "Anyway," she finished lamely, "it's all very nice."

They drove out of Bath in silence and then Andrew said, "How was the dress rehearsal?"

"Ghastly! The whole thing is a shambles. Don't come and see it."

"Try and keep me away. How's poor old Martin coping with Maxim?"

"He's good." She felt a familiar stab of irritation. Martin was neither poor nor old.

Andrew laughed. "I gather he's madly in love with you!"

"Martin?" Sarah stared incredulously at Andrew. "You must be joking!"

Andrew grinned. "I promise you I'm not. Howard says everyone's noticed it."

"If that's what Howard's been telling you, then he has a rich imagination! Martin's been seeing a very glamorous woman called Sally-Anne Furlong, as Howard knows very well. Martin was very upset when she broke it off."

"Is that what Martin told you? Sarah, you're wonderfully naive. You never were able to tell when someone came on to you."

"Andrew, Martin has never 'come on to me.' "

"Of course he wouldn't. That man doesn't have the guts to come on to any woman he really likes. That's why the only women he ever gets are the predatory ones who are prepared to make the first move and the second and probably the third as well. But trust me, the man is mad about you. Sally-Anne Furlong told Howard that the moment you got back from your Majorca trip, he lost interest in her. They were supposed to be going to Devon for the weekend. He canceled it because he wanted to go for a walk with you. Sally-Anne was terribly upset. They had a quarrel. She waited for him to apologize and he never did."

Sarah said, "He was very good to me when I got back from Majorca. He found me in a bit of a state. He's been a very good friend. Howard wouldn't understand something like that."

"I'm sure Martin's been a wonderful friend."

"Andrew, why are you so rude about Martin?"

Andrew shrugged. "We don't have a lot in common."

"There's no need to be rude about him. Oh look!" Sarah craned her head forward. "That is the most beautiful moon!" She sat back in her seat, good humor restored. "It's very good of you to give me a lift home."

"It's a pleasure. And I'm sorry I was rude about Martin. I know how fond you've become of him. Perhaps I'm a little jealous."

"You're jealous! Excuse me if I give a hollow laugh!" She

frowned. "Have you ever tried to give a hollow laugh? Why do people say that? It can't be done!"

Andrew tried a large, disdainful cackle. "What about that?"

"No. It didn't sound hollow at all." She glanced up at the moon. It looked as if it were chasing them across the sky.

"Sarah," Andrew said, "it's nice being with you like this. I've missed you."

Sarah eyed him cautiously. "Have you?"

Andrew kept his eyes fixed firmly on the road ahead. "I'm not trying to excuse myself. I know Hyacinth threw herself at me but I should have resisted. Things spiraled out of control and I didn't know how to stop them. But you and I, we were a good team, weren't we?"

"I thought so," said Sarah. The moon seemed to be losing pace now, its warm, gentle light partially obscured by the trees.

"And then, tonight," Andrew said, "I was so proud of you. It felt like the last few months had never happened. It was you and me taking on the world like we used to. Andrew and Sarah." He changed gears abruptly and slid into a turnout on the side of the road. He switched off the ignition and turned to face her. "I've been an idiot," he said, "but if nothing else has come out of all this, it's shown me that I love you." He took her face in his hands and kissed her. "I do love you, Sarah."

"Do you?" Sarah asked. "What about Hyacinth?"

Andrew touched her cheek with his hand. "It's you," he said simply. "It's always been you."

Take the Initiative

Sarah was not looking forward to telling Martin. The fact that she was about to earn universal ridicule for her ludicrous attempt to portray herself as a sweet young bride seemed totally irrelevant. All her concentration was directed on what she was going to say to Martin and how she was going to tell him. The day seemed to stretch endlessly ahead of her. Exasperated by the endless dialogues going on in her head ("Martin, can I have a quick word?"; "Martin, you know I saw Andrew last night?"; "Martin, I won't keep you a moment but . . ."), Sarah decided to clean the house. By six o'clock she had swept, scrubbed, dusted, vacuumed, and polished until the place gleamed. Her house reminded her of her grandfather, who had always put on his best suit for church. He had scrubbed up well but he couldn't wait to get back into his comfy old cords and woolly sweater.

She arrived at the village hall to find everyone in a state of barely suppressed excitement. Audrey was dressed in her traditional first night outfit, a long floral dress with a violently turquoise, tasseled shawl. She was doing her best to calm her cast. "Now I want you all to enjoy yourselves this evening! Just do your best and project, project, project! We have a full house tonight but don't let that worry you. Just be your parts! I will be in the wings, ready to prompt if necessary but of course there will be no need to prompt anyone. Now, before you get ready, we need to practice the final lineup. Can I have you all on stage?"

Everyone dutifully filed onto the stage. "Where," Audrey demanded, "is Martin? People will be arriving soon!" She raised her face to the ceiling and shouted, "Martin!" as if hoping to see him floating in the air.

"I'm here!" Martin came through the front doors of the village hall. He was wearing his old denim trousers and a white T-shirt and appeared to be remarkably calm for a man who was going on stage in less than half an hour.

"Martin," Audrey said severely, "do you know how late it is? Come up here and get into line. Now listen carefully everyone. At the end of the play, when Frith leaves the stage, Martin will give Sarah The Kiss. After that, he will take her hand and raise it to his lips. When Steve sees Martin kiss Sarah's hand, he will close the curtains. Whatever you do, Martin, you must not forget to kiss Sarah's hand, because Steve won't do anything until you've done that. You will then line up and be ready when the curtains open again. Martin, I want you to stand next to Sarah in the middle. I want everyone to hold hands. Sarah, you will count to three and then bow. The rest of you will take your lead from Sarah."

Martin hauled himself up onto the stage, fell into place next to Sarah, and took her hand.

"Now," said Audrey, "that's right. One, two, three, and bow and smile at the audience. Thank you. Go and change and get ready to give your all!"

It was going to be impossible to speak to Martin until the interval. Sarah bit her lip and retired to the women's dressing room. Now that the Martin ordeal was temporarily shelved, she could allow herself to get scared about the play. There was going to be a full house! She was going to forget her lines! The audience would laugh at her as soon as she stepped on stage!

Claire was still grumbling about the safety pin. "I'm not happy with my costume," she said. "I'm not happy at all. If I could wear my shirt over my waist it would help. Look," she demanded of Sarah, "is the pin noticeable?"

"Hardly at all," said Sarah optimistically.

"Oh well, it will have to do. Is Andrew coming tonight, do you know?"

"Yes," said Sarah reddening, "he is."

"Oh, good. At least he'll tell us the truth. If he likes the play, we'll know it's worked. Nothing can be worse than the dress rehearsal."

Sarah wasn't so sure. Her heart was beginning to pound uncomfortably inside her. She opened her script and then wished she hadn't. She wished she could be like Margaret, who was sitting placidly in the corner doing her knitting. There was a Tannoy monitor system in the dressing rooms, connected to the stage. Sarah could hear the low murmur of a host of people. "They're coming in!" she said. "They're here!"

Claire said, "Let's go and have a look through the side curtain. Are you coming?"

Anything was better than staying in the dressing room. Sarah followed Claire through. She could see the vicar and his wife near the back. Luke Everseed and Tracy were reclining in their chairs at the front, chewing gum and looking bored. Jennifer and George were three seats back, talking to the colonel and his wife. Andrew was sitting in front of them. He was talking to Simon and Clementine while on his other side, Sally-Anne Furlong was giving him an appraising glance. Sarah moved away. She had seen enough. Her heart was about to disintegrate with fear. Now the music came on, which meant that the play was starting in five minutes. Audrey had chosen Mozart's *Requiem,* which was very beautiful but pretty depressing. Audrey took up her position in the wings, the actors cleared their throats and took their places. The music stopped and the curtains opened.

The play began. Sarah, watching from the wings, envied the easy confidence of the players on the stage. Now the butler was announcing to the family that Mr. and Mrs. de Winter were driving through the gates. Sarah was joined by Martin, who gave her hand a brief but comradely squeeze. Then suddenly, Martin became Maxim, talking offstage to the butler. And then they were on.

It was a bit like diving into a pool and finding she could swim. The audience did not laugh when she entered, she did not forget her lines, and even the erratic spotlight failed to discompose her. The only moment of panic came when she had to leave the stage to change into her fancy dress for the ball. At the dress rehearsal she had discovered she had only seven minutes in which to change. Now, as she put the dress over her head, she could not pull it down. Sarah swore loudly. Fortunately Claire was on hand to tug it into place for her.

"Thank you!" Sarah said, and surprised them both by giving her a hug.

"You look great," Claire said. "On you go!" And on Sarah went. When the curtain came down for the interval, the clapping from the audience was loud and unforced. Sarah could hear George bellowing, "Good show!" and smiled.

Backstage, Audrey told her cast to get changed for the next act and announced that she wanted to speak to them all in five minutes in the ladies dressing room. Audrey's granddaughter came in, bearing coffee and biscuits. Audrey sailed up to Sarah like a galleon. "Against all the odds," she said graciously, "you are doing an excellent job."

Sarah celebrated with a chocolate bourbon.

The rest of the actors trouped in and cast anxious looks at their director. Audrey smiled at them all. "So far," she said cautiously, "we are putting on a performance in line with the high quality of all previous productions. I am proud of you all. I am sure"—her face darkened for a moment as her eyes rested on Martin—"you will not disappoint me in the final act. Martin, I will say only two words to you: The Kiss." Martin looked at his shoes. "You may drop the first kiss in scene one but you have to kiss Sarah at the end of the play." She looked earnestly at Martin, who continued to look at his feet. "I'm sure I can depend on you. Now, as for the rest of you . . ."

"I'm sorry." Sarah broke in suddenly and at a volume that

surprised herself as much as it did everyone else. "But I have something very important to say to Martin. Will you please excuse us for a moment?"

The effect was extraordinary. It was, Sarah thought, as if a mouse had just roared. Audrey's mouth fell open but failed to say any words. Howard and Claire exchanged quizzical glances. The last two stitches Margaret had made fell from her needle. Martin's face was unreadable. He didn't say anything but stood up and followed Sarah out. Sarah led the way into the men's dressing room and closed the door behind them.

"Martin," she said, "why didn't you tell me Andrew slept with your wife?"

Martin pulled out a chair and sat down. "He didn't."

"Please don't lie to me," Sarah said. "I can't bear it if you lie to me."

"I'm not lying." He looked straight at her. "I caught them kissing in the kitchen. Andrew did not sleep with her. I'm not at all sure he would have. Anyway he didn't get the chance because I . . . I ejected him. Why did you think he did?"

"I've been trying to work out why he disliked you so much."

"Now you know. I wasn't as polite as I should have been." Martin stood up. "Is that all? Can I go?"

"No. Please sit down." Sarah gripped her hands tightly together. "I'm about to say something very embarrassing and if I don't say it now I will never have the courage to say it again. Andrew asked me to go back to him last night. . . ."

"Congratulations."

"Please be quiet, Martin. This is really difficult for me and it doesn't help if you interrupt. He asked me to go back to him

last night. And I said I couldn't. I said I had feelings for someone else."

"Barney," Martin murmured.

"Will you please be quiet? The funny thing is I didn't
know it until I said it. It never occurred to me until then. And
as soon as I did say it, everything became clear. The very first
time Audrey told you to kiss me, I really wanted you to. I
thought it was because I was a sad, desperate woman when in
fact it was far more simple: I just fancied you. I was so busy
wondering why Andrew had stopped loving me, I never wondered why I was so happy when I was with *you*. As for Barney:
he was sexy and he was fun, at least he was fun for a while. He
made me miserable because he made a fool of me, not because
he broke my heart. These last few weeks, I've been really
happy because I finally feel that I know myself. And you and I
were friends again and I was glad you weren't seeing Sally-
Anne anymore. I'm telling you this because now that I've
worked it all out, I can't unwork it again. I like going for
walks with you, I like talking to you, I like being with you, I
like the way you look at me, I like the way you make me feel
about being alive. Andrew seems to think you might . . . you
might like me a lot. I'm pretty certain he's wrong and I'm
pretty certain I'm making a complete ass of myself and you
don't need to say anything and I'll certainly never mention it
again. But I want you to know that I love your kindness and
your strength and your honesty and that I think you're a
pretty remarkable man. And that I'd miss you like anything if
you weren't around anymore. So now you can go and I wish
you'd please stop looking at me."

Martin's face had remained inscrutable throughout Sarah's

confession. It was as if he had closed the shutters. He said, "Sarah . . ."

There was a very loud knock on the door and Margaret popped an apologetic and frankly curious face round the door. "I'm sorry," she said, "but Audrey wanted you to know the play is starting and she's beginning to panic."

"Thank you," Sarah said, and fled past both of them onto the stage. For a little while at least she could stop being Sarah who always got things wrong and concentrate on being Mrs. de Winter who had unforeseen nerves of steel.

She could tell that the final act was going well. The audience followed all the twists and turns with an intense silence that was very satisfactory. It was only as they got near to The Kiss that Sarah, aware of what was coming or rather what was not coming, could feel herself going rigid with tension. She waited for Martin to come forward and lob a kiss in the direction of her chin.

In the wings, Audrey was getting worried too. "Kiss her, Martin," she whispered furiously.

Martin stood up and walked toward Sarah. Then he smiled at her and it was a Martin smile, not a Maxim smile. He took her in his arms and he kissed her. He kissed her with a strength that made Sarah melt like butter in a sizzling pan. She forgot she was Mrs. de Winter. She forgot she was in the village hall in front of the villagers of Ambercross. She was only aware of Martin. She could have kissed him forever and it was clear that Audrey thought she was going to because she began to hiss desperately, "Very good, you two, very passionate, but that's enough now. You can stop now, Martin, do you hear? Martin, you can stop. You have to kiss her hand and then Steve will close the curtains! Did you hear what I said? You can stop!" But Martin did not stop and he kissed her with a confidence and a passion that had the audience rise to their feet and cheer with one accord. Someone, almost certainly Luke Everseed, gave an energetic wolf whistle.

Offstage, Audrey screeched, "Stop kissing her!"

The hero released his heroine at last.

Offstage, there was a stunned silence and then Audrey, pushed beyond endurance, cried, *"Will someone please close the curtains?"*

UP CLOSE AND PERSONAL

WITH THE AUTHOR

WHERE DO YOU SEE SARAH AND MARTIN FIVE YEARS DOWN THE ROAD?

I see them taking a three-month break to go backpacking round Australia. Sarah has had three successful solo exhibitions of her work much to the chagrin of Andrew, who has never quite forgiven her for choosing Martin instead of himself. She is enjoying the novelty of a slowly burgeoning confidence. This is due to her artistic success and to her happiness with a partner who both loves and respects her. Neither of them are in the Ambercross Players any more.

WAS ANDREW WRONG TO INITIATE A DIVORCE? SHOULD HE HAVE TRIED TO WORK THINGS OUT WITH SARAH BEFORE LEAVING HER FOR HYACINTH?

Andrew was wrong to succumb to temptation in the first place. He was also wrong to initiate divorce proceedings so soon after the children's departure from the family home. To be ready to abandon so easily a good marriage of twenty years is an indication of both carelessness and callousness. Sarah was right not to take him back. Andrew saw her as an appendage who reflected his opinion of himself. Martin sees Sarah as a woman who he loves for herself.

NOTWITHSTANDING THE EMOTIONAL UPHEAVAL, IS SARAH BETTER OFF WITHOUT ANDREW?

As Andrew's wife, Sarah had always felt inferior to her husband: he had the charm, the looks, and the charisma. She and Martin share a similar sense of humor as well as a love of travel. Their partnership is based on mutual respect. The confidence this gives Sarah colors her life.

WILL YOUR FRIENDS SEE VERSIONS OF THEMSELVES IN THESE PAGES OR ARE YOUR CHARACTERS PURELY IMAGINARY?

Some of my friends will recognize bits of themselves and one will certainly recognize her kitchen! I'm glad to say that the less agreeable characters are imagined. Jacko, however, is based on a terrifying dog I once had the misfortune to look after.

DO YOU SHARE ANY OF SARAH'S PASSIONS: ACTING, TEACHING, TRAVEL, AND/OR PAINTING?

I do love amateur dramatics. I once played the same part that Sarah did. Also, like Sarah, I was a teacher but my subject was history rather than art. I have a daughter who is a very talented artist but I have no skills in that direction. I wish I did! As far as travel is concerned, there are masses of places I still wish to see. I know Majorca well and I love it dearly.

WHAT ARE YOUR SECRETS FOR LIVING WISELY AND INDEPENDENTLY?

As I get older, I am more aware that change is a natural part of life and that adaptability is therefore an important quality. I try to live within my income, to nurture my friends and my family, to appreciate what I have, and to know that happiness is something to work for rather than to find.

DO YOU BELIEVE PEOPLE CAN REINVENT THEMSELVES, NO MATTER THEIR AGE OR THEIR RELATIONSHIP?

I know they can! I've seen it happen many times, the most glorious example being that of an older friend. After the death of her very controlling husband, she discovered new friends, new enthusiasms, and new confidence at the age of eighty-three.

HOW DO YOU BALANCE YOUR FAMILY LIFE WITH WORK?

As a mother of five who did not want to be a slave to the house, I long ago decided that an untidy house was not the end of the world. I am also blessed with a husband who is a very good cook.

DO YOU HAVE ANY ADVICE FOR ASPIRING NOVELISTS?

Accept that rejection is a necessary part of your chosen career. Read widely. Always be open to new ideas from conversations, films, papers, etc. Read your dialogue out loud: you can instantly hear if it sounds phony.

There's nothing better than the perfect bag...
Unless it's the perfect book!

Don't miss any of these fashionable
reads from Downtown Press!

**Happiness
Sold Separately**
Libby Street
Too bad life doesn't come
with a money-back guarantee.

Younger
Pamela Redmond Satran
She's old enough to be his
mother. Too bad she's having
too much fun to care...

**Confessions of
a Nervous Shiksa**
Tracy McArdle
In Hollywood, when your
well-scripted romance
ends up on the cutting room
floor, it's time for a new
leading man.

Rescue Me
Gigi Levangie Grazer
Sometimes love
needs a lifeboat...

**Love Will Tear
Us Apart**
Tara McCarthy
They're rich.
They're fabulous.
And they're joined at the hip.
Literally.
Sometimes two's a crowd....

Did the Earth Move?
Carmen Reid
She's looking for a man to
take her all the way.

Great storytelling just got a new address.

**DOWNTOWN
PRESS**
A Division of Simon & Schuster
A VIACOM COMPANY

Available wherever books are sold or at www.downtownpress.com

13459

Want it ALL?

Want to **read books about stuff *you* care about**?
Want to **meet authors**?
Heck, want to write stuff you care about,
want to *be an author*?

Want to **dish the dirt**? Sound off? Spread love?
Punk your boss? Out your mate?

Want to **know what's hot**? Want to *be what's hot*?
Want **free stuff**?
Want to do it **all at once, all in one place**?

18-34 year olds, there's only one stop… one spot.
SimonSaysTheSPOT.com

Visit us at http://www.simonsaysTheSPOT.com